TAKE ME HOME

TAKE ME HOME

Jerri Corgiat

A SIGNET ECLIPSE BOOK

SIGNET ECLIPSE
Published by New American Library, a division of
Penguin Group (USA) Inc., 375 Hudson Street,
New York, New York 10014, USA
Penguin Group (Canada), 90 Eglinton Avenue East, Suite 700, Toronto,
Ontario M4P 2Y3, Canada (a division of Pearson Penguin Canada Inc.)
Penguin Books Ltd., 80 Strand, London WC2R 0RL, England
Penguin Ireland, 25 St. Stephen's Green, Dublin 2,
Ireland (a division of Penguin Books Ltd.)
Penguin Group (Australia), 250 Camberwell Road, Camberwell, Victoria 3124,
Australia (a division of Pearson Australia Group Pty. Ltd.)
Penguin Books India Pvt. Ltd., 11 Community Centre, Panchsheel Park,
New Delhi - 110 017, India
Penguin Group (NZ), 67 Apollo Drive, Rosedale, North Shore 0745,
Auckland, New Zealand (a division of Pearson New Zealand Ltd.)
Penguin Books (South Africa) (Pty.) Ltd., 24 Sturdee Avenue,
Rosebank, Johannesburg 2196, South Africa

Penguin Books Ltd., Registered Offices:
80 Strand, London WC2R 0RL, England

First published by Signet Eclipse, an imprint of New American Library,
a division of Penguin Group (USA) Inc.

ISBN 978-0-7394-8782-2

To my own Greek Chorus of Optimism:
Pam Cyran, Ann Handelman, Jill Meradith,
and Nancy Phillips

Acknowledgments

One of the pleasures of writing is the research; I enjoy gaining new knowledge and very much appreciate the people who are willing to share theirs. . . .

Dr. Ted Rosentreter's contribution was invaluable. Any errors contained in the diagnosis, explanations, and treatments espoused by the fictional Drs. Rosen and Treter are mine alone; the real doctor took pains to help me understand unfamiliar territory.

As did Cathy Macek, of Macek's Auto, patiently answering my clueless questions about car mechanics. (Sorry, I had to edit out the part of the book where they would have applied, but at least I know more now than I did then.)

Mary Rohr . . . a special and heartfelt thank-you for sharing your experiences with me.

Once again, a lot of people held my hand through the process, including my writer buddies, wonderful talents all: Karen Brichoux, Nancy Parra, and Libby Sternberg (aka Elizabeth Malin).

Claire Zion and Marcy Posner . . . hats off to you as always.

Mike . . . may your light continue to shine. Mac . . . always the light of my life!

Chapter 1

When Florida Jones opened the door on that sweltering Friday afternoon in July, she didn't know who she'd expected to see.

Maybe Eddie or Freddie Steeplemier. The twins, a matched set of bowling pins in overalls, had gotten on—way on—in years, but still served the Cordelia, Missouri, post office. Although it was more than two months away from the wedding, gifts were already trickling in, early senders currying favor from her fiancé, she supposed.

Maybe Alcea. Although, living next door, her best friend, business partner, and sister-in-law rarely used the doorbell. Or even the front door.

Or maybe—probably—eight-year-old Joey Norsworthy, who had recently moved in across the way, just down from Beadler's Feed and the Rooster Bar & Grill, into the last house on the street before

Main turned into highway and threaded south into the blue mist of the Ozark Mountains. A short block the other direction, Main formed one side of a square lined with brick buildings. Their narrow windows, topped with cut-stone eyebrows, stared out at St. Andrew's Church, which watched over the green in the middle of the square where the youngsters sometimes played. Fitting, since Joey treated Florida's daughter, Missouri, as if she were God in pigtails.

But it wasn't Joey, Alcea, or the postman.

It was her mother.

She stared into the same crystal blue eyes she saw when she looked in the mirror. Even though the years had rounded the jut of sharp shoulders and etched lines on the face and honed an already-thin frame . . . even though the gold hair was now cropped short and obviously came from a bottle . . . that screw-you glint in the eyes was the same.

The same as the one in the dog-eared photograph she'd cried over for a dozen years, and then hated for another couple decades plus a half. It had been only since Missouri had been born that she'd finally let go of the pain of abandonment. Or that's what she'd thought.

Now it all rushed back. She wanted to curse. She wanted to cry. At the very least, she wanted to just slam the door and pretend nothing had happened. But instead she just said, "Hello, Tamara." She and her half brother had never called Tamara *Mother*.

"Florida." Her mother didn't make a move forward, just stood there, looking her over.

Acting as if she didn't notice—as if her mother showing up on her porch wasn't any big deal—Florida glanced next door where her half brother's Jeep sat out front. She wondered if he knew Tamara was back.

Displaying a really annoying talent for telepathy, Tamara said, "Dak knows," and, even though she hadn't been asked in, stepped past Florida into the foyer. Lit by a skylight by day and a Crate and Barrel light sconce by night, the tiled entryway opened to the great room on the left, and the kitchen in the rear. Tamara's movements were accompanied by the clink of wide bracelets and a mingled fragrance of spiced citrus and smoke.

Florida sneezed. Sneezed again.

Tamara glanced back, a penciled eyebrow raised.

Florida waved a hand. "The cheap perfume."

Tamara's mouth quirked.

Disappointed she hadn't drawn blood, Florida stayed put in the doorway, making it clear there wouldn't be any hearts-and-flowers reunion. She felt little surprise to see Tamara. Somewhere, somehow, she'd known this would happen. Once upon a lifetime ago, she'd even hoped it would. She felt still less surprise Tamara had found them. They were right where she'd left them. Besides, this was Cordelia. All a body had to do to find someone was stick a head in a few places and ask.

But why now? Right when she'd reached the

top of her world? Forty was approaching in another five months, but held no horrors. She was still knock-'em-dead gorgeous, didn't need Clairol on her mane of strawberry blond hair, shunned Retin A, and had retained her slim figure. She was a savvy businesswoman raising a wonderful daughter, and engaged to a wealthy hotel magnate, Daniel Davenport.

Lightbulb. *That's* why Tamara had shown up now. Money. Daniel was building hotels with the frenzy of a Donald Trump wannabe. Although he was still an up-and-comer, he was making a splash, not just in his hometown, Kansas City, but across the region. Their engagement had received some press. Very little press and in very obscure papers, but press just the same. Her mother had probably seen it, come looking for proof her daughter was striking it rich, and found it in her brand-spankin'-new BMW Z4 convertible. Tamara couldn't know she'd depleted her nest egg buying that car, since eggs were no longer such a worry, considering her engagement. Besides, that car . . .

Well, thinking of how it soothed the soul to fly down Highway 52 in the lap of 215 horses, she knew it was worth every cotton-pickin' penny. Evidence of her success, it sat in the driveway, hot sun glinting off its red enamel. Right next to evidence of Tamara's lack of it: a Ford Focus, dusty, dented, and held together by rust.

Of course if it was need for money that was spurring a display of maternal devotion, it begged the question of why Tamara hadn't returned when

Dak's fame as an author had grown. She shrugged. What difference did it make? If she had anything to say about it, Tamara wouldn't be here long. Although the way her mother was lingering in the entry, staring up the stairwell that led to the bedrooms above and ignoring the hint of the open door, she was in no rush to be gone.

Florida slammed the door and followed her in.

"Things have certainly changed," Tamara murmured.

The last time Tamara had graced this property with her presence, this building had housed Cowboy's Tow and Service. That last time, Tamara's father, Cowboy, had still been alive. And about to get the pants shocked off him when Tamara paused only long enough to drop off her two illegitimate brats, both named for the states where his wanderlust daughter—heavy on the *lust*—had birthed them.

First Tamara, then Florida had grown up in the tall, pinched house that was adjoined to this one by a long breezeway. A decade older, Dak had spent only a couple of years there before he'd skedaddled off into a career as a wandering scribe. But life had brought him full circle—and straight into the arms of Alcea O'Malley. He still wrote, but he didn't wander as much.

"Did you think they wouldn't?"

"Not this much," Tamara said, still looking around.

Not long after they'd married, Dak and Alcea had transformed that shadowed house into an airy home, then offered Florida, who had moved into a trailer at the rear of the property, the funds to convert the service garage. The former three-bay space was now filled with light and high ceilings and blond oak floors hugged by a railed porch out front that was scented by lilacs in spring and roses in summer.

"Must have cost a pretty penny. You do it?" She glanced at Florida. "Or your brother?"

"Both." Which was shaving the truth. Back then, she'd been a new mother with a fledgling business, and in need of some help. Dak hadn't minded providing it, feeling it only fair, since he'd inherited the bulk of Cowboy's estate, not that it had been much of a fortune. In fact, it had taken her brother's bank account, stuffed with spoils from his popular *On the Road* series and a best-selling novel, to put the place back into order. But she'd organized all the remodeling and it was her taste that filled the house.

Tamara had moved onto the wool rug that occupied the center of the great room; its stylized border reflected the Chinese Red and lime that provided an accent to the room's medley of natural colors and textures.

Crossing her arms, Florida watched her, wondering how Dak had taken her return. While Florida had never, ever, never doubted that a black stone substituted for a heart in Tamara's chest, Dak had somehow managed to grow into adulthood seeing their past through rose-colored lenses. When he'd finally learned the truth—that

Tamara's abandonment was motivated by cold calculation and not some claptrap about being unable to provide for her children—he'd suffered. At least for a while. Dak did "Live and let live" as well as Florida did "Vengeance is mine."

Tamara turned a slow circle, taking in the rich leather of the Manhattan sofa, club chair, and ottoman, as well as the Chihuly glass sculpture Daniel had bought at an art auction last year, an engagement present that cost more than her car. Throwing a rainbow onto the floor, it stood on a pedestal next to the native-stone fireplace. A collection of Willow Tree angels gathered near one end of the mahogany mantel; a contemporary original acrylic blossomed on the wall above them.

"You've done well."

"Yes." Florida grasped her arms tighter, glad Missouri was still at the swimming pool with Joey, and that Julius, Cowboy's once best friend and now Dak and Florida's surrogate grandparent, was asleep in the suite of rooms Dak had built beyond the kitchen when the old mechanic had become confined to a wheelchair. They wouldn't be witness to the violence pulsing under her skin.

"What do you want?"

"I don't want anything—"

. . . Florida's eyes rolled . . .

"Except to see you."

. . . so far back in her head they almost got lost.

Dropping her Dooney & Bourke purse—a knockoff, Florida noted from the stitching—on the sofa, Tamara lowered herself beside it before Florida could protest. She crossed her legs, straightened the crease of her white pants, polyester masquerading as linen, and dipped into her purse. When Tamara bent her head, Florida saw her hair had thinned. She did the math; Tamara was hovering somewhere past seventy.

And the last time Florida had seen her, Tamara would have been younger than Florida was now. A number of emotions churned, none of them pretty. Pity wasn't among them. "Right."

"No, really." Tamara straightened, a long cigarette in one hand, a lighter in the other. Of course, she wouldn't ask.

"No smoking." Not just because she didn't like it, but Julius had an oxygen tank. "Feel free to step out on the porch."

Undoubtedly realizing the door would be locked behind her, Tamara shrugged and tucked the cigarette back. There was a beat of silence. "What if I said I was dying?"

"Are you?"

"No."

"That's too bad."

That finally got a reaction. Her mother's eyes flew to hers. She felt a jolt at her callousness herself. Well, what in hell's bells did they both expect?

Then Tamara laughed. Florida remembered that laugh. Breathy, like butterflies winging in the breeze. But this time it ended in a cough. When Tamara recovered, she continued to stare up at her daughter, a smile curving her lips. "You're right. I shouldn't expect—nor do I deserve—anything from you. I'm here to say sorry, before I really do pass into the great beyond. Bound to happen sooner or later." She shrugged again. "Probably sooner."

"I won't forgive you." There was no heat to it. She'd simply stated a fact, like the sun sets in the west.

"I don't expect forgiveness."

"Then what do you expect? Or, rather, *how much*?"

Tamara didn't answer. Her gaze roved Florida's face. "You're beautiful."

"I know."

"Like I am. *Was*. And I hear you have a daughter." Tamara smiled, this time without cynicism. "I have a granddaughter, imagine that. *Missouri*."

Florida suddenly regretted that a burst of postpartum insanity at seeing her newborn had led her to name the child the same way her mother had named her and Dakota. "Let's not get sappy. It's an accident of blood. You don't know her. You *won't* know her."

The smile twisted. "Dakota told me she was a *planned* baby."

Dak told her? Florida flushed, anger melting the ice in her veins. The mother that had abandoned them had shown up at his door and he'd invited her in for coffee and sugar cakes and a bit of chit-chat about the family history? While she was overjoyed to have Missouri, that episode of her life wasn't one she wanted broadcast. Especially to their mother.

"Yes," Tamara continued. "Seems we share more than the color of our eyes, don't we? We share a parallel history."

And it seemed Dak hadn't left out any details. She wanted to smack Tamara. No . . . she wanted to smack Dak.

Ten years ago, Florida had purposely seduced her then boss, bank president Stanley Addams III, on the verge of his second marriage, knowing it likely she'd end up pregnant. Desperately *wanting* to end up pregnant because she desperately wanted Stan. The part of her plan where she got pregnant had worked; the part where Stan flew back to her arms hadn't. He'd married Serena Simpson. Florida had borne Missouri.

After Missouri had been conceived, Florida had discovered that, years before, Tamara had used the exact same ruse on Dak's father. Not such a huge coincidence, considering that for ages idiot women like she'd once been—and like her mother undoubtedly still was—had tried to use pregnancy to entrap some man.

But in one of those cosmic jokes that always makes you wonder what kind of sick sense of humor God really has, there had been another outlandish similarity.

Florida had seduced Stan. Just like Florida's mother had once seduced Stan's father. No, no, *no* . . . not resulting in Stan—thank God for small favors—but in her half brother, Dakota.

Stan's father, S.R. Addams, was now long deceased, gone in Stan's early adolescence, and probably rolling in his grave from the confusion of trying to keep the whole story straight.

The unholy connection between their actions still appalled Florida even more than what either of them had done. "I was young and stupid."

"So was I."

"But there's a difference."

"How so?"

"When my plan didn't work, I didn't extort money from Stan like you did from his father. And I didn't dump Missouri on somebody else before I ran off to God knows where in tarnation. I stayed the course. I *wanted* to stay the course. You didn't." Arms still crossed, Florida dug her fingernails into her skin. She'd come a long way from that bewildered and scared little girl. But it still hurt. It would always hurt. "And I didn't stay silent for nearly three decades. No letters. No phone calls. Not even a God-falutin-damned post-card. In short I wasn't—I'm not—a coldhearted bitch. So whatever you want, you aren't finding it here. Get out of my house. Get out and stay—"

"Dakota's house."

"What?"

"This is your brother's house. At least that's what he told me."

Tamara was right. But what in the devil did that have to do with anything? As business had blossomed, Florida had taken over every expense associated with the house, although the title remained in her brother's name. It was all one property with the house next door.

"A technicality. So what?"

"So, he said I could stay here. After you get married and move, of course."

"Dak said—? I don't believe you."

Tamara shrugged. Reaching into her purse, she drew out the cigarette again and this time she lit it. "Go ask him."

"Oh, you bet I will." And then she'd kill him.

But first things first. She advanced on her mother, plucked the cigarette out of her fingers, turned, and stalked through the door. "Y'all stay put," she ordered over her shoulder.

She threw the cigarette into a puddle of water left when Julius had watered the pots of impatiens anchoring each corner of the front porch this morning. *Her* impatiens. *Her* front porch. Her heels almost punched holes in the concrete as she crossed the breezeway that connected her brother's house with hers.

Hers.

She didn't care whose name was on the title— there was no way Tamara was moving in, before she left, after she left, or when hell froze over.

She threw open the door to Alcea and Dak's kitchen, a long room lined with no-nonsense stainless steel that reflected the light from a bank of windows overlooking a broad deck attached to the back and shaded by silver maples.

At the counter, Alcea turned around. "Florida! You scared the crap out of me." She brushed pale hair out of her dark eyes. A couple of years ago, when she'd reached forty-five, Alcea had cut her hair into short curls that set off her fine bone structure. She wore the silver that now threaded the gold with the same ease with which she'd don a tiara. "Have a seat."

She motioned at a scarred oak table holding its own in the contemporary atmosphere. After Alcea's folks had moved from their sprawling bungalow on Maple Woods Drive to a retirement community southwest of town, Alcea had co-opted their table, the one where her family had once gathered for boisterous meals and infamous family meetings.

"No, thanks." Florida moved toward the doorway on the far side of the kitchen that opened to the back stairs.

Alcea shrugged. "Then have a scone." Near her elbow was a tray of the Blueberry Bright Scones that had helped make the business they ran together a regional success. Alcea's recipes combined with Florida's acumen had grown Cordelia's Peg O' My Heart Café and Bakery into a must-stop for the tourist trade that trundled through town on their way to the lake region farther south; they also provided the primary attractions for the franchise arm that Florida had launched.

When she bypassed the scones, as well, Alcea frowned. "What's wrong?"

Florida paused at the doorway. "Don't give me that innocent look. You know damn well what's wrong." Turning away from Alcea, she hollered into the stairwell. "Dakota Jones! Prepare to meet your Maker!"

Chapter 2

But Dakota had vamoosed.

"He drove the Jeep off into the hills some-where," Alcea said, busying herself with emptying the scones onto a cooling rack. Her voice was calm, her movements steady, but she kept her eyes averted. "You know him. Part of his creative process."

"Bull-honkey." While she understood the lengthy research trip Dak took each fall with Alcea in preparation for writing another *Road* book, she scoffed at Alcea's claims that Dak's solitary sojourns into the hills were part of his artistic temperament. "It's not creative process. It's that fat stripe of yellow that runs down his back whenever he has to deal with anything he doesn't like."

Ignoring the scones, Florida stepped to a window that looked out to the driveway between their houses. Not that she didn't trust her best friend, but she didn't trust her best friend. Alcea had a strong will, but an even stronger love for Florida's half brother. But Alcea wasn't lying. Florida had raced over so fast, she hadn't noticed. Dak's Jeep was gone.

"What do you know about Tamara popping up on my doorstep?"

Still that avoidance. "Why, I—" The phone rang, and Alcea snatched it up. "Mother!" she said into the receiver with far more enthusiasm than Florida had ever seen Alcea give Zinnia O'Malley. "Mother," she mouthed at Florida in case she hadn't caught it the first time.

Florida sighed. Zinnia could talk paint off siding; there was no such thing as a short conversation where the matriarch of the O'Malley clan was concerned. And no getting information out of Alcea if she didn't want to give it.

Besides, it wasn't Alcea she wanted to rake over the coals; it was Dakota.

Frustrated to near popping, she returned home, each footfall flashing with a different emotion: hurt, resentment, anger, rejection. And relief when she saw the Ford Focus was gone. Forever, she hoped, although she thought it unlikely. If Tamara wanted money—

Good God, she'd left her alone with the Chihuly. Picking up the pace, she yanked open the door and hurried to the great room, pulling up short in relief. The glass sculpture still gleamed on its pedestal. Thank God. Daniel would skin her alive if anything happened to the thing.

Shit. *Daniel.*

She checked her watch. He'd arrive for the weekend in only a few hours. By now, he would have already stepped out of his office and onto the private plane that would carry him to Sedalia, the nearest town with an airstrip. It was too late to call and beg off, even if she could think of a reason that would make sense. Besides, she'd just be postponing the inevitable. She'd need to tell him about her mother—not just part of the story, like she had before, but all of it. *Damn* Tamara. And damn Dak.

Plucking anger out of the stew in her head, she used it to propel her activities for the next few hours, aiming to keep to the schedule she'd planned, hoping busyness would barricade Tamara back in the farthest corner of her mind, where she usually lodged. But even through a stint in her upstairs office answering business e-mails and preparing bulk orders for the franchisees, a sortie to the laundry room to make sure Missouri had clean leotards for ballet tomorrow, and a flurry in the kitchen, where she prepared an early supper for Julius—thank God he liked grilled cheese, which, along with fried eggs and hamburgers, about rounded out her culinary expertise—Tamara refused to stay put.

As she worked, Florida kept an eye out for Dak. But, smart man, he stayed missing. His Jeep finally pulled into the drive—just moments before Daniel was due to arrive on her doorstep. She doubted the timing was coincidental. Dak knew Daniel was always prompt. Seriously prompt. Moguling required an efficient schedule and Daniel maintained a strict one. It didn't have room for Prodigal Mothers and backstabbing half brothers, nor did she want it to. She didn't want her past intruding on her new life. Intruding on Daniel. It was the reason she'd shared only selected samples of her history with him.

And now she'd have to serve up the whole meal. Dammit.

When the doorbell rang, she greeted Daniel with a measure of calm she wasn't feeling, despite having grabbed a brief soak in the Jacuzzi tub that dominated her bathroom, an oasis of taupe tile and black marble and fluffy Egyptian-cotton towels adjoining her bedroom. Not wanting him to sense anything out of the ordinary, she was now jasmine-spritzed, hair-styled, legs-shaved, and wearing a flirty Maggy London dress cinched at the waist, bare-shouldered, and cut down to there. She'd present Tamara's return with nonchalance. Nothing he had to bother his head about. Nothing *she* had to bother *her* head about. Even if her head had other ideas.

"Hey there." She moved back to let him in.

As usual, after his flight landed, he'd driven the near-fifty miles from Sedalia to Cordelia in the Lincoln Town Car he normally rented. He'd unlatched his cuffs and rolled up his sleeves, but he was far from rumpled. Daniel didn't do rumpled. His trousers still held a sharp crease, his shoes a high polish. His golf-course-tanned forearms glinted with gold that matched the wavy hair on his head and an even golder Rolex, only adding to an air of casual elegance.

He smiled, revealing the perfect teeth that only money could buy. "Mmm. You look great." As soon as the door had shut, he pulled her against him and kissed her thoroughly, before drawing back and giving the air an appreciative sniff. "Smells like you've outdone yourself."

The house was filled with the heavenly scent of chicken breasts stuffed with mushroom caps, cheeses, shallots, and other good stuff she hadn't—actually couldn't have—identified.

"Actually, Alcea did all the outdoing." She might shave the truth by omission, but she'd never led him to believe she was Emeril. The deception would have been way too hard to maintain. "I swiped the casserole from Peg O' My Heart."

She led the way to the kitchen, a sleek Scandinavian affair of blond wood and black granite. He followed her like a hound on scent, accepting the martini she handed him with a satisfied sigh. She watched him with equal satisfaction. So far, so good. The Stepford-wife effect was intentional, designed to lull him while she filled in the missing pieces of her past.

It wasn't that Tamara's tale was so sordid, really. It was just . . . well, since their engagement, she'd been pinching herself at her good fortune, afraid he'd wake up one morning and change his mind. In her experience, the people you counted on didn't always stick around.

"So." Daniel palmed some nuts from a bowl on the counter and leaned back against it, crossing his long legs at the ankle. "What's up in your world?"

Well. No time like the present. Taking a gulp of her martini, she dived in, her voice casual. "You'll never guess who showed up on my doorstep today. . . ."

Turning her back to pull the chicken from the oven, she proceeded to stumble through a tangle of explanations. All the while, Daniel watched her, his gaze growing sharper until it had the same unblinking intensity he'd give a minion under the gun.

Really, he did know a lot about her past—the worst bits, in fact. He knew she'd been a near orphan from an early age, and he knew she'd once lured Stan into her bed with the hopes of conceiving a baby. (A tidbit she hadn't been thrilled to share, but Grandpa hadn't raised a fool. In a town like Cordelia, it would have been only a matter of time before someone let news of her long-ago affair with Stan fall into his ears if she didn't drop it there first.)

The rest of it . . . she hadn't bothered to explain the convoluted relationships that existed among her family. He didn't know that the same man who had begotten her half brother, Dakota, had also sired her ex-lover Stan, the father of her own daughter. Different mothers. Same father. Dak and Stan had formed a casual friendship since finding out they were half brothers a decade ago, but treated their relationship more like a genetic accident than anything else. They rarely brought it up. She never brought it up. And even the normally loose-lipped townsfolk hardly thought it worth a mention.

Partly because it was old news. Partly because it was a brain bender to find a coherent explanation. But mostly because all that siring and begetting through two generations made the passel of them sound uncomfortably akin to *The Dukes of Hazzard*.

A town had to have its pride.

But now that Tamara was back, Daniel was bound to encounter renewed gossip about her sooner or later—if not the woman herself; Florida needed to sully hers.

"So," she concluded, throwing a salad together in a teak bowl with more bustling than was needed, feeling she'd overdone the explanation part, neglected the coherence part, and totally failed in making her family seem more than the punch line of an Ozarks joke, "Stan and Dak are half brothers. One legitimate, one not. Skip to the next generation and Stan has two daughters that are half sisters: Kathleen is legitimate, the result of his first marriage, while Missouri is mine and—" Her tongue tripped on *illegitimate*.

But Daniel wasn't one to quibble over niceties. "Illegitimate," he completed.

She bristled. The word was diminishing. Missouri had never been labeled and Florida didn't want to start now. Since the day Missouri had been born, she'd been embraced not only by her half sister, Kathleen, sixteen years her senior, but even by Kathleen's mother . . .

Who just happened to be Alcea. Yep, Stan's ex-wife. And now her best friend.

Taking a gander at Daniel's expression, she knew he'd cycled through the same set of facts. Florida stopped bristling. He wasn't thinking *Dukes of Hazzard*. He was thinking *Deliverance*.

"Why didn't you mention this before?"

She licked her lips. She *should* have mentioned it before. She sorted through various excuses: shame, denial. Fear that if he learned about these shenanigans, coming on top of the shenanigans he already knew about, he'd look at her exactly like he was looking at her now?

She turned back to the chicken, added serving utensils, and deposited the dish into a wicker carrier for its trip to the table. "Until Tamara turned up, it was just . . . family trivia."

"Trivia? Florida, this woman could make trouble. The press could have a field day with that kind of background."

She barely withheld a snort. "She's not going to sell our story." Daniel Davenport and Florida Jones weren't the stuff of *The National Enquirer*, no matter what Daniel might hope. But it was likely wiser not to point that out. "She just wants to make amends."

Not believing it for a second, but wanting the subject closed, she stepped past him, carrying the chicken.

Daniel did snort. "Right. When she heard about your engagement, she undoubtedly decided to see if she could hop on the gravy train."

Exactly what she'd thought. But at his words, the bristles popped back out. It'd be nice if Daniel would focus more on the jolt Tamara's return had given her system rather than on what demands her mother might make of his fortune. "If that was the case, she would have hopped on Dak's a long time ago."

"She probably doesn't know the extent of Dakota's celebrity. Until recently, he's operated under the radar."

True. Dak aimed for low-key as much as Daniel sought high profile. Her half brother had always used a pen name, but in the age of the Internet, he'd eventually been uncovered. In fact, the revelation had caused a bit of a stir because of his best-selling status. One that his publisher, seeking to bolster sales in a soft market, now insisted he use to his advantage on a publicity tour or he might just find himself without a contract. Liking the laid-back lifestyle publishing had allowed him, Dak had reluctantly gone along.

Daniel picked a carrot out of the salad and

munched. "Hmm. Two birds with one stone. I imagine that's what she was thinking."

Again, she agreed, but a thought flashed into her head. Who cared what Tamara was thinking? Daniel should be thinking about her, not her mother.

Suddenly needing his attention—and knowing just how to get it—she paused in front of him, plucked the carrot out of his mouth, and slid her arms around his waist, tilting her face up to his. "Let's not talk about her. Let's talk about us," she murmured.

He was still frowning somewhere over her head. "I wonder if she'll want to be bought off or—"

"Daniel." Her voice was sharp. She softened things by pressing against him, relieved when she felt him growing hard.

"Hmm." He finally looked down and smiled. "What do you want to talk about? This?" He dipped his head to nuzzle her neck. "Or this? . . ." His hand cupped a breast.

Kissing him, she warmed to his touch, but thinking that Julius or Missouri might wander in, she drew back. But not too far back. "How about our wedding plans?" She traced his lips with her finger. "Have you heard anything from Jenna lately?"

Jenna was the wedding planner Daniel had hired. They'd made a decision to limit their list to their nearest and dearest. By a stretch of the

definition, Florida's side of the aisle would number about sixty. Daniel's would populate Chicago.
So he was footing the bill. No fool she, Jenna always consulted with Daniel first. Accustomed to
making rapid-fire decisions, the groom often forgot to consult the bride. And given that Jenna had
dreams of gold and Daniel dreams of grandeur,
the two of them alone were a sometimes lethal
combination. So far, the bride had deflected plans
to have peacocks wandering among the guests at
the reception and an orchestra the size of a
battalion.

"Almost forgot," Daniel said, capturing her
hand and kissing her fingertips. "She wants us to
pose for more pictures. Let Rita know your schedule next week. She'll set it up." Rita was Daniel's
executive secretary.

Still distracted by her hormones, she was watching his mouth. It was an amazing mouth. It could
do amazing things. "More pictures?" she murmured. "For what?"

"The ice sculpture."

Her mind made connections and her hormones
stilled. "Of us?"

"Of course. What else?"

She examined his expression for humor and
didn't see any. "Swans?" she said hopefully. "A
heart?" Even cupid peeing into the punch bowl
would be preferable to their likeness carved in ice.
Look up *tacky as all get-out* and you'd see just what
she meant.

"Everyone does that. This will be unique."

She couldn't quibble with that.

"Do we have to invite her?" Daniel asked.

She didn't hear him. She was consumed by a vision of her iced image . . . melting. By the end of the reception, she'd look as old as she was beginning to feel. "Huh?"

"Your mother," Daniel said impatiently. "Do we have to invite her?"

"No!" The mention of Tamara woke her like a slap. "Make that a *hell*, no."

"Good. C'mere." Daniel pulled her against him again.

His kiss was thorough, his embrace strong, and things grew heated as they usually did. His hands slid over her back and cupped her buttocks until she fit snugly against his hardness. Dropping her head back, she gave his lips access to the plunge of her bodice. He nuzzled the material aside and everything else started to fade from her head. Julius. Missouri. Tamara. . . . His tongue grazed a nipple. . . . Ice sculptures. She shivered. He moaned. And she shivered again. It was archaic, she knew, but having this kind of power over a powerful man was more of an aphrodisiac than a truckload of oysters. It also gave her a cheap thrill because Daniel was a good six years younger than she was.

Not that a hint of inexperience showed. Probably because he wasn't. His tongue traced a line from her cleavage up to her ear. His fingers slowly gathered up the skirt of her dress until he could slip his hands into the back of her panties. Her breath coming lickety-split, she managed to hang on to a thread of decency and turned slightly to put his back to the door, effectively hiding her from intrusion.

Just as she'd thoroughly relaxed, anticipating the oblivion brought by a new high (the counter), he murmured into her neck, "It'll be all right, you know. Your mother can't touch me."

Me again.

Ardor dampened, she gently pushed him away. "Missouri might come in, and the chicken's getting cold."

He frowned. "What's with you?"

She didn't wonder at his disgruntlement. He understood—at least, he'd say he understood—why she'd make Missouri a priority. But chicken? Why was it men—especially the self-made kind—seemed to have a decided ignorance of the nuances of sensitivity?

In any case, Missouri chose that moment to burst through the door, making the point for her. A nine-year-old windmill of knees, elbows, and wet, tangled hair, her daughter had Stan's coloring—the dark hair, the dark eyes, the tawny skin—and Florida's wide smile.

Which faded as she took in her mother's companion. "Hi, Daniel."

"Hello, Missouri."

As usual, they were polite. And that was about as good as it got. Florida pardoned Daniel on the grounds that he'd spent no time at all around children. And she pardoned Missouri because . . . well, just because. She had hopes that once they were all under one roof, familiarity would breed affection, not contempt.

Duty completed, Missouri skipped over to the table and peered dubiously at the chicken. "Can I have grilled cheese?"

"We want you to eat with us." She smiled at Daniel, hoping he'd second the motion.

Missouri switched her dubious gaze to Daniel. "No, you don't," she decided. She looked back at her mother, all soft puppy eyes. "Grilled cheese? Puh-lease?"

"Daniel," Florida said lightly, hating that she had to say anything at all, "tell her how much we'd like to have her join us."

"Have you seen that sweatband I bought Daddy? I need to wrap it. His birthday's today, remember?" Missouri angled her eyes at Daniel, then away.

Well, that tore it. Daniel went stiff and Florida sighed. No matter how much—and in what ways—Florida reassured him, Daniel still got uptight over her past relationship with Stan. Missouri knew exactly what buttons to push.

"I remember," she said, giving Missouri a Look. She'd never forgotten Stan's birthday once in the years since their affair, but for the last two, she'd bought him nothing in deference to Daniel's sensitivity. Sometimes she wished her fiancé had just a little more maturity. "And you know right where it is. On your dresser."

Having saved up her allowance to buy Stan a fluorescent orange sweatband he could wear jogging at night, Missouri had hardly let it out of her sight.

"Oh, yeah." All innocence, Missouri raised her eyes to her mother's. "Grilled cheese?"

"Please," Daniel added, with a pleasant smile and gritted teeth.

"Oh, all right."

Missouri whooped and ran off to find Julius. Now disgruntled herself—at Missouri, at Daniel, and at herself because she'd just been played by them both—Florida reached into the dishwasher for the griddle. "Daniel, once we're married, I want us to be a family."

"Missouri already has a father."

"You know what I mean."

"We will be," Daniel said. "Just not right now." He reached for her again.

Sidestepping, she tossed his words back. "Not right now." Giving him a playful smile to hide her pique, she ran a hand along his cheek. "But I promise, I'll make it all up to you later."

But later that night, for the first time in their relationship, she didn't.

Just as they'd done every Friday night whenever Daniel came to Cordelia, they finished supper, made sure Julius and Missouri were settled in for the evening at a card table with one of the model-car kits the old man loved, asked Alcea to keep an eye on things, then went out. *Out* being only as far as the Cordelia Sleep Inn.

And just like on every other Friday night, Daniel's motel room door had barely closed behind them before he was hauling her against him, one hand twining into her hair to pull her head back so his mouth could cover hers, the other hand freely roaming her body. She met his urgency with her own, her breath rasping, her hands loosening his top buttons, his belt, freeing his shirt to push it up. He took it the rest of the way, yanking it off his head and tossing it aside before curling his fingers around the strap of her dress to bare a shoulder. Fabric ripped. The sound fueled his impatience. Wrenching down her bodice, he freed a breast. Finger and thumb toying with a nipple, he captured her mouth again and they thudded back against the door. His other hand ran up her inner thigh until he could push her panties aside to find the softness between her legs. She moaned. He slid to his knees. She panted. He nuzzled. Seconds later, she came.

He rose to tear off the rest of her clothes while she shoved at his; then they tumbled naked onto the bed, where she stoked his fires but good. But she couldn't fan her own into flames anymore. Thoughts of Missouri, of the small scene before supper, and of Tamara all numbed her nerve endings. As he slipped inside her, she stared up at the ceiling, made a gasp here, a moan there, and he finally shuddered and rolled off.

She'd thought she'd faked things pretty well, but she could see a frown in his eyes—maybe even disappointment—before he cuddled her against him. She opened her mouth on an excuse, but his breathing had already settled into a steady rhythm. Her mouth closed. Daniel wasn't one for talk postlovemaking. He was a true time-and-place-for-everything kind of guy.

Wishing he were more inclined to sweet nothings, she waited a few beats, then gently rolled out of the bed so she could go home to her own. Also on par for Friday nights. Daniel always objected, but while Julius would move the moon for Missouri, what he couldn't move was himself up the stairs to her daughter's room. She never left them alone very long. And never overnight.

Besides, there was a matter of pretenses. Not that important to her, but they were to Joey Norsworthy's mother. Within three days of the last time Florida had failed to pick up her Saturday paper from the front walk before eight, her across-the-street neighbor had lent her a book: *Parenting Children into Moral Maturity*. Barb Norsworthy was a pill.

Florida collected her clothing from the floor and her purse from a chair, and slipped into the bathroom. Closing the door, she flipped on the light and blinked at the harridan with the smeared makeup and ratted hair who looked back from the mirror. Another good reason to leave. Before she scared Daniel out of his ever-lovin' skin.

Instead of making her smile, the thought prodded a worry that had gotten increasingly twitchy as the wedding grew closer.

Ever since they'd met, heat had been a constant by-product of her relationship with Daniel. Intro-

duced at a cocktail reception for an ABWA confer-
ence, "Success Strategies for Entrepreneurs," at
the Hotel Davenport KC—she, a guest; he, the
keynote speaker (as well as the owner of the
hotel)—they'd been shaking hands in the Blue
Ballroom at six. By midnight, they'd been ensconced in the penthouse suite, amazing each
other with their sexual gymnastics. Normally,
she'd said, she wasn't that hasty. Usually, he'd
said, he wasn't, either. But she'd jumped on those
boyish good looks coupled with that aura of
power. And he'd jumped on the Anne Klein chif-
fon she'd just splurged for at Nordstrom.

Now, in the motel bathroom, she pulled her
Maggy London dress over her head and examined
the tear at the shoulder. The Anne Klein had been
the first dress he'd ruined; the Maggy London the
latest. In between, there'd been quite a few more.
Although a few hours lay between his Mission
Hills home in Kansas City and her renovated garage in Cordelia, they managed to spend most
weekends together, usually alternating between
KC and Cordelia, but occasionally taking his private plane to St. Louis or Minneapolis or Tulsa.
Not top-drawer destinations, but as each was
seeded with one of the Hotel Davenports that
were rooting in the region, there was nothing low-
brow about the treatment they received. And
nothing tired about the passion they shared.

Until tonight.

She looked back into the mirror and saw worry
lines creasing her brow. She rubbed them away

with her fingers. Enough of that. What had happened was completely understandable. Only a matter of time, after all, before the fireworks failed to ignite. It was only once, and fortunately, she'd been the only one who had failed to launch. But . . .

But once she was living under Daniel's roof, once familiarity settled in, would the flames be banked?

The worry lines returned, this time disappearing when she snapped off the light. But the concern followed her home and disturbed her dreams. She dropped off only as dawn neared.

When she opened her eyes again, it was closing in on eight, a late hour for her. Just as though she'd never fallen asleep at all, thoughts rushed back in. Daniel. The wedding. Tamara.

Groaning, she threw back the covers. One thorny problem at a time was enough. Last night's performance with Daniel was an aberration. Her fears of future problems were just prewedding jitters. The ice sculptures could wait (boy, could they wait). She'd deal with Tamara first—or, rather, with her half brother. Then *he* could deal with Tamara.

After a quick shower, she threw on white shorts and a shirt appliquéd with bright flowers, paid some attention to her makeup and hair, then went to check on the rest of the household. Daniel reserved Saturday mornings for business with his laptop before freeing the afternoon for her, so she wouldn't see him till later.

A glance into Julius's suite of rooms at the rear of the house revealed a mug rinsed and upside-down on the drainer in the tiny kitchenette, and a bed with neatly tucked corners, but no Julius. Although he functioned from a wheelchair and with only one fully usable hand, the other having been injured long ago in a tussle with an engine block, he took care of his own needs as much as he could.

Out in the great room, Missouri sat on the otto-man in front of a television set tuned to cartoons. A bowl with an inch of milk and a few Cheerios floating on top sat next to feet clad in Mary Jane Crocs—purple, with her name markered on the bottom, since she usually kicked them off wher-ever she was. The rest of her slight frame was sheathed in the pink leotard she wore to Miss Tal-lant's (no joke) School of Dance on Saturday mornings. Her dark hair had been pulled into a scrunchie, forming a none-too-neat knot on top of her head. Florida would bet she hadn't brushed it first.

Florida gave a lopsided smile. These days her daughter seesawed between frilly femininity—the ballet lessons and pink leotards and occasional brush with lipstick—and tomboyish abandon—hair a continual tangle, escapades with Joey. On occasion, a *heart-stopping* escapade with Joey. Last week they'd gotten caught using a fraying rope swing—forget the footbridge, way too tame—over Navajo Creek from the woody bank on one side to a bump of an island in the middle that held a tumbledown duck blind no longer in use. *Creek* was a misnomer, considering the stream was more rock than water in summer. She shuddered thinking about what could have happened if the rope had broken.

As Florida paused at her daughter's side, Missouri tipped up her face. In the shadows that moved beneath the high cheekbones she'd bequeathed to her daughter, she caught a glimpse of Tamara in her face. She pushed away the thought and dropped a kiss on Missouri's nose. She would *not* think of her mother while looking at her own daughter. "Where's Julius, hon?"

"He went with Uncle Dak to Peg's."

Dang. Dak had effectively stayed his execution again. On Saturday morning, Peg O' My Heart would be packed. Throughout the weekend, there was steady traffic through Cordelia as out-of-towners motored to vacation homes in the lake regions to the south. A good percentage of them stopped at Peg's to stock up on Tropical Blend Muffins and Blueberry Bright Scones and mouthwatering brownies for the weekend.

And mornings were busiest. Along with the tourists, locals would stuff the red vinyl booths. Paddy O'Neill, grizzled owner of O'Neill's Emporium; Erik Olausson, the Swedish yardman with a tuft of hair as fine as a dandelion at seed; and erstwhile postmen Freddie and Eddie Steeplemier

would be playing sentry in their usual booth—
the one with the sweeping view of the windows
fronting Main, the entrance, and everything in between. The oldsters spent so much time planted
in Peg's that Florida was tempted to charge them
rent. The quartet made it their life's mission to
chew over every scrap of gossip with the same
thoroughness they gave the blue plate specials.
Then they'd serve it up on their afternoon rounds.
Dak knew she wouldn't dare raise her bloomers
in there.

Well, first things first. She needed to drive Missouri to lessons anyway; she'd confront Dak later.
But just as she'd picked up her car keys from the
occasional table near the stairs that held a telephone and notepads, a horn honked out front.

Missouri jumped up. "There's Joey."

"Hold on there. What about ballet?"

"Joey's mom said she'd take us."

"*Us?*"

"Yeah." Missouri threw her gym bag over her
shoulder. "Joey signed up for ballet last week."

It *was* true love. Amused, Florida dropped her
keys into her pocket and followed Missouri out to
the front porch. It was another hot day. A few
coral roses were tentatively opening in a burst of
sun near the drive, but the blooms of spring had
long since given in to the heavy hand of summer.

"Do you have your dancing slippers? Your dad
said he'd pick you up. Do you have his present?"

"In my bag. *With* my slippers."

"Don't forget and traipse off somewhere else."

"I won't."

"Especially not the park."

Tucked back into the woods at the rear of Memorial Park, Navajo Creek meandered down the hill to feed the park's duck pond before wandering off into greener pastures. Since Joey and Missouri's Tarzan and Jane imitation, they weren't permitted to play there without supervision.

"I *know*. I'll come right home." Missouri's tone said she thought her mother a hopeless neurotic. "I *want* to come right home," she added. "Aunt Alcea's baking cookies."

Aunt Alcea's cookies were a powerful draw, but her daughter also had a powerful short memory. "Well, I mean it."

As she hopped down the stairs, Missouri's answer was a big sigh. Florida stood at the top, arms crossed, as her daughter got into the backseat next to Joey. Even from here, she could see the adoring look Joey bestowed on her daughter. And the long-suffering one on Barb Norsworthy's face. Barb wasn't as infatuated with Missouri's charms as her son.

The Norsworthys had moved to Cordelia last year—Jim Norsworthy had been a management transfer from somewhere up north to PicNic Poultry Processing Plant outside Cordelia. Barb Norsworthy was an accountant at the H&R Block outlet next to the bank on the square. But despite their short tenure in Cordelia, it was long enough to pick up all the local lore. Florida wasn't sure if Barb's less-than-enthusiastic attitude toward Missouri was due to the girl's less-than-blue-blooded lineage or to Barb's conviction that any prank the kids pulled must be Missouri's fault.

Barb Norsworthy flapped a hand at her as she pulled out of the drive. Bemused, Florida waved back. Since the Navajo Creek incident, Barb's demeanor had been decidedly cold; looked like a thaw had finally set in. Well, just wait until she got a load of the latest addition to the family.

Florida watched the car drive off, smiling as Missouri made a goofy face at her out the window. As she turned to go inside, sadness swept through her: Why had her own mother purposely missed out on moments like this?

She shoved the thought away, and took refuge in activity—the in-basket was never empty— checking periodically to see if Dak had returned. More laundry went into the washer. The kitchen floor got swabbed. Then she settled into her home office and flipped on the computer. She'd complete the bulk orders she needed to make for Peg's franchisees, a number somewhere so far below McDonald's you couldn't see there from here, but healthy enough now that royalty payments had finally started outstripping their outlays, thank the heavens.

She and Alcea had sunk a ton of money into the start-up of the franchise business not long after Missouri was born. Okay, it had mostly been Dak's money with an assist from Missouri's father. With an eye for a good deal, Stan had not only arranged a loan for them before he'd left the bank to start his own business; he'd invested some of his own money, as well. His vote of confidence had fueled her own. But money and confidence weren't the whole ball game. God, they'd worked like Trojans those first few years. Still did, but most of the work had now fallen into routine.

And routine being what it was, while she waited for the PC to come alive, newly awakened memories took advantage and crowded back in.

Resting her chin in her hand, she stared out the window. Her office faced east just shy of where Main slid into highway that twisted up into the hills. In the distance, the mist had burned off, leaving the dark green of the woods etched against a sky faded from too much sun.

Whether the view was dulled by summer's sun or winter's gloom, or bright with spring's hope or fall's farewell, she loved it. She'd miss it. And she'd miss Cordelia. Especially Peg O' My Heart Café and Bakery, from its nosy patrons to its signature orange and red uniforms (which should have looked ghastly but somehow didn't).

After she moved to Kansas City, she'd continue to run the franchise operation, but the flagship store would rest entirely in Alcea's hands. Except for a mental math block that contracting a bookkeeper would solve, Alcea was beyond competent, a fact that should make leaving easier, but didn't. The original Peg O' My Heart was more than a hometown diner. It had been Florida's inheritance.

Her grandpa's longtime paramour, Peg, the original owner and childless—always waiting for Cowboy to come up to a mark he couldn't reach again after his wife had left him—had willed the place to Florida. The place was all Florida had left of Peg. Special because Peg had been more mother to her than . . .

. . . her own mother.

She shifted in her seat, memories suddenly sharp and painful. The first time she'd seen Cowboy's house, it had been a day like this—so hot and humid that her hair was a halo of frizz, refusing to surrender to the restraints of pigtails. But the atmosphere had weighed on her less than the heaviness in her heart.

As Tamara had driven her children to Cordelia, in a rattletrap car she'd borrowed from one of her commune friends, she hadn't uttered a word about leaving them behind. But somehow six-year-old Florida had sensed this time was different from the other times when they'd packed up and moved on. Maybe it had been something to do with the pinched look around her mother's mouth—the kind of look she sometimes saw on Missouri's face. The one that said she knew what she was about to do was wrong, but she was determined to do it anyway. The image was clear—more clear than the montage from the first years of her life, a series of different scenery, different beds, different people. Dak and Tamara had been her only constants.

And then Tamara had been gone.

Two years later, so had Dakota.

Brilliant, despite an erratic history of home-schooling in the series of scruffy motels and communes and collectives they'd landed in, he'd caught up and then bypassed his Cordelia High peers, graduating with honors and the scholarships his English teacher had sponsored. He'd joined the Ivy League in the East and he hadn't looked back. For twenty years, although he'd kept in touch by letter and later e-mail. Florida hadn't blamed him—while she'd embraced her pain, he'd run from it. It had taken his wife, Alcea—and her daughter, Kathleen—to show him that family ties were worth the occasional knot.

While Dak understood her past anguish far more than anyone else could, except for a brief period at their reunion, they'd never really hashed through their feelings together. He, because he preferred to relegate the past to the past and live in the moment. She, because, at some point during her childhood, she'd carved Tamara out of her heart.

She hadn't wanted to waste one tiny thought on her mother.

She still didn't.

Movement below scattered her reflections. Dak's Jeep bumped into the driveway. Sitting up straight, she watched as he pulled to a stop, got out, and unloaded Julius's wheelchair. Nearing fifty, Dak still cast a lean shadow and still had a full head of dark hair, and still preferred clothing that stopped just this side of aging hippie. Today's glam outfit consisted of fading denims, a black T-shirt, and a favorite pair of Doc Martens.

After he'd unfolded the chair, Dak opened the passenger door and helped Julius out. The old man's hair was a blush where it had once been bright red, his freckles faded into age spots. Congestive heart failure necessitated occasional oxygen cocktails and had turned him frail, his frame no longer filling his overalls, but he could still stand, could even walk if he had some support. And he certainly still had plenty of spirit. As soon as he'd grasped one of the armrests with his one good hand, he shrugged off Dak's continued assistance.

" *'Get thee to a nunnery'!"*

Even through the glass she could hear him. It'd take more than ill health to mute Julius's boom of a voice, which had gotten louder in direct proportion to his failing hearing.

"No contest. *Hamlet,"* Dak replied, also speaking loudly. He stepped back as Julius settled himself into the chair.

"Not *Camelot!"* The old man scoffed. *"Hamlet!"*

Florida mirrored her brother's fond smile. Named for Caesar by a mother who had loved the Bard and read him plays in place of bedtime stories, Julius played Name That Quote with anyone who would play back. Dak was a favorite contestant.

A thought floated through her mind. She couldn't remember Tamara ever reading her anything at all.

Her smile faded. Waiting until she saw Dak return from helping Julius into the house, she set her chin and stood up. It was time to confront her Judas of a brother.

Chapter 3

This time, when Florida threw open the door to her half brother's house, Alcea didn't bother pushing food her direction, just took one look at her face, yelled up the stairs for Dak to come back down, muttered something about needing to get to Peg's, and disappeared through the back door, car keys jangling.

Now who wore the stripe? Yellow-bellied coward. Florida seated herself at the kitchen table and waited, drumming her lacquered nails. Today the kitchen was fragrant with vanilla and cinnamon. A plate of Snickerdoodles rested by a bakery box that undoubtedly held several dozen Alcea had meant to cart to Peg's, but had forgotten in her headlong flight. Alcea did most of her baking in the industrial appliances of the bakery that adjoined the restaurant, but occasionally she'd work her magic here.

A clock on the wall ticked off the seconds with maddening slowness. Just as she was about to rise to do some yelling upstairs herself, she heard Dak's tread on the stairs. Moments later, he appeared in the kitchen. As he moved toward the counter, he raised dark eyebrows at her in inquiry. *Pffbt* . . . like he didn't know what she was there for?

"It's about time y'all came out of hiding."

"Hiding?" Dak picked up a coffeepot and poured two mugs, then fixed her with his gaze. He had a sharp gaze to match a face of shadows and angles that time was carving into even sharper relief. He set a mug in front of her, then took the chair opposite, turning it so he could stretch out his long legs. "What am I hiding from?"

"Me."

He locked his legs at the ankle. "You. Why?"

"Tamara."

"Oh, her." He took a drink.

"Like you forgot. C'mon, Dak. What in blue blazes possessed you to, one, push her over to my house without even warning me—"

"I'd planned to tell you." He set his mug down. "I didn't know that's where she was headed when she left—"

"—and two, tell her about Missouri's paternity—"

Dak raised a brow. "This is Cordelia. It'd only be a matter of time before—"

"—and three, and worst of them all, tell her she could stay at my house!"

His expression stayed reasonable. "Not until after you've moved to Kansas City with Daniel."

"That doesn't matter! It's *my house*, no matter who holds the title. You know how much love and thought I put into it. I don't want her there. I don't want to picture her there. She was never here for us before and now—"

She stopped. The emotion that suddenly crowded her throat made her madder than a wet hen. She didn't want to rehash the past. Not now. Not ever. She'd hashed plenty in the past and she was *over* it, dammit. Done. *Finis!* She just wanted Tamara gone. If Tamara stayed, she'd spoil the wedding. She'd spoil the time that remained to Florida in Cordelia. She'd . . . At the thought of leaving, her tears immediately spilled over. She wanted to go—certainly she did—but she'd grown up here. Her half brother was here, her friends . . . and now her mother, damn her. . . .

She covered her eyes with her hand.

"Ah, Florida." Dak's voice was soft. "I'm sorry. You know me; I don't always think things through . . ."

"You're a big fat lunkhead," Florida said, getting up to grab a Kleenex. She wiped her nose.

". . . but Tamara's getting old."

"No *getting* about it."

"And she wants to make amends."

Florida snorted.

"You're moving out soon, so let her move in. No matter what happened in the past, she's family. We're family. Look on this as an opportunity to heal the past."

Florida snorted louder.

Dak stared at her thoughtfully. She could almost hear the wheels turning as he looked for a way to change her mind. "I know she sucked as a mother. But you're not heartless. If you turned her away, you'd feel guilty." *Not like her.*

He didn't say the words, but the implication was there, the little shit. Dak knew a mission in her life was to be as different from her mother as possible.

"No, I wouldn't."

"Yes, you would."

She abruptly stood up. "Where's the gin?"

A corner of Dak's mouth quirked. "Bit early, don't you think?"

"I don't care how early it is." Florida started rummaging through the cabinets. "And I don't care how Tamara would feel if we booted her out on her heinie." Dak had a point, but she thought she could live life just fine all riddled with guilt.

"She'll help us with Julius after you've left."

"Some help. It won't be long before she's as feeble as he is. Besides, Julius is movin' with me. He doesn't need her." At first Daniel had been reluctant to accept Julius into their household, but he'd eventually relented. She wished she could shake the feeling that his generosity stemmed not from understanding that she could no more leave Julius behind than she could Missouri, but from the realization that in a six-bedroom Mission Hills Tudor and with enough money for round-the-clock help if it ever was needed, he would likely be oblivious to Julius's presence.

Dak was quiet, but she could feel his gaze following her. "But maybe," he finally said, voice soft, "Tamara needs Julius."

Florida went speechless. Julius had been Cowboy's newly hired, still-wet-behind-the-ears mechanic when Tamara was born, and as she'd grown, so had the men's friendship. He'd been there when Cowboy's wife had deserted him, then later his daughter, and finally his health. Along with Peg, Julius had helped raise Florida, helped her tend Cowboy in the months before his death, and mourned with her when Peg had passed on not long after. In his early nineties now, he was the only one left of the trio she'd considered her family.

Her family. Not Tamara's.

"Who the hell cares what she needs?" Florida turned around to glare at Dak. "What is *up* with you? Tamara gave up even the teensiest right to claim us as family a long time ago. I thought you felt the same way."

"Julius wants to make you happy, Florida. He's always wanted to make you happy."

"What in tarnation does that have to do with anything?"

Dak leaned back in his chair. His eyes were an odd shade, shimmering between gray and pale green, sometimes blue. Sea foam that changed with the weather. As, it seemed, did his mind. "He doesn't want to leave Cordelia."

Florida turned her back on him again to rummage anew. She knew Dak was right, but she was hoping that once Julius got to Kansas City, he'd learn to be happy there, as well.

Realizing Dak had dodged her question—and having found nothing more than a bottle of cooking wine—she turned around, determined to force the issue. "How come you're suddenly so reconciled to Tamara? I know before she showed up, you felt the same way I did about her." Or close to it. Her half brother had a tendency to go all woo-woo about life. *Let go. . . . Love what is. . . . Accept what can't be changed. . . .* All that rot. It must be a burden having such a hard time holding a grudge.

Dak looked away. Suddenly suspicious, she frowned. He was always so damned self-assured, never felt a need to explain himself. Yet here he was, avoiding her eyes.

Her own narrowed. "Or was it sudden? It seems you've given this a lot of thought."

Before she could prod further, the back door swung open. Her daughter traipsed in, a few damp locks curling on her forehead. She dragged her bag behind her, as well as her father.

Seeing Florida, Stan halted on the threshold. Even though they saw each other frequently, Stan always looked thrown whenever he encountered her unexpectedly. He wasn't the only one. The sight of him could still give her a twinge.

Just a little twinge, she assured Daniel silently. And not because he was attractive, although he was. Even more so than when they'd had their affair. Time and Serena had influenced him to trade gold chains for a silver watch and occasional understated cuff links; black hair that curled over his collar for a bimonthly trim; and the tropical shirts he'd left open practically to his navel for crisp polos usually paired, as they were today, with Nike track shorts and Air Max running shoes.

But the looks weren't the twinge maker. It was because he was—and always would be—the first big, outsized, colored-by-fantasy love of her life. Despite the fact that when they'd met, he'd been her boss.

And despite the fact that he'd been married.

To Alcea.

(Any wonder Daniel was drawing comparisons to Ozark hillbillies of yore?)

"Happy birthday, a day late," she said. He'd just turned forty-eight.

Just like every year, Stan looked disconcerted that she'd remembered. He shouldn't be. He'd once been the center of her life; she remembered a lot about him. Both good. And bad.

"Thanks." He motioned at the plate of cookies. "Missouri said cookies. We stopped by to steal some. Better than cake."

"Did you have any?" Florida asked.

"Any what?"

"Cake."

"No." He frowned at her, obviously wondering why she'd care what he'd been eating.

"I meant, did you celebrate?"

Stan's frown deepened. Now he was obviously wondering why she was wondering what he'd done for his birthday last night. She glanced at her half brother. And Stan wasn't the only one. Dak was watching her, brows at half-mast. She felt her face heat. Oh, c'mon. It was an idle question. She didn't really care. It was just that ever since Serena had died two years ago, Florida was curious why Stan didn't go out much. He could if he wanted; plenty of women would stand in line.

"No, I worked." Stan looked down at Missouri and smiled. "I waited to celebrate with my favorite girl."

Stan switched his gaze back to Florida and the puzzled expression surfaced again. She realized she must look more pleased than his preference for their daughter's company warranted. And fact was, she wasn't just thinking of Missouri. What was the matter with her? Why should she be glad he'd spent the night working, not partying? Her unsatisfactory night with Daniel must be bothering her more than she'd thought.

"Want milk with that?" Dak asked his niece.

When Missouri nodded, Dak half rose, but Stan waved him away. Casting another glance in Florida's direction, he reached for the fridge, looking relieved he had something to do.

While Missouri chattered about her ballet lesson—Miss Tallant had been in a "bad, bad mood" and had made them practice the basic positions "over and over and over and over"—Stan watched her, his expression soft. And Florida watched him, thinking of how much he'd changed since the start of their involvement with each other.

At the ripe old age of thirty-three, Stan had been the older man to her young, and admittedly foolish, twenty-five. They'd shared a lot of things: work—he, the bank president; she, the managing assistant. Vulgarity—his gold chains, her short skirts and screw-me heels. And a selfish disregard for everyone else. Their affair, started while Stan and Alcea were married, had flared on and off for half a decade after they'd ultimately divorced, and had finally, irrefutably ended before Missouri was born and Stan married Serena.

Serena had been an airhead, but a sweet airhead with good intentions and a pliable nature—the polar opposite of first-wife Alcea and Florida the mistress. But still Serena had done what neither Alcea nor Florida had been able to do: She'd ended Stan's life as a serial adulterer.

Despite the passing of a near decade since Stan, Florida could still feel shame for her past. But she couldn't regret everything about their affair. It had brought her Missouri.

And Alcea.

When Dak had bounced back to Cordelia a decade ago after Cowboy had died, leaving Florida bereft of family, Florida had been ecstatic to have her long-lost half brother within reach. Until she'd watched him tumble knees over elbows for the four-years-divorced and newly broke woman who had once been her archrival for Stan's attention. Florida had known even then that in order to preserve her ties to her brother—a flimsy connection in those days—she'd have to learn to at least tolerate Alcea. Just as Alcea had known she'd alienate Dak if she couldn't be at least civil to his half sister.

So a chilly tolerance had come first, friendship much later. When Peg had died and left the diner to Florida, she'd had the business acumen to run the place, but not the flair the restaurant required nor a thimble of skill in a kitchen. Floundering, panicked that she'd destroy the legacy Peg had put into her safekeeping, she'd realized she needed someone who knew her way around a kitchen and whose name wasn't mud in most households. Home wreckers weren't that popular, even ones who had wrecked the home of the then-snooty Alcea.

Having sped through her divorce settlement, Alcea had desperately needed a job and had few friends to provide one. Mutual need had turned into grudging respect, which had ultimately led to understanding and friendship.

Over the years, for the sake of Stan and Alcea's

daughter, Kathleen, and Stan and Florida's daughter, Missouri, not to mention for the sake of their own peace of mind—Cordelia was a small place and who wanted to be the butt of nudges and gossip forever?—they'd reached détente with Stan through Serena's guileless maneuverings.

There was still an edge of discomfort, though. Big surprise.

And when Alcea stepped in from the back again, the discomfort was, though well hidden, complete.

Alcea looked startled. "Hey, Stan. Still training?"

Stan looked stiff. "I thought you were at Peg's."

Dak looked amused. "That marathon comes up pretty soon, doesn't it?"

"Two weeks." Stan relaxed, eyes lighting at the mention of his passion. Florida would scoff, except she admired his dedication. And envied the fact that he'd run next in Hawaii. On the rim of a volcano, no less. "Not sure I'll be ready. It's a tough course."

She gave him a once-over. He looked ready. When Serena had been diagnosed with cancer several years ago, Stan had taken up a regimen that had sculpted away the paunch he'd started developing even before Florida's affair with him had ended. Eventually his involvement in all things fitness had led to a change of career. The former bank president now dedicated his time to ownership of a gym and participation in marathons.

Alcea motioned at the counter, where nothing

much remained except the box and a few crumbs. "I forgot the cookies. And, uh"—she glanced at Missouri—"Tamara is on Florida's front porch."

Cookie in hand, Missouri took a chair next to Florida. "We saw her. Daddy said, 'Race for the hills!' He said she might be"—she took a bite—"a Yahoshas Inness."

"Don't talk with your mouth full." Raising a brow at Stan, Florida got up to look outside. "A what?"

He followed. "A Jehovah's Witness. What do you think?"

From this angle, she couldn't see the porch. But a Ford Focus sat at the curb.

"Oh, for God's sake."

He nodded. "Thought so."

"No, it's . . . nobody."

He didn't argue. He rarely did.

When they returned to the kitchen, Alcea had picked up the box, but hadn't yet moved for the door. Obviously curiosity over what would transpire between brother and sister was now at war with self-preservation.

Missouri looked up. "So who is she?"

Florida paused to brush a sprinkle of sugar off Missouri's lips, then stooped for a hug, savoring the smell of Powerpuff Girls toilet water and sweat. She'd watched Alcea and Stan's daughter grow up, along with Kathleen's bevy of O'Malley cousins, and knew it wouldn't be long before it was Missouri's turn. Every moment was special.

And not to be shared with Tamara. Tamara

hadn't earned the right to be Missouri's grand-mother.

She squeezed her hard and straightened. "No-body. Just someone coming to steal the silver, then she'll be on her way."

Missouri giggled. "You're silly. Who is she really?"

"No, really. Your uncle Dak and I . . . owe her some money." Like hell. They didn't owe Tamara a thing. "Once we give it to her, she'll be moving along. I just came over to get Uncle Dak's share." She smiled brightly at Dak. "So pony up, Uncle Dak."

"Florida." Dak shook his head.

Missouri looked between them, her face a study in confusion.

Okay, it was stupid to try to keep this from Missouri. Florida sighed and pulled up a chair. "Well, honey pie . . . that woman is your grand-mother. My mother."

Missouri's eyes went round. "I have a real grandmother?" With Stan's parents gone, Flori-da's father a mystery (even to Florida's mother), and her grandmother previously MIA, Missouri hadn't ever known a grandparent.

"Yes." Unfortunately.

"Will she stay with us?"

"No! I mean, she's staying with Uncle Dak." Until she convinced him to throw her out.

Stan leaned against the counter. "Damn. So that's Tamara Jones."

Of course he'd be more curious than incensed.

Lucky man, Stan had never known Tamara; her affair with his father had ended when he was *in utero*.

"And you might get to visit with her some," Florida said to Missouri, wondering how she could keep that from happening, "but don't get too excited. She probably won't stay long. Right, Bro?"

Dak didn't respond. He'd found something to study on the tabletop.

"Dak?" Florida looked over at Alcea. Her best friend was chewing her lower lip. "Okay, what's going on?"

Unlike Alcea, Stan wasn't a slouch in the self-preservation department. Curiosity apparently morphing into a sudden urge to be gone, he pushed away from the counter and addressed Missouri. "How about we head next door, kiddo? After you change, I'll take you across the street to the Rooster for a burger."

"But Tamara—" Florida stopped. How to tell your child she can't go home because she might run into her grandmother?

Missouri had hopped up from the table. "Hot dog instead. And ice cream, after?" she said, hopeful gaze on Stan.

Sin-Sational Ice Cream Parlor—specialties: a mind-numbing Chocolate Death, sub sandwiches, and hot dogs ladled with enough onions to level Chicago—was on the corner of the square a few doors up from the Rooster.

"Sure."

"Can Joey go, too?"

"Joey the lovelorn? Why not?"

Missouri frowned. "Joey doesn't *love* me. Gross."

"Sure, he doesn't," Stan said, putting a hand on her head to steer her out the door. "He just plans to build you a shrine."

The frown turned to puzzlement. "Why would I want one of those?" Then, "What's a shrine?"

Smiling, Stan looked back at Florida. "Don't worry. I'll steer her clear."

She knew he was talking about Tamara. Except in business—nobody knew his way around a balance sheet better than he did—Stan had never been much of a take-charge kind of guy, usually more bluster than substance up until the last years. But something in his expression calmed her worries. An odd feeling to associate with Stan.

After they'd left, Alcea set down the cookie box, apparently just now struck by a powerful yen to clean out the coffeepot. Florida's suspicions grew. Was Alcea sticking around—had she returned—to defend her husband? From what?

As if cued, Dak picked up his mug and carried it to the counter. He would have taken Florida's, too, but she snatched it back. On his way past, he paused to drop a kiss on his wife's neck. Alcea turned her head slightly and gave him one of those follow-you-to-the-end-of-the-earth smiles. It was a fleeting look, but Florida felt a stab of envy. They had the whole ball of wax. Love, affection, and simpatico natures, even if they had the occasional flare-up that nearly set the house on fire. They gave each other space to grow, but at the same time, give one a cause and the other would jump on the bandwagon.

Florida wished, not for the first time, that she and Daniel were more like that. There *was* love, of course. And lots of sex. But maybe not a lot of cuddly affection. And if she ever espoused a cause . . . well, Daniel was likely to have a roomful of accountants measure profit and loss before he jumped anywhere.

She frowned into her mug and told herself to stow the prewedding angsting, already. Never married before, she'd expected shaky knees as the date neared, but if she didn't keep a handle on herself, she'd need Julius's wheelchair and a push to get up the aisle. Every bride felt like that.

Right?

Having deposited his mug on the counter, Dak was heading toward the hallway.

She rolled her eyes. "Hey, where you going, bub? We're not finished here."

Looking resigned, Dak reversed course and sat back down. Behind him, Alcea scrubbed the carafe hard enough to fuse glass.

Suddenly feeling grim, Florida fixed Dak with a stare. "Let's have it."

He sighed. "Florida—"

"Look, I'm sorry Tamara is old and lonely. And without friends. Or family. But she did it to herself. It's her problem, not ours."

"You know Cowboy was an old man when she left us here."

She shrugged. "So what?"

"He was soft with us. Wanted to do his best by us, felt sorry for us. But with Tamara—"

"Are you going to tell me he was some kind of heavy-handed patriarch? Not Grandpa." Cowboy had been bewildered by their sudden presence in his life, but while he hadn't been a demonstrative man, he'd never been harsh.

"I've been talking to Julius," Dak said. "After our grandmother left Cowboy, he came down hard on Tamara. Julius said he was afraid she'd turn out the same way as her mother."

"Well, he knew what he was talking about, didn't he? You're not the only one who's talked to Julius about Tamara, Dak. He said she was a slut."

"Julius wouldn't say—"

"Okay, he said she was *a little too free with the milk*. Hell, she doesn't even know who my father is for sure. Look. Who cares what happened? The fact is, she left us. That's unforgivable. She has no right now to make her problems ours. Let's just give her some money. It's what she wants. And then she'll leave and be out of our hair."

"She's not after money, Florida."

"Tamara is all *about* money."

"You can't concede that maybe she's changed in the last few decades?"

"If she changed so much, she would have contacted us before now."

"She had reasons. She—"

Florida blew out a breath of exasperation. "Sure she had reasons. She was afraid. She'd extorted money from Stan's father—your father; she'd signed papers saying she'd give him their baby— give him *you*—if he paid her. Then she took the money and ran. Even when she found out S.R. was dead, she'd know his widow might make trouble for her. Or even Stan. Of course she had reasons. She didn't want to go to jail!"

Dak was silent. "She said you wouldn't listen."

"Why in the hell should I? And why are you? She hurt the bejesus outta you, too."

He opened his mouth and she glared at him. "If you say anything remotely close to 'Let by-gones be bygones,' I'm gonna crack you upside the head with Alcea's cast-iron skillet."

At that, Alcea put down the pot and turned, looking grim herself, but Dakota spoke first. "That's enough, Florida."

His voice, never sharp with her, was sharp. Surprised, she sat back.

"I want to make peace with my past"—Dak's voice was measured, but firm—"and I've told her she can stay. If you don't want anything to do with her, that's okay. She'll stay with us for now and I'll talk to her. Ask her to stay out of your hair. And later—you won't be here to care. I hope you can accept that; I don't want problems between us."

She felt betrayed, as though Dak was taking Tamara's side against her. It wasn't that long ago that he'd felt very much like she did. Okay, maybe not quite that murderous—Dak could hardly bring himself to squash a bug—but close. And he always mulled things over ad nauseam before acting. So why had he suddenly . . . ?

The pieces fell into place. "You know her pretty well for such a short acquaintance. And you've thought this through."

"I—" Dak broke off. The man who never looked guilty actually looked guilty.

"How long?" she asked flatly.

"How long what?"

She stood up. "How long have you been phoning her? Visiting her? E-mailing her?"

"I—" Dak repeated.

"How long?" Her voice rose.

"Florida, calm down." Alcea spoke up. "Dak didn't look for her or anything like that. Tamara called several months ago. And then last month, when we went away that one weekend?"

"Alcea . . ." Dak's voice held a warning.

"No, Dak. She should know. We went to see her. It took Dak time to come around himself and knowing how you felt, he wanted to be sure of her sincerity before he said anything to you."

"Several *months*?" She wouldn't even bother to comment on how ludicrous it sounded to put *Tamara* and *sincerity* into the same sentence. "You lied. Both of you lied. You said you were going to Arkansas. Neither of you thought maybe I might want to know something before she turned up on my doorstep?"

"I wanted to tell you, Florida. Honest. But . . ."

But Alcea had been torn between loyalty to her husband and her best friend, and whenever that happened, Dak always won, hands down. Florida couldn't really blame her, but she could blame her brother. The snake.

When she opened her mouth again, Dak held up a hand to stop her. "I'm sorry you're finding out this way. She wasn't supposed to arrive until after your wedding. After you were long gone. But her lease was up, so she came early. I tried to keep her from seeing you, but she insisted—"

"*She* insisted? It's all about what *she* wants? And you were just going to move her into my house—*my* house—as soon as you'd seen my back end, without saying a word until it was a done deal?"

"Not exactly. I—"

"*Goddammit*, Dak. You're taking 'Live and let live' too far, don't you think?" Florida realized she was crying. Tears of frustrated anger. Seeing Tamara had more than awakened the sleeping hounds she'd laid to rest; it had set them snapping at her heels. And Dak had to have known how this would affect her. Yet he'd let Tamara waltz next door. . . .

She turned to leave. She couldn't believe his insensitivity.

"Florida—" Alcea laid a hand on her arm.

"Don't *touch* me." Florida pushed her away and then pushed through the door. Once outside, she realized she had no place to go. She couldn't go home. She didn't want Missouri to see her like this. And she especially didn't want to see *her*.

Remembering she still had her car keys, she pulled them from her pocket and stalked toward the BMW. Behind her, she heard the door open again.

"Florida!" Dak called out.

"Give her some space." Alcea's voice.

Florida ignored them both and slid into the car, oblivious to the hot leather against the bare backs of her legs. Out of the corner of her eye, she saw a figure on the porch stand up. She ignored that, too.

She revved the engine. With a squeal of tires, she roared out of the driveway.

Chapter 4

Hearing tires screech, Stan looked out a window from Florida's great room. Beyond the shadowed front porch and the woman silhouetted at the railing, he saw the tail end of the BMW as it raced up Main. He shook his head. God help anyone crossing the square. His gaze returned to the woman. Staring after the car, she stood straight, but her age showed in the slight bow of her narrow back.

Tamara Jones.

Gold digger. Extortionist. Bane of his mother's existence . . .

His parents had died a long while ago: his father in a car accident when Stan was thirteen, his mother two decades later following a lengthy illness. When Ellen Addams had realized her days were numbered, she'd told him about his father's affair with "a gold-digging tramp," Tamara Jones, the woman his father, S.R. Addams, had impregnated in a last burst of wild oats, then spurned for a life with Ellen Van Stassel.

Probably not an issue of true love, Stan had surmised then, remembering the powerful man his father had been, which just about completed all the impression he had of S.R. Addams. Their communication had largely been limited to S.R.'s admonishment to "sit up straight" or the ever-affectionate "Close your yap." No, his father's choice had likely been a matter of economics: Ellen's family had owned a chunk of Cordelia, while Tamara's had owned only a square patch of scruff on the edge of town and Cowboy's Tow and Service.

News of his father's affair hadn't disturbed him—I mean, really, considering his own past, how could it?—but Ellen *had* surprised him with news that he had a half brother, not that he'd known what he'd do with one. It hadn't been dreams of a teary reunion weighing on his dying mother's mind, though; she'd told him because she'd feared the love child would one day appear to claim half of Stan's inheritance.

He smiled ruefully. Except for Serena, he'd always been surrounded with women who knew the value of a dollar.

And his mother had been right. Some years later, Dak *had* shown up, but with plenty of money of his own and no aspirations to extortion. Unlike Tamara, who had wrested a wild sum from his parents, promising them the son she didn't want, then keeping both to punish Stan's father. Until S.R. had passed into the great beyond, Ellen had told Stan, his father had never stopped looking for Dak. Given their father-and-son relationship, Stan figured it was more a matter of S.R.'s pride than paternal longing—Tamara had been sharp; she knew how to hit S.R. where it hurt— although it was still a matter of debate whenever the gossip revived.

Learning his father's history had filled a few gaps. Despite Ellen's agreement to adopt S.R.'s illicit progeny were he ever to find him, S.R.'s affair had cut her deeply, as witnessed by her near-rabid support of "family values," her dedication to the church . . . and, despite her suffocating affection for him, her threat to disinherit him after he married Alcea if he so much as looked at another woman.

Something he'd increasingly done as his marriage wore on. He and the former beauty queen had married for a lot of reasons—for example, her itch to possess a big house on a hill and his to possess Miss Cordelia. But even though they may have fooled themselves about many things, love hadn't been among them.

His mother's threat hadn't deterred him, but it *had* made him the soul of discretion until after his mother died. It was that fanaticism (all right, all right—along with his own cowardice and suck-up-ishness) that had kept him so long in a first marriage that never should have happened. And that had led him, in what could only be called immature idiocy, to take refuge in alcohol and other women.

Notably Florida.

They'd grown up in the same town, but the eight-years-younger Florida hadn't registered in his brain until she'd joined the staff at his bank, a vibrant Venus amid pale faces and gray suits. She'd mesmerized him with her passion, intelligence, and spirit, qualities his first wife also possessed in abundance. But unlike Alcea, Florida had loved him. Really loved him.

He'd known it. And he'd used it. Never knowing—or even trying to examine—how he really felt about her.

Their five-year affair, on and off, filled with passions he'd never explored with Alcea—had never, truth be told, wanted to explore with Alcea—had been an addiction, one he'd tried to break with forays into other women's beds, finally finding peace in Serena's. When Florida had bushwhacked him in an attempt to win him back with a deliberate pregnancy, despite the pull he'd still felt for her, the parallels between mother and daughter, father and son, had doomed any possibility they might have had at reconciling.

He'd never met Tamara Jones. But she'd certainly impacted his life.

He stared at the figure still standing at the railing. She hadn't given any indication she'd seen him and Missouri enter the house or heard them inside. Maybe she'd done neither.

He shrugged and went to the bottom of the stairwell. "You ready, kiddo?" he called to Missouri.

"My hair is *hopeless!*" she called back. Footsteps thudded down the hall from her bedroom to the bathroom.

He smiled, thinking that he'd need to get used to these lightning shifts from little girl into full-female throttle, wondering what else he'd need to adjust to as she grew up. Knowing her primping would take time, he started to lower himself into the easy chair, then changed his mind.

Tamara Jones. Bane of his mother's existence. Source of Florida's pain. And, let's not forget, his daughter's grandmother . . .

Like it or not, she was back. Curiosity and paternal concern spurred his footsteps as he moved to the door.

When he stepped out on the porch, the first thing that struck him was a fistful of heat. The second was the resemblance to Florida that showed in the face Tamara turned toward him. Same eyes, fine bones, hollow cheeks, and generous mouth but with thinner lips. And same way of raising an eyebrow.

He smiled and nodded toward the street where the BMW had left rubber. "Didn't take you long to stir up trouble again, did it?"

The eyebrow went higher. "Do I know you?"

"No."

Florida's porch was adorned with pots of flowers, a wind chime, and wicker furniture thick with rose-splashed cushions. Expression more interested than puzzled, Tamara seated herself on the settee and plucked out a cigarette from the purse she'd left there. Her hands tremored briefly and he felt a small twinge of pity. But only a small one. She might be growing old alone, but she'd caused a lot of people a lot of pain. What in the hell had Dakota been thinking when he'd asked her here?

He almost snorted. Like he'd ever understood what went on in Dak's head?

Then . . . what had Alcea been thinking?

He did snort. Like *he'd* ever figure that out?

At the sound, Tamara only lit her cigarette and blew out a stream of smoke. "Then you must know me."

She was a cool one. Thinking of Florida's past, he felt a protective surge and amended that to *cold* one. Then abandoned the surge. Florida had never wanted or needed his protection. Missouri, though, that was a different matter.

But before he could reply, Missouri appeared in the doorway. Her hair piled over her shoulders, she was holding a ribbon.

"I can't get this stupid bow—" Gaze landing on Tamara, she stopped and edged all the way out. "Hi."

Stubbing the cigarette out in a pot, Tamara sat up straighter. "Hello."

"I'm Missouri. You're my grandma."

"And you're well informed. I don't like the word *grandma*, though. Sounds like an old lady."

"But you *are* an old lady."

A half beat behind and wondering how to get Missouri back inside before Florida showed up again, Stan frowned. "Don't be rude."

Tamara laughed, a breathy sound. "I like you, Missouri. But think of something else to call me."

Missouri's forehead wrinkled. "Like what?"

"Tamara. Tammy . . ."

"No, it needs to be a grandma name."

". . . Duchess . . . Queen . . . Empress . . ."

Missouri giggled.

Too much camaraderie too soon. Stan's instincts kicked into gear—for his daughter and for himself. Florida would not be pleased. "Missouri, go finish getting ready."

Missouri glared at him, apparently wondering what would happen if she spouted a *Don't be rude* of her own. But she only raised her chin and looked back at Tamara. "Well, I wish I could talk longer," she said graciously, "but Daddy and I are gonna go get hot dogs." Her face brightened. "Hey, do you want to go with—"

"Missouri." Stan held open the door.

"Okay, okay!" She stomped back inside.

When he turned around, Tamara was eyeing him with new interest. "Daddy?"

"Yes, and take it easy on the buddy stuff. She's got a soft heart and I don't want it broke."

"I'll be damned. You're Stanley Addams the

Third, am I right?'' Reaching down, she withdrew another cigarette from her purse, lit up, leaned back, and puffed out a cloud. "Well, well. How's your mother?''

"Dead.''

"At least you don't beat around the bush. If you're holding a grudge''—she shrugged—"get in line.''

With more speed than he would have thought possible, Missouri appeared again. She'd given up on the ribbon in favor of other accessories. A small canvas purse hung from her shoulder; heavy plastic bands encircled her narrow wrists. And if he wasn't mistaken, she'd borrowed her mother's lipstick. He thought about making her go upstairs to wash it off, then thought about it again. Missouri had a quick temper. Like her mother. And a disgruntling way of outtalking him. Also, like her mother.

He'd lose any argument he started. So why start one? Cowardly, but he decided if they were to get away from Tamara, he'd need to give the lipstick a pass.

"I'm ready,'' Missouri said to him, although her gaze was pinned on Tamara.

"Then let's go.'' He tugged her down the stairs before she could invite her grandmother again. From Tamara's amused expression, he knew she'd say yes.

Missouri hung back, looking over her shoulder at the woman on the porch. "I can't believe I have a real grandma.'' Pulling her strap over her shoulder, she faced forward. "That's really cool. Wait'll

I tell Joey. He thinks it's weird I don't have any grandparents, but now I do."

At least until the woman decided to take off again. Stan's mouth thinned. He'd been serious about one thing: Tamara had better not break even a teensy piece off Missouri's heart.

Almost to the car, Missouri halted, looking struck. "Mom's car is gone."

"She . . . had an errand."

"Well, we can't leave Julius alone."

Damn. She was right.

"I'll stay with him." Tamara had followed them down the walk. Car keys in hand, her walk was stiff. Some arthritis, he'd bet. "I was leaving, but I can stay a while longer."

Missouri brightened. "You know Julius?"

"He was my father's best friend."

"Oh." Missouri considered this. "That's right. You would've lived here, wouldn't you? I've lived here all my life. Well, not here, exactly, because this used to be a garage. But you know that. Mom and I used to live in that funny pink trailer out back, but that was before she made enough money that we could—"

Tamara had crossed her arms and was watching Missouri with pure enjoyment. And an almost proprietary air. Stan tugged on Missouri again. "C'mon, kiddo. Hot dogs are awaiting."

Missouri resisted. "So *she's* staying with Julius?"

Julius. Stan sighed. "No, *we'll* stay with Julius." He looked pointedly at Tamara. "*She's* leaving."

Just as he and Missouri were turning back to

the house, a sleek (like a shark) Lincoln Town Car slid to the curb heralding Daniel Davenport. Stan's sigh was aggravated and loud. The day was just getting better and better.

When Florida had first told him of her engagement to the budding hotel mogul, he'd been distracted, torn between his continuing grief over Serena's death and the frenzied energy he'd put into changing careers once she was gone. But as he'd emerged from the hole life had pitched him into two years ago with Serena's death, he'd realized he didn't like the idea.

And the better he got to know the man, the more he *really* didn't like the idea. For one thing, the guy was a show-off. Stan had once owned a Hummer, but that was before he'd realized he didn't really *need* status symbols. Which was somewhere around the time he'd sunk a small fortune into first Peg's, then his own new business, sold the Hummer, and bought a Suburban, roomy enough to seat one of the groups he sometimes took to marathons. Practical . . . but no cool factor. He looked at the Lincoln. Absolutely zero cool factor.

But worse—far worse—than losing the battle of the status symbols was the fact that the schmuck would soon spirit off his daughter. And her mother. His train of thought suddenly derailed.

Except where Missouri was concerned, whom Florida chose to marry was none of his business. It disturbed him how often lately he'd wished that it was.

The man unfolded his length from the car and Stan glowered anew. That was another thing. Daniel was taller than he. Without moving, Stan flexed an arm and was reassured.

"Addams." Daniel gave him a cool nod, gave Tamara a curious glance, then smiled at Missouri. With a sideways glance at Stan, he held out his arms, as stiff as his smile. "Hey, pumpkin!"

Pumpkin? Disgruntled, Stan watched his daughter. She hung back a nanosecond, then approached Daniel and gave him a halfhearted hug. "I thought you wouldn't be here till later."

"Why, I couldn't stay away from my best girls, now, could I?" He released her and touched her lips. "What's this? Are you bleeding?"

Missouri stepped out of reach. "Just some makeup. All girls wear makeup."

"When they're old and decrepit, they do. But pretty young things like you don't need it." He smiled at her again. For a minute, Stan thought he'd actually wag a finger. "Why don't you go wash it off and you'll see?"

What a fake. Couldn't Missouri see through him?

Missouri was glowering. "Mom wears makeup and she's not old and . . . whatever you said."

Good girl. She could.

Daniel touched her nose. "No, she's cute like you. Must run in your family. Just run up and wash it off, okay? And I'll take you and your mom out for a steak."

"I want a hot dog. And she's not here." Missouri's chin was out.

"Where is she?"

"She won't be back till late," Stan said, not knowing what devil had just juiced him.

Daniel frowned.

"Very late." Watching silently until now, Tamara spoke up. "She must have forgotten."

Daniel turned the frown on her. "Who are you?" he demanded.

At his tone, Tamara's eyes narrowed. "Why are you asking?"

"If you're the Prodigal Mother, I want to talk to you."

"That's nice. But I don't believe I want to talk to you." She drew herself up. "In fact—"

Despite the new respect Stan had for Tamara's ability to read character in a single glance, before she could say any more, he took her elbow. Florida didn't need her mother and fiancé coming to blows in her front yard. Nor did Missouri need to see it. "You were just leaving, remember?" He steered Tamara toward her Ford.

Before they'd gone two steps, though, a clatter rose from the house. Something fell with a crash, a curse sounded, then bumping ensued. Another curse sputtered forth.

Stan rolled his eyes.

Missouri clapped her hands. "Julius is up!" She tugged on Tamara's hand. "He'll be glad he didn't miss you."

Tamara followed Missouri to the door. Brow still lowered, Daniel held it open. Feeling any semblance of control slip away, Stan brought up the rear.

As they stepped inside, the phone rang. Stan flopped down on the sofa and wondered how he could have ever run a bank or started a business when managing just a few people eluded him. Giving Stan a triumphant look, Tamara took a seat at the other end.

Missouri skipped toward the table by the stairs where the phone still trilled, but before she reached it, a wheelchair shot from the hall. Missouri made a practiced side step.

Tamara inhaled sharply. "That's Julius?"

"That's Julius," Stan agreed.

When she didn't answer, he looked over. Supercilious look gone, her face was filled with pain. "He's . . . old." She looked down at her hands, raised veins, bumpy knuckles. "So much has changed."

Julius gave Missouri a broad wink. She stepped back and he snatched up the phone. " 'Peace here,' " he boomed into the mouthpiece. " 'Grace and good company!' "

Stan begged to differ. But the quote brought a small smile to Tamara's face.

"That's Isabella," Julius continued. "From Shakespeare's fine work *Measure for Measu*—" Apparently interrupted, he paused and listened intently. "I beg your pardon. Isabella is *not* trashed. She's a character in—"

The voice on the other end of the line grew almost audible across the room.

Julius's face paled. "Oh. *Crashed.*"

Stan felt a tremor of alarm and stood up. "What is it?"

Julius held up a hand, then hung up the phone without saying good-bye. Sending a be-patient look at Stan, he reached for Missouri. "C'mere, little lady," he said gently. He hefted her onto his knees like he had when she was little. Missouri looked worried, but didn't pull away. "We've had a mite of bad news, but I just know everything will be okay, so be brave. It's your mama," he said. "There's been a little accident. But she's fine. She's on her way to University Hospital."

Ashen, Daniel said, "Where's that?"

"Columbia," Stan said, his heart dropping into his stomach. University Hospital was a level-one trauma center almost two hours away. "If she's going there, they'll transport her by helicopter."

Adrenaline pumping with alarming speed, he started toward the door. He'd get Dak. With luck, they could make it in less time than that.

"Go grab Dak." Daniel crowded behind him, face pale, chin set. "Sedalia's the opposite direction, so the plane's a waste of time. We'll take the Lincoln."

Stan almost told him to shove off, then realized Daniel had more right to take charge than he did.

Missouri pulled out of Julius's arms. "I want to go!"

Looking shaky, Tamara pushed herself up. "Me, too."

Julius looked at her for the first time. "I'll be damned. Tamara?"

"We can't all go," Daniel said, impatient now. "We won't fit."

Alarm for Florida, concern for Missouri, disgruntlement with Daniel . . . Stan's emotions all rolled into a ball of sudden helplessness. Until Missouri burst into tears.

Suddenly knowing exactly what to do, Stan plucked her out of Julius's lap, and her arms twined around his neck. Her feet dangled near his knees, her face burrowed into his neck, and he could feel the warm dampness as she cried.

"I want my mommy!"

He held her tight. "*You* go get Dak," he said to Daniel. "Alcea'll want to go, too. Missouri, go put on some lipstick. We'll all fit in my car."

Chapter 5

"Mommy?"

Surfacing out of murky depths, Florida started to turn her head toward the sound of Missouri's voice, then stopped when somebody stabbed a spear into her skull. She groaned.

"Mom!"

Someone made a shushing noise. Florida opened one eye. Light lanced in. She closed it.

"She's awake!" Missouri's voice again, high with excitement.

"Florida?" It was Daniel.

She tried to say something, but only a croak came out.

"Don't try to talk," he said.

"What's this young lady doing in here?" Another voice, deep but female, one she didn't recognize.

"She needed to see her mother." Daniel's voice was firm.

"That may be as may be, but only one visitor at a time in ICU. And *no* children." The voice brooked no argument. Florida peeked from one eye again, shut it almost as quickly, but not until she'd glimpsed a uniformed woman as big as a battleship standing at the base of the bed.

"Sorry," Daniel mumbled. If she could have smiled, she would have. She'd never heard him give in.

There was a rustling; then the scent of Powerpuff Girl brushed her nose, and soft lips touched her cheek. "I'll be back again later," Missouri whispered. Her voice went even softer till it was almost just breath against her face. "Daddy will sneak me in. You get well. Promise me."

Florida tried to smile through the pain, and hoped the grimace she managed didn't scare her daughter. "I will, hon." *I'yull hunh.*

"C'mon, missy." The nurse again. "I'll take you back to your family."

As their footsteps trailed off, Florida became conscious of the beep and whir of machines. She couldn't remember . . . didn't know what she was doing here.

"Daniel." It came out "Dunnah."

She heard a scrape as he pulled up a chair; then she felt his hand on hers. "You're at University Hospital in Columbia."

Alarm bells joined the ringing in her ears. If they'd brought her here . . .

He squeezed. "You were in a car accident and hit your head. You've been unconscious, so they brought you here just in case—" Aggravation joined the relief in his voice. "I'm glad you're awake. But what in the hell were you thinking, driving that fast?"

Car accident? She couldn't remember what she was thinking. She couldn't remember any of it. "Anyone else?" *Inny-un elsh*? God, please, let nobody else be hurt.

"No. You lost control and went into a ditch. The car's a loss."

Her BMW. Her beautiful BMW. She turned her head away and regretted it immediately when pain lanced again. But not as much as she regretted having skimped on the insurance. She wouldn't get nearly as much as the car had been worth.

"The doctor says concussion. Your head will hurt for a while, but you'll heal. You'll be okay."

"Time's up, Mr. Davenport." The nurse had returned.

"Time's up when I say it's up," Daniel said.

Florida opened her eyes.

The nurse ignored him. "I've called the doctor to let him know she's awake. He'll be up to see her shortly. You can see her again once he's gone."

Daniel blinked, but rose.

"Way!" *Wait.* Feeling another spurt of panic when the word came out wrong just like the others, Florida reached out to capture Daniel's arm before he left. The movement sent pain arcing through her head. *Why couldn't she talk?*

"What's wrong with her speech?" Daniel asked.

Yes, what's wrong with my speech?

"Sometimes if the brain gets rattled around like that, things can get a little mixed-up for a while. I'm sure she'll be fine."

She released the breath she didn't know she was holding.

Thank God. She relaxed and sleep overcame her.

When she woke, it was morning. From the way the sun sloped through a six-inch gap in the curtains onto the linoleum floor, leaving a small pool on the floor, it was still early. The room was mostly shadowed. Staying still, remembering pain, she stared at the only corner of the room within her vision. The room . . . it was different. Sometime during the day . . . night? . . . she remembered being trundled through the halls. To a whirring and clanking warhorse of a machine. Then they must have brought her here. Wherever here was. Her head still throbbed, but it felt less like it would fall off her shoulders.

"Good morning."

She turned her head toward the voice, winced. She was wrong; it *would* fall off her shoulders. A short man wearing half-glasses, a tie under his white coat, and carefully combed straight sandy hair stood next to her side, holding a chart. His hands were long-fingered and freckled.

"I'm Harold Fitzsimmons. Neurologist. You had

a nasty bump on the head. Do you remember how it happened?" While he was talking, he set the chart aside and examined her, pulling up an eyelid and flashing a penlight in front of her eyes.

Florida thought. "Daniel said car accident." Thank God. Her voice was raspy, but her words were no longer slurred.

"But you don't remember it yourself?"

"No." Just that it had been Saturday morning. Missouri in her pink leotard. Julius out with Dak. Alcea. Dak . . . she'd had an argument with him . . . about what?

Apparently noting her frown, Dr. Fitzsimmons patted her shoulder. "A spot of amnesia surrounding an accident that causes head trauma is common."

"Head trauma?" That didn't sound good.

"Concussion. Because you passed out, we put you in the ICU for a while. Just a precaution. You're looking good, don't worry. Do you know what day it is?"

She thought of her car. Not her lucky one. "Sunday?"

"Right. And what's your name?"

"Florida Jones."

"Where do you live, Florida Jones?"

Dr. Fitzsimmons continued in this vein for a few minutes as he carried on his examination, checking reflexes, asking questions, checking her memory, her concentration, jotting notes on the chart. Finally he slipped his pen back into his jacket pocket.

Reaching behind him, he pulled up a chair. "You're doing well. The scan looked fine." The noisy machine. "But there are a few things to watch for." He looked toward the corner of the room. The one she hadn't been staring at. "Mother, you might want to take note of this, too."

Mother? Florida followed his gaze. Until now, she hadn't noticed the still figure sitting in the guest chair in the corner of the room. *Mother.* Omigod. The memory of yesterday morning came crowding back. Tamara met her eyes and gave a slight shrug, an apology for being here. Her bracelets clacked when she moved.

Florida opened her mouth to order her out, then realized Dr. Fitzsimmons was talking to her.

". . . postconcussive syndrome."

She focused back on him. "Huh?"

"PCS," he said, displaying no impatience. It was probably a commonplace event for him to have a patient zone out. "In about ten percent of cases like yours, there are some aftereffects. Dizziness, persistent headache (you can use pain meds like Tylenol), some problem-solving difficulty or trouble concentrating. Nausea. Sometimes some vision problems."

Lovely.

"These usually go away on their own given time. Make an appointment for your GP to look you over in about a week; let him or her know what's going on. Meantime, if anything comes on suddenly—headache gets more intense; vomiting

becomes severe; blackouts; extreme confusion—
you get yourself to the ER. Okay?"

She nodded. Then wished she hadn't.

"And no driving for a few days. Longer if
symptoms persist."

No problem. No car.

He patted her shoulder again, stood up.

Tamara did, too. "We'll keep an eye on her."

We? She snorted.

Both Tamara and the doctor ignored her.

"Good. I'll get her discharge going. The nurse
will be in soon to give you instructions. You can
get her home?" He addressed Tamara.

Tamara nodded.

Like hell. Daniel would take her home.

"You've got quite the . . . entourage." Dr. Fitzsimmons smiled at her. "You're lucky."

Yeah, lucky. When he left, there was silence.
Tamara didn't move, just continued standing
there, looking at her. As if of its own volition, one
hand toyed with the corner of a blanket. Smoothing, patting, pulling straight, then pushing into a
little mound.

Determined to act like Tamara wasn't there, at
first Florida ignored her. But after two minutes,
she felt like screaming. Screaming was out of the
question. "Would you stop that?" she whispered.

"Sorry." For a brief moment, Tamara looked
chastened. For a brief moment, she looked like
Missouri.

Florida averted her gaze. "What did the doctor
mean, *entourage*?" She didn't want to talk to Ta-

mara, but questions teemed through her head and there was nobody else to ask. Where was everyone? Where was Daniel?

"Alcea, your brother, Stan . . . they're here. People were coming and going all night. Some of Alcea's family checked on you, too. Her daughter—Kathleen?—wanted to know if she should fly in."

"From New York?" Good God, had the doctor told her everything? "I'm not . . . Am I dying?"

Tamara snorted. "No more than anyone else."

"Thanks, *Mom.* Your compassion is touching."

"Alcea told her to stay put." Tamara didn't look at all abashed. "But a few O'Malleys drove up late yesterday from Lake Kesibwi and created chaos. A nurse finally shooed them off. Zinnia O'Malley didn't go quietly."

Alcea's mother, a fireplug of a woman, always took *no* as *maybe.* Florida retained a vague memory of the battleship-sized nurse. A smile tugged at her mouth. That must have been quite a face-off.

"Zinnia . . ." Tamara's mouth curled. "Some things don't change. Same busybody she was over a half century ago when we were both girls. Always had a poker up her butt where I was concerned. She had good—"

"Y'all shut up about Zinnia O'Malley." Florida's voice was low, but fierce. "She's been more mother to me—and more grandmother to Missouri—than you ever even thought of being."

Although now that Zinnia and Pop had moved out to Gentle Slopes Retirement Community, she rarely saw them anymore. When they weren't mixing it up at the retirement community, they were traveling to visit family. She missed them. All of them. Alcea's middle sister and her husband had retired early, sold their home in Cordelia, and moved to the family cabin at Lake Kesibwi. Her youngest sister and her husband, plus their twin toddlers, were off in the wilds of Kansas. The twenty-something grandchildren were scattered around the country. Florida knew a few lived in San Francisco and Kathleen in New York; she wasn't sure about the others.

Tamara gave her a look of long-suffering patience. "Before I was interrupted, I was about to say she had good reason. I didn't—don't—like her. Big Goody Two-shoes. But I wasn't exactly Sandra Dee. I came on to Tom O'Malley more than once when they were pinned; if I were her, I wouldn't have trusted me, either. Although *she* could have trusted *him*. Tom never looked twice at anyone else. Not even me, and I was something to see."

"I'll just bet. Where's Zinnia now?"

"They drove back last night after the doctors said you were out of danger. They had a plane to catch today for San Francisco—visiting family there. And Alcea wanted her niece—what's her name, another damned bloom of some kind?—to be at work this morning." Her tone said she didn't appreciate the O'Malley inclination to name their girls after flowers.

"Daisy. And you named yours after states," Florida pointed out.

"So did you," Tamara countered. "So don't act so smug. Alcea wanted Daisy at work this morning."

Deciding she'd need another pair of hands once Florida had married, Alcea had recently hired Daisy O'Malley Mastin, her niece, for the position of assistant manager at Peg O' My Heart. Over Florida's objections. It wasn't that she didn't like Daisy, but she was—well, the kindest way to put it was brain addled. But Alcea said all she needed was someone to keep an eye on things when she couldn't be there.

Florida thought it all sentiment. Daisy's husband was a local lawyer, but local lawyers made about as much in chicken eggs and chopped wood as they did in actual fees. Hardly enough to stretch to cover a family with two young girls. Pop and Zinnia O'Malley had bestowed their big ol' bungalow on Maple Woods Drive on Daisy when they'd moved to Gentle Slopes, but from what Florida overheard, the family still struggled.

"Daisy should get her tubes tied," she'd muttered. Baby three was on its way.

"Florida! Where are your priorities?" Alcea's hard look had made her feel like a pea.

But, she thought now, it wasn't her fault she hadn't much experience with families looking out for one another. In fact, she decided, eyeing Tamara, she wasn't even sure she wanted to start now. What she wanted was . . .

"Find Daniel for me."

"I would, but he's not here."

"When will he be back? I want *him* to take me home." In that pretty little plane of his.

"He said he couldn't miss some meeting in Kansas City this morning, that he loved you, and knew you'd understand." She shook her head. "Asshole."

"He is not!" Florida said. "Of course, I understand. He's got a big business to run and—"

"And a fiancée in the hospital who could use his support. Asshole, just like I said."

"What do you know? He needs to set priorities and he knew I was fine and . . ." Feeling like weeping, she let the sentence trail off.

Tamara relented. "Okay. He said he'd call later. He probably loves you—in his own way. I'm sure he'll call."

Probably? His own way? "I don't need your reassurance." If that's what you'd call it. "And I don't need you."

She broke off as Nurse Battleship steamed in, pushing a wheelchair. "Alley-oop, missy. Doctor says you can be up and on your way, so let's get going. I saw the rest of your family outside, and told them to go fetch the car."

Even though she rose to a sitting position slowly, the nurse's arms helping support her (after she'd batted her mother's away), Florida felt a wave of dizziness. Followed by a wave of nausea. It was a whole damned ocean of discomfort. She didn't think she could make it across the room, let alone all the miles back to Cordelia. What had that doctor been thinking? Another wave of dizziness crested, then ebbed. What had *Daniel* been thinking?

"How good is Fitzsimmons, anyway?" she grumbled.

"Dr. Fitzsimmons is *very* well respected," Nurse Battleship said in offended tones. "Now, here's your instructions." She thrust some papers into Tamara's hands, then addressed Florida. "As Dr. Fitzsimmons probably told you . . ."

While she helped Florida dress and then wheeled her to the entrance, the nurse repeated almost verbatim everything Dr. Fitzsimmons had already said, then rattled off the instructions on the sheets she'd handed Tamara. By the time they reached the hospital entrance, Florida's head was buzzing.

When she found out Daniel had driven off in the Suburban last night, apparently thinking his meeting trumped everything else, and that in the jostling of cars coming and going, only Dak's Jeep and Tamara's Focus were left in his wake, the buzz turned into a clatter. Her immediate thought was . . .

(asshole)

. . . that she'd suffer any amount of jouncing in her brother's vehicle as long as she didn't have to ride with Tamara. They weren't halfway to Jefferson City, though, before the clatter turned into a roar. They stopped and shifted her into her mother's car.

Tamara solicitously lowered the seat and kept the pace steady and her mouth shut all the way

back to Cordelia, but still, by the time she reached
her bed, Florida thought her brains would burst
out her ears. She'd never experienced a headache
like this in her life.

After Julius had dosed her with pain pills, Tamara with tea, and Missouri had sat for a half
hour (an eternity in a nine-year-old's life) tracing
her fingers over her mother's forehead, Florida finally fell into a fitful sleep.

So it wasn't until morning that she realized
Daniel hadn't ever called her at all.

Chapter 6

"But I did call," Daniel said, his face a mask of patient reason that made her itch to smack him. "I called Dak and Alcea, who told me you were resting. I didn't call you because I didn't want to disturb you. And haven't I phoned every day since then? Two, three times a day."

Several evenings later, Florida lay marooned on her king-sized bed amid a nest of pillows and a plush comforter, squares of olive brocade and scarlet silk and high thread counts, watching Daniel as he paced around her bedroom. To accommodate her head, the wood blinds were closed against the rays of sunset. Even with the bedside lamps on low, bronzing the teak furniture, the room was shadowed; Daniel's pale hair was the brightest spot against the Chinese Red walls.

Following him was like watching Pac-Man

bounce across a computer screen. If he didn't sit down soon, she'd have another doozy of a headache, and the last one had just subsided. Since she'd returned home, intermittent dizziness and nausea had kept her close to her bed while the headaches came and went. Mostly went, but they stirred back up at the slightest little thing.

Like the thought that Tamara was inhabiting the room down the hall.

Even if Florida hadn't been confined to her bed for the longest stretch of time she could remember since a bout of pneumonia when she was ten, just that alone was enough to lend a surreal cast to life since the accident. She hadn't had the energy to fight Tamara's presence.

But she had enough brain capacity to resent it like hell, no matter the arguments Alcea put forth: Julius wasn't spry enough; her sister-in-law needed to be at the restaurant; Missouri was too young; and Dak—her treacherous sage of a brother and the root of all her evils—was racing to meet a deadline before he ran off to hide himself in a monthlong publicity tour, which would include pit stops on *Oprah* and *Regis and Kelly* and the *Today* show—la-di-da—before he started his annual research trip for his next book. In effect, in typical Dak fashion, he'd leave everyone else to deal with the mess (in the form of Tamara) that had started with him.

She watched Daniel continue to pace and explain and wondered if there was a man alive who didn't forever dish up excuses. She sighed and plucked at a piece of brocade. Probably not. And maybe, she thought grudgingly, some of that reasoning was valid. While she'd like to throw all the blame for her accident on Dak—as well as demand he replace her poor baby of a BMW, which would shortly turn into a chopped-up hunk of rusting metal—she knew it was her own lead foot that had landed her here. Choices—it was all about choices. And Dak's was to have a relationship with their mother. Just as hers was not.

So having Tamara foisted upon her was maddening.

Even though she understood the necessity. That rusting hunk of metal had eaten up any savings she might have spent on an aide to help her and Julius. Still, if Alcea ever mentioned Tamara's name in the same sentence as she uttered *godsend*, Florida would bean her but good.

"Besides," Daniel said, "you had a whole crew of people dying to help you. Addams practically moved in here."

Suddenly she understood Daniel's behavior. If he couldn't be quarterback, he didn't want to play at all. Especially if he'd been relegated to second string. But this time . . . this time, he should have thought of *her* first and been a good little linebacker. In fact, knowing how she felt about Tamara—surely that had registered, since she'd groused at every phone call—*he* might have suggested footing the bill for home health care. But he hadn't. And she wouldn't suggest it, knowing his ever-present suspicion that anyone who came close was mining for gold. His gold. She'd always been careful not to ask for more than he wanted to give, and she planned to sign without a murmur the prenup his lawyers were preparing.

Sometimes she wondered if she was proving to him—or to herself—that her attachment to him was about more than just money. *God.* She'd never been a bride before. Was there no end to the pre-wedding doubts?

Tears welled, blurring his face. She hurt; she felt useless; she was confused; she wanted Tamara out of her house, and Daniel to shut up and just hold her. Tired of slogging around in self-pity, she blinked them away, but it took a few moments before she saw clearly again. This wasn't the first time things had briefly gone hazy, but remembering how the knock on her head had caused her speech to slur, she didn't panic. Dr. Fitzsimmons had said this might happen; eventually it would pass.

"I'm here now, aren't I? Damn, Florida. I rushed through the afternoon and left work early to board my plane. Spent another hour driving in from Sedalia so I could be here midweek. And now all you can do is bust my chops?"

Yada yada yada. Daniel hadn't noticed her tears. She watched him continue to stride around in an injured snit, and kept a tight rein on her own temper.

Sometimes Daniel acted like a spoiled child.

*   *   *

In Missouri's room, next to Florida's, Stan got up to close the door on Daniel's ranting, wondering if the man knew how stupid he sounded.

"That happen a lot?" He poked a thumb at the door.

Sitting at a French Provincial dressing table, a recent addition to the room, Missouri twisted her hair into a knot and made a stab with a fluorescent orange hair comb. Her tongue poked out between her lips. The comb slipped and her hair tumbled over her shoulders again. She growled but started twisting again.

"Sometimes. Daniel can be *such* a child."

Resuming his seat on the bed, Stan choked back a laugh, feeling glad, then guilty that he was glad about any trouble in Eden. Not that Florida didn't deserve happiness. He'd had his with Serena and he wished her all the best, but Cordelia wouldn't be the same with her gone. With *Missouri* gone, he amended.

Leaning against the headboard, he folded his arms behind his head and gave himself up to delight watching his daughter. Like on every evening since Florida's accident, he'd left work to spirit her off to supper, taking advantage of the situation to soak up the time she had left in Cordelia.

Also because he was uncertain how far he could trust Tamara. Even though she belonged more to his parents' history than his, she had absconded with a chunk of their money and managed to hide for sixteen years, returning only long enough to dump her kids and spit on his father's grave before she'd taken off again. Not exactly the stuff guardians were made of.

Although if it hadn't been for the grace of the gods and his second wife, he wouldn't have been much better. Through Serena, he'd gotten another chance, not just as a husband, but as a father. And this time he hadn't screwed it all up. It was too late for him and Alcea, but he'd done his best to make Serena happy, and his utmost to involve himself with his oldest daughter, Kathleen. He'd come late to the table, but she'd learned to love him anyway before she'd moved on to college and then to the Big Apple, relegating him mostly to holidays and a weekly telephone call.

Which was as it should be; she had her own life. But now he felt Missouri slipping through his fingers, as well. Way too soon.

As she took another stab at her hair, his gaze wandered her bedroom. The dressing table was a piece of feminine fluff among sturdier fare. Bunk beds hugged one wall. A bookcase crammed with a model-car collection leaned against another.

From the age of four, Missouri had been Julius's avid apprentice and she was still the only female Stan knew who knew a crankcase from a camshaft. Actually, except for Julius, the only *person*. God knew, he didn't.

Despite ill health and a disabled hand, Julius had continued to work up until the time he was forced to admit he needed the chair. Once he had, Missouri hadn't been the only one to notice his increasing listlessness, but she'd been the first to jump on a solution. She'd begged money from Florida, rooted through Harvey's Hobby House, an outpost of models, games, and trinkets just around the corner, and, after a lot of debate Stan had difficulty following, picked out a box containing the die-cast metal parts for a 1955 Chevrolet Bel Air convertible.

Julius's eyes had lit up like Christmas when she'd put it in his hands. A new partnership had been born. With Missouri providing the sharp eyes and nimble fingers, and Julius the patience and entertainment, several evenings a week now found the two bent over the newest die-cast model, each one sparking Julius's memory into reminiscences of cars loved and lost.

Stan's daughter was a marvel.

He wondered how Julius would survive without her. Florida seemed to be the only one who didn't realize that no matter how much she schemed, Julius intended to stay put in Cordelia. As he'd told Stan, "Florida's a granddaughter to me, that girl, but *'crabbed age and youth cannot live together.'* " He'd waited a beat, but when Stan (who remembered only *Romeo and Juliet* from high school) stayed silent, he'd sighed with obvious dismay at Stan's lack of education. *"Passionate Pilgrim."* Then a little later, "Besides, I don't cotton much to that new beau of hers. Seems she's been blinded by more flash than substance."

Hear, hear.

Thinking of how much Julius would miss Missouri, how much *he* would miss Missouri, his ire at Daniel Davenport, unreasonable though it might be, increased. It'd been two years since Serena had passed, and three since Kathleen had graduated and moved, but damn if he didn't sometimes feel like life was taking away everything he loved.

Paybacks were hell.

"You don't like my hair this way?" Missouri was watching his face in the mirror.

"I like your hair any which way."

She rolled her eyes and went back to her primping, tongue jutting out in concentration, head tilting so she could see every angle. He smiled, a sad smile, wishing he could spend every remaining second with her until her mom up and married. But he couldn't. He glanced at his watch. In fact, he had precisely one more hour today before business intruded.

As Serena had neared the last stage of her life, he'd realized the stark truth in that old chestnut "Life is short." And he realized that, for most of his, he'd been toiling at the bank like his dad had before him and *his* dad had before *him*. Feeling like he'd been handed the family heirloom for safekeeping, it had never occurred to him to question what he was doing.

But when Serena fell sick, he questioned a lot of things. His job. Fate. God . . .

All while working his body and working out his anger and grief. Early mornings found him at the local Y before he joined Serena for breakfast;

nighttimes when he couldn't sleep saw him pounding the path that circled the duck pond in Memorial Park, once, twice, four times . . . and ultimately more circuits than he wanted to count. By the time hospice workers were haunting their home, he was running miles along the wooded, uneven trails of the surrounding Ozark hills in a futile effort to stem the unrelenting approach of a future he couldn't control.

During those bleak hours, he'd considered his own future without his wife. The long and empty hours he'd need to fill. Some years before, he'd invested heavily in Florida and Alcea's franchise endeavors—no cheap enterprise—rather amazed he'd done so at the time. But pounding the pathways, he'd realized it had been a vicarious venture—he'd enviously and avidly followed their dreams instead of living his own. Before Serena had drawn her last breath, while she was still capable of encouragement, he'd given up the bank, plowed his money and efforts into planning a new business. Not long after her death, he'd opened the door on Strides, the largest fitness facility in the region and slowly becoming its best. Plans were progressing for outlets elsewhere. It had required hard work and long hours: Strides opened at dawn . . .

And closed at ten. And he'd told his second-in-command, a bundle of muscle named Jess, he'd handle the night deposit.

He pushed up from the bed and stretched. "I

don't have much time left, cutie, so if you still want ice cream . . ."

"Yes!" She twisted around. "I'm having Chocolate Death. What'll you get?"

"No-Guilt Napoleon."

Missouri grimaced at the mention of the only fat-free flavor Sin-Sational offered and turned back to the mirror. "You *always* get that."

Yeah, not much excitement in No-Guilt Napoleon, but—he patted a flat belly that had once had the consistency of a down pillow—he had to stay in shape for the marathon. *The* marathon. The Kilauea Volcano Wilderness Run, a twenty-six-mile test of endurance known as one of the world's toughest.

When he'd started running, his only goal had been escape from pain; once that had dulled to a throb, he'd hunted down new challenges. First had come some local runs—to benefit the library at Cordelia High School, to raise money for St. Andrew's outreach programs, to assist the Ladies' Auxiliary, the Masonic Lodge, and Brownie Troop 1411. When small runs palled, he'd involved himself and finally Strides in regional efforts for the American Cancer Society.

To make a promotional splash, he'd not just entered himself. He'd planned and promoted team participation, stirring local interest, drumming up funds for charity, and increasing membership in Strides. Over the short history of his new business, his groups had joined throngs in Des Moines,

Kansas City, St. Louis, and had capped last year with the Chicago Charity Run.

But Kilauea was the biggest of them all and the challenge of his lifetime. Originally he'd intended to enter one of the run's lesser counterparts, the ten-mile Rim Run or even the Kilauea Caldera run or walk, tame by comparison at a mere five. But when he'd filled out his application, he'd hesitated only a moment before checking the wilderness run.

It was time to see what he really could do.

As the date approached, despite his fitness, he wondered if he'd stretched too far. Not just because of the punishment his body would take, but because of the hit to Strides's bottom line at a time when he needed capital for expansion. Travel to Hawaii wasn't cheap, so he'd deep-discounted the cost, expecting a loss, but figuring that with the right press releases, his group could get mentions in local papers where he planned to open new outlets next year. But half-price tickets to paradise had proven irresistible. Thinking he might get a dozen participants if he was lucky, he'd lured four times that from across the state, with a loss now in the tens of thousands and counting. He'd held his breath as applicants had finally trickled to a halt, leaving him with a meager cash flow, but no need to assume more debt.

Missouri finally lost patience, wadded her hair in a knot, and wrapped a band around it. "Horrid," she pronounced.

"Nah. You always look like a princess."

"Oh, Daddy." Missouri shook her head.

Stan was again hit by melancholy. The roll of the eyes. The exasperated tone . . . the universal female expressions—ones perfected by his ex-wife and ex-mistress, and even, on occasion, used by Serena—for the cluelessness of men. Missouri was growing up. And away.

With Daniel. Who was still grousing in the room next door.

Abruptly, Stan stalked to the door and yanked it open. "Can it!"

Silence fell.

Rubbing his hands together in a job-well-done gesture, he turned around. Staring at him wide-eyed, Missouri clapped her hands over her mouth before laughter escaped. But her efforts were futile. A snort sounded through her fingers, and she went off into peals.

And that did it for Stan. He joined in.

And a short heartbeat later, he heard a burst of laughter from the room next door. Florida had caught the wave.

That night, for the first time since the accident, Florida fell asleep with a smile on her face. She hadn't meant to laugh at Daniel, but the look on his face when Stan had shouted down the hallway had been . . . priceless. Daniel was so accustomed to issuing orders himself, the idea someone else would take umbrage at his bitching . . .

. . . because it *was* bitching . . .

. . . had completely blown his mind.

The look on his face had combined with the sounds of hilarity coming from Missouri's room. She'd tried to hang on to an expression of disapproval, but her lips wouldn't stop quivering. When she'd finally let loose, Daniel had turned fire engine red. She'd managed to stop almost as fast as she'd started, but hadn't been able to talk again without a quiver in her voice.

He'd gotten disgusted and left, muttering something about not being appreciated.

She felt rather bad, but *really*. Who was the injured party here?

Still, she thought, snuggling into her pillows, she'd call him in the morning, tell him she was sorry, stroke his ego, and remind him of how well she stroked other things. She smiled. He'd forgive her.

But when she woke up in the morning, calling Daniel was the furthest thing from her mind. Because when she opened her eyes . . .

She couldn't see.

Chapter 7

Thinking her vision was just temporarily blurred like it had been before, she blinked. Blinked again. But all she could see was a milky haze, somewhat like early-morning sun rising behind a band of thick gauze. Her hands flew to her face and she felt her eyelids to see if they were open. They were.

Trying to stem her rising panic, she turned her head. The haze grew darker when she twisted toward the interior of the room, lighter toward where the windows would be. But she couldn't make anything out. Nothing.

"Omigod, omigod, omigod."

Her voice was a whisper. She swung her legs out of bed and stumbled forward, holding out her hands. Her foot hit the leg of the chair Daniel had pulled up near the bed, but had forgotten to put back before he'd stalked out of the room. She sprawled forward. The chair clunked against the wall as it toppled over.

Breath coming fast and hard, she rolled over onto her back. She needed to calm down. Hadn't Dr. Fitzsimmons warned her she could have some vision problems? This was simply some aberration because of her concussion. Something that would pass. Like the slurred speech she'd experienced before.

The thoughts failed to reassure her. "Omigod, omigod."

"Florida?"

She heard the door open.

"What the hell—"

Footsteps rushed forward. The smell of oranges. Tamara. "Are you okay?" Hands felt her limbs. "I was getting the paper; Julius said he heard a crash."

Florida pushed her away. "Stop it. I can't see!"

"You can't—things are blurry?"

"No, things are not *blurry*. I. Can. Not. See." Disoriented, she needed Tamara's help to rise. She didn't want to need Tamara. Once on her feet, she tried again to push her away. "Call Dak. Or Alcea." *Anyone but you.*

Tamara didn't let go. "Sure, honey." Tamara guided her forward.

"And don't call me honey."

"Sure, honey." Hands released her, left her standing uncertainly. There was a rummaging; then something bumped the backs of her knees.

She realized Tamara had uprighted the chair. Hand grappling to feel it behind her, she sat.

More footsteps. "What in Hades is going on in here? Julius called—" The scent of vanilla. Cinnamon. Hands gripped her knees. Alcea had knelt in front of her.

Florida clutched at her. "I can't see. I can't *see*!"

"You mean *nothing*?"

"Some light. Where light should be. But nothing else." Her voice rose. "Nothing else!"

"Shh. Shh," Alcea crooned. "I'm sure it's something temporary. I'll call your doctor."

Running feet down the hallway.

"Mom!" Missouri, breathing heavily. "Julius told me to see what happened. Are you okay?"

No. I'm not okay. I'm far from okay. "I'm okay. Right as rain." Florida managed to steady her voice. "Come here." She held out her hand. Missouri's slipped into it, warm and vibrant.

"Then what's wrong?"

"I . . . I seem to be temporarily sightless."

"You mean like Helen Keller?"

Dear God, no! She swallowed. "Yes, like Helen Keller."

"But just for the moment," Alcea said, giving Florida's knee a pat.

Florida's ears were picking up every nuance. Despite the confident words, she heard the worry. "Yes, just for the moment." Nausea churned her stomach. "Will someone point me to the bathroom?"

Hands reached, led her forward. Cinnamon. Alcea. She gripped her friend's arm.

"Wait here with me, honey." Tamara's voice, summoning Missouri.

Hearing her daughter's chirrup of agreement, Florida felt a new stab of unease. This wasn't right. None of it was right. Beneath her feet, carpet gave way to tile, then to the thick fluff of red shag in front of the vanity. Her stomach convulsed again. "Alone. I want to be alone."

"Sure you'll be okay?" Alcea asked. She placed one of Florida's hands flat on the marble vanity. "Sink here. Toilet straight behind."

"I know the damn room, Alcea." She couldn't keep the undertone of hysteria out of her voice.

"I know, I know." Alcea's distraction heightened her alarm. Alcea never got flustered. Florida heard rummaging; then Alcea moved her hand again. "I put your toothpaste and brush right here."

"I can manage."

"I'm going to call the doctor and try to track down Dak. He's out somewhere. Tamara is right outside, so call when you're ready to come out."

Florida didn't respond.

"Promise?"

Florida let out a breath. "Promise." She'd lock herself inside until Alcea returned.

The door closed. Florida waited until she heard Alcea's footsteps recede; then she flipped on the overhead fan, felt her way past the shower stall and Jacuzzi tub to the commode, carefully lowered herself to her knees, and threw up.

Omigod. Omigod.

Unable to locate Dak, Alcea had summoned Stan from Strides right after Florida had locked herself in the bathroom. Dropping everything at the note of hysteria in his usually calm ex-wife's voice, he'd left Jess in charge of the matrons who dropped their kids in the on-site day care facility before joining the Thursday Morning Moms' Makeover workout, and rushed over, bounding up the stairs to hear Alcea assuring Florida that, yes, absolutely, she, and not Tamara, would watch Missouri, while Stan drove Florida to Columbia. She'd called Dr. Fitzsimmons, who had made an emergency appointment for her with an ophthalmologist he'd said was top-notch.

Having vowed after Serena's illness to avoid all medical facilities forever and ever, amen, Stan had entered the room ready to protest that it made more sense for *him* to watch Missouri—he could even take her back to Strides—while Alcea drove Florida.

But then he'd seen Florida. She'd sat stiffly erect on the edge of her bed, eyes directed straight ahead. Pale. Silent. White-knuckle. Her fear had filled the room. The feeling that had swept him had been as familiar to him as breathing; he'd no more been able to turn away from the task Alcea had assigned him than he would have refused help to Serena.

But now, sitting in a thinly padded chair next to Florida across from an empty desk in an expensively appointed office not far from the hospital she'd left only a few days ago, he felt another familiar feeling. One of doom. They were waiting for the ophthalmologist, Dr. Treter, to come in and explain the results of the umpteen tests Florida had just been through. And while he was trying to keep an optimistic outlook, he couldn't count the times he'd spent hearing bad news delivered in quiet voices in quiet offices just like this one.

At the sound of muffled voices in the corridor, he felt a sudden urge to run. His legs even twitched.

But instead he reached for Florida's hand and held tight, hoping his grip gave her some comfort. He was all she had right now. And, despite her silence, he knew she was scared shitless. Hell, *he* was scared shitless. They still hadn't reached Daniel, largely because Florida refused to let anyone give his secretary a reason urgent enough for him to be interrupted. She didn't want to tell him anything until there was something to tell.

Given Stan's primitive dislike of Florida's chosen, a sudden testosterone-laden satisfaction that she was relying on him instead of her fiancé spiked in his blood, then turned to shame. Juvenile. And proof that the exasperated-woman look he'd seen on his daughter's face yesterday had justifiable origins. This wasn't a competition. Of course he'd do whatever he could to help. Because she was Missouri's mother. Missouri's *engaged* mother. No more, no less.

The voices drew closer, paused outside the door, then faded off down the corridor. Florida had tensed, but now her shoulders slumped. He glanced at his watch. It had been only fifteen minutes since Dr. Treter's assistant had led them away from the stands of equipment they'd used to test her and into the office where the doctor had initially taken Florida's case history, referring frequently to the documents Dr. Fitzsimmons had messengered over. But it felt like forever. Waiting was the bitch. Worse than any news.

As the doctor had studied Florida, preferring to conduct all the tests himself in this case, the assistant had explained the examination in excruciating detail, most of which Stan had forgotten: intraocular testing for a pressure reading, an ophthal-something-scope to look inside the eye, and a retinal camera to capture pictures. They'd injected dye into her arm to photograph the network of veins that fed her optic nerves, her retinas . . . her eyes. But neither the doctor nor his assistant had been nearly as forthcoming about what conclusions they might be drawing as they jotted down notes and twisted dials, Dr. Treter saying only that he hesitated to draw any until "all the evidence is in."

Stan glanced at Florida. He'd been the one prodding (gently, gently—in his experience, impatience only upped a doctor's dander); Florida had sat silent throughout, responding only to direct questions. She was still voiceless, her eyes black against her white skin, pupils still dilated from the drops they'd used.

"Everything will be all right," he murmured, giving her hand another squeeze.

They were the same words he'd used with Serena. Empty ones. Because, of course, everything wasn't going to be all right and they'd both known it. Still, somehow, it had helped Serena to hear him say them.

"Yeah, right."

Obviously they didn't mean much to Florida. Her dry tone reminded him she wasn't Serena. Like Alcea, she was made of sterner stuff, two peas from the same very frightening pod, when you got right down to it. Except—he glanced down at Florida's hand linked with his, her grip tight, her knuckles white pebbles—Florida hadn't shaken off his hand. Maybe today's reality was a little too much even for her.

Another voice came from the corridor. Only this time, it stopped at the door. Dr. Treter entered, holding a file.

Florida straightened, her expression growing sharply intense, as though her sightlessness might affect her hearing unless she concentrated hard.

Dr. Treter pulled a couple of films from the file. "Sorry for the wait. I wanted to consult a colleague." He clipped the films to a light box and flipped it on.

He nodded to Stan. "We'll leave the office dim because of Ms. Jones's dilation. Don't want any further injury."

That sounded good. If the situation was hopeless, why care about that?

The doctor addressed Florida. "You may want to wear a pair of sunglasses when you're outside. I know that makes things even more difficult, but it'll protect your eyes until it's habit not to look toward the sun."

Florida licked her lips. "Habit?" she repeated.

That didn't sound good.

The doctor sat down in a leather chair behind his desk. "I'm getting ahead of myself. Ms. Jones—"

"Florida."

"Florida. Your case history, the exams, the films . . . they're diagnostic for a condition we term Purtscher's Retinopathy."

Stan frowned. "Purtscher's what?"

"Retinopathy. The retina is an extension of the optic nerve, which fans over the back of the eye— the retina—to receive images. Retinopathy is the term used to indicate the retina is shortchanged of blood."

Florida's mouth moved, but nothing came out. She closed it and swallowed.

Stan filled the silence. "How would that happen?"

"This condition is rare, so not well documented." The doctor leaned back and steepled his hands. "But the theory is that impact to the head or chest can generate an intravascular hydrostatic reaction that transmits to the retinal vasculature. Another school of thought is—"

Another doctor who had flunked Laymen's Language 101. Stan stopped him with a raised hand. "English, please." Voice pleasant but firm.

"Sorry. The theory is that a sharp impact sends a shock wave, if you will, through the vascular system, and ultimately through the veins and capillaries that, in turn, affect the eye. Another school of thought is that frontal head trauma can stretch the optic nerve. Other possible causes—and you'll be tested, Florida, to rule these out, although at your age, I doubt they're a cause—could be an underlying pancreatic or vascular disease. You see—"

Stan interrupted again. They didn't need a course in the subject, just some straight talk. "Doctor."

Dr. Treter paused. "Sorry, again. Another theory—and to me the most reasonable—is that the impact dislodged a small embolism—could be fat, air, bacteria. . . . In other words, whatever it was traveled through the bloodstream and eventually lodged in a narrow artery, where it caused occlusion—" Stan opened his mouth, but the doctor caught himself first. "I mean, where it obstructed the blood supply to your eyes, resulting in what you're experiencing now." He motioned to the films. "It's visible in the dark areas on the angiography."

Stan looked at the films. There were multiple dark areas. He looked over at Florida. Chin set, she sat silent. His gaze moved back to the doctor. "Then you'll—what? Surgery? Drugs? How do you *un*obstruct things?"

Dr. Treter hesitated. "I wish it were simple. There's no routine standard of care—in other words, no accepted proven treatment—because the condition is rare. There's some anecdotal evidence that high doses of corticosteroids—powerful drugs with anti-inflammatory properties—can produce some improvement. The steroids would be administered continuously through an IV over the next few days, so the treatment requires hospitalization. On Monday, once you've completed the course, Florida, we'll look at things again and probably put you on an oral dose for a while."

"Downsides?" Stan asked.

"Possibly increased appetite. Maybe some weight gain or upset stomach. Or headache, mood changes, trouble sleeping. The drugs will also temporarily lower Florida's resistance to infection, but she'll be on them only a short time, so we wouldn't expect any of the side effects associated with long-term use. All the rest will go away when she stops taking them."

Florida continued to remain silent.

Stan cleared his throat. "And there are no other options?"

"No."

The doctor gave him a look. He knew that look. Part pity. Part helplessness. On the scale of effectiveness, Dr. Treter's proposed treatment fell into the realm of Hail Mary.

Stan rubbed a hand over his face. "Florida?"

She gave a barely perceptible nod. He addressed the doctor. "Then let's do it."

"Fine." Dr. Treter rose. "Give us a few minutes to call University."

"Wait." Florida finally spoke up.

Halfway to the door, the doctor paused. "Yes?"

"You said . . . *some* improvement. There's only a chance for *some* improvement?"

"I'm afraid so." Dr. Treter's face softened. "I'm so sorry. . . . The chances for a complete recovery are almost nonexistent."

The chances for a complete recovery are almost nonexistent.

Dr. Treter had returned with more information and more encouragement, but she'd hardly heard him. Those were the words that were stuck in her head, the ones still knocking around in her skull a half hour later. Her thoughts smacked together with such force, she was surprised the noise wasn't echoing through Stan's Suburban as he drove them toward the hospital she'd left a few days before. Only a few days. It seemed another lifetime. From the warmth in her lap, the sun was slanting in through her window. Late afternoon. Maybe early evening.

I can't see the sky. I can't read a clock. I'm blind, blind, blind. . . .

She held herself straight, hands clenched together in her lap, afraid if she moved, she'd crack into pieces.

Stan's hand covered her fists and squeezed. "Let's get something to eat. You've only had breakfast."

"I . . . I'm not hungry."

Her stomach was hopping all over the place,

keyed up by next-to-no breakfast, the dye from the angiogram, and fear. It chose that moment to growl.

"Uh-huh," Stan said. "There's a Perkins up ahead."

"No! Really."

Remembering breakfast, she cringed. Becoming almost hysterical over Tamara's attempts to help her with a bowl of cantaloupe chunks, she'd slapped her mother's hands away while Alcea was on the phone. She'd picked up her fork and tried viciously stabbing for the fruit, missing and finally firing the fork into a corner, where she'd heard it clatter to the floor. Crying and frightened at her unusual display, Missouri had run from the room.

"Good job, Florida," Tamara had said. "You've got good reason to be upset; I don't blame you. But for Chrissake, around your daughter, get a grip."

Get a grip? She'd been stunned into stillness. She'd awakened blind and that was Tamara's best advice?

She'd swiveled toward the sound of the voice. "Get out," she'd forced through her teeth. "I don't want to see you. I don't want to hear you. I don't want to *smell* you. *Get out!*" Her voice had risen to a near screech.

Upstairs, she heard Missouri wail and immediately felt ashamed. Tamara's footsteps had sounded on the stairs as she went to her granddaughter.

"No, really," she repeated now to Stan. "They'll give me something at the hospital."

Stan snorted. "I was thinking along the lines of something edible."

As the car slowed and turned, she gripped the armrest. "Stan. I . . . I can't. I need help eating." Like a baby. Like a goddamn baby . . .

Like a blind person.

The car eased to a halt. "Florida," he said gently. "We'll manage. I won't let you embarrass yourself."

She thought of the fork. "That's what you think."

"And nothing you do will embarrass me. And if you're uncomfortable—quit worrying. At this time of day, the place will be deserted."

As he led her to the door, careful to murmur to her about any obstacles before she encountered them, she flashed on an image of Stan and Serena in Peg's, a time after illness had weakened Serena, but before it had consigned her to bed. Stan's wife had looked exhausted, but her dark eyes had glowed; it was obvious she'd enjoyed being out. Stan had been the picture of consideration, helping her with whatever she couldn't manage, but doing it unobtrusively and preserving Serena's dignity. He'd used the very same tone with her. A comforting tone.

Inside, the restaurant was quiet. They were seated quickly and she heard the clatter of silver and glassware as someone slid their place settings in front of them. Afraid she'd knock over her water glass, she carefully kept her hands in her lap.

There was silence across the table; then Stan said, "If you put your hand on the edge of the table . . . yes, there . . . and walk it forward about eight inches, you'll find your glass." Hesitantly, she tried, her fingers stopping at the feel of cold glass. She picked it up and drank. "Now. What'll you have? For salads, they have—"

"Just a hamburger." She set down her glass—carefully.

"Are you ready to order?"

A chipper voice sounded to her right and she started, hand knocking the glass. Fortunately, though, it didn't topple. She slid her hand back to her lap and, not knowing if the waitress had addressed her or Stan, sat silent. After a beat, the waitress said, "What'll she have?"

Florida suddenly felt tiny, invisible . . . worthless.

"A hamburger. With—" He stopped. "Florida? What'll it be?"

"Just mustard. Nothing else." The better to keep from making a mess.

She heard pen scratching on paper. "And what'll she have to drink?"

"What'll she . . . ? You know, why ask me?" Stan's voice wasn't unkind, but it held a hint of annoyance. "Obviously she's not deaf and mute."

Flushing but finally locating some pride, Florida sat up straighter.

There was a moment of hesitation. "I'm sorry, ma'am," the waitress said. "What would you like to drink?"

Such a simple question, yet it made her feel like she'd regained a little control over her life. Not much, but a little.

The rest of their meal passed without incident. An hour, and a full half of a hamburger, later, her stomach felt better. As did her spirits, which had risen a few degrees above rock bottom. Stan had steered the conversation away from her condition, anticipating her needs with matter-of-fact instructions interspersed between other topics, as though her lack of sight was a mere inconvenience.

It was, of course, impossible to forget her situation—impossible not to be horrified by her situation—but for a little while, between moments of stark clarity that almost had her climbing the walls in panic, she'd been able to pretend what was happening to her, well, wasn't happening to her. That this whole ordeal was temporary. That she *would* be cured.

When they left Perkins, she felt less like a freak.

At least for a few minutes. As they pulled out of the parking lot, as the distraction of the restaurant faded, her anxiety again careened toward terror. She couldn't see. How could she manage if she couldn't see?

As Stan steered the car toward the hospital, his voice, still keeping steadfastly to mundane topics, receded, and other noises intruded. The wind that rushed past the windows held an ominous edge. The radio announcer's tone grew strident. The whine of the tires over asphalt held menace. Every sound, so familiar, so commonplace, took on the timbre of a nightmare. Traffic surged by and she drew her arms inward. A car honked and she jumped.

The chances for a complete recovery are almost nonexistent.

Fumbling in her purse, she pulled out her cell phone and thrust it toward Stan. "Try again."

About every half hour throughout the day, she'd had Stan punch Daniel's speed dial code, then hand her the phone. So far, she'd reached only voice mail. Not uncommon. Whenever Daniel had a full slate of meetings, he left the phone with his secretary, Rita, so he wouldn't be distracted. This time, though, it rang through. Twice, three times. And when he finally picked up, she panicked and flipped the phone shut. Then fumbled for the off button before he could call back. He wouldn't think it odd; despite the cell phone towers that had proliferated in the Ozark hills like giant silver thistles, sometimes reception was still erratic.

"Still not answering?" Stan said. "Leave a message. Or talk to his secretary. She'd interrupt him if she knew what it was about."

"It's . . . it's just not something you leave in a message." It was just not something she could bring herself to say at all. *Hi, hon. Just wanted to let you know I'm blind. Blind, blind, blind . . .* Telling him would make it all real. Too real. "Besides, we're doing everything we can, so there's no point in makin' him drop his business and come running."

There was a beat of silence. "But he'd want to, Florida."

Would he? She thought of how little time he'd given her concussion. She was afraid to find out.

"I just . . ." Her resolve not to break down . . . broke down. She threw the phone on the floor and covered her eyes. Why did she cover her eyes? She couldn't see anyway. A laugh escaped her. It was too high.

"Florida?"

The car slowed. She swayed as Stan made a turn, then slowed further.

"Don't stop. I'm okay." *Drive forever. I can manage if we just drive forever*. Her breath was coming fast and shallow.

"Right. You're hyperventilating."

The car stopped. As she'd done so many times today, she tried to open her eyes so she could see where they were before it hit her that her eyes *were* open.

A sob hitched her chest. "I said *don't stop*."

"Take deep breaths. Hang on."

Stan's door opened and closed. What was he doing? She strained to hear his footsteps over the running motor and the hum of the air conditioner. Panic rose. *What if he fell? What if someone else got in the car? How could she tell? Stan shouldn't leave her. She needed to hear him. She needed—*

"Goddammit, Stan!" She felt hysteria crowding up her throat. "Where are you? Where are—"

Her door unlatched and warm air rushed in. "Florida."

Despite her best efforts, a sob burst forth. She groped for him, her fingers finally wrapping around his collar.

"It's okay. It's okay. Scoot."

Stan's body crowded hers against the console. Turning sideways, he pulled her close. It was damn uncomfortable, but she didn't loosen her grip. She wanted to. She wanted to push him away. But she couldn't make her fingers follow her brain's command.

"I don't want—" Another sob loosened her chest.

"I don't care what you want. What's happened sucks. Big-time *sucks*. Quit with the stiff-upper-lip act and let it all out."

Pressing her lips together, she resisted the pressure building inside.

"I'll bring Missouri to see you tomorrow at the hospital. You don't want to fall apart in front of her, do you?"

"That's hitting . . . below the . . . belt." Her breath hitched between words. The pressure increased.

"Cry, Florida. Cry."

She burrowed her face into his neck and cried.

Chapter 8

The next four days passed in a—*ha-ha*—blur. Over the weekend, they'd pumped her full of corticosteroids. She'd lain there—when she wasn't eating; *increased appetite* didn't quite cover it—straining to shift through the shadows of light and dark for any signs of improvement. She detected some. But not enough. Nothing less than full recovery could ever be enough.

A therapist dropped by a few times to give her some pointers, but until they knew how much vision would return, there would be little therapy. She'd been told that once her vision had stabilized, an assessment would be conducted and then the real therapy would start.

She gritted her teeth whenever Daniel or Dak or Alcea admonished her to buck up and believe things would get better. They were her own personal Greek Chorus of Optimism.

And they were friggin' tiresome. Dak, the worst.

On Saturday morning, he'd shown up with a caramel *macchiato* and two of Alcea's Tropical Blend Muffins, which she'd accepted with much more enthusiasm than she did the *Everything happens for a reason* monologue that he launched into after a few pleasantries and before she'd had time to let the first sip of sweet coffee slide down her throat.

She could see him in her mind's eye, lounging in the single chair in the room: jeans, shirt open at the throat, Doc Martens up on the side of her bed, the picture of casualness. But she could feel the way his body had tensed, feel his gaze fixed on her, his eyes sharp with concern.

Tempted to tell him to shut up, she refrained. Maybe from sugar euphoria. Or maybe because under the philosophical words, she heard pain in his voice.

". . . Tragedy shifts our lives in unexpected directions, often to a better outcome. But we usually don't grasp that at the time, we—"

"Dak."

He stopped. "What?"

She knew where the tension and pain came from. "It wasn't your fault."

There was a beat of silence. Then his voice quietly carried to her. "I'm the one that upset you."

No, Tamara had upset her. Tamara had always

upset her. But tell Dak that, and he'd continue to blame himself. She'd like to let him, but . . . *damn* some lingering sense of justice; she was unable to carry bitterness that far. "And I'm the one who reacted by jumping in the car and driving off like a bat out of hell. I'm just glad . . ." Oh, this was taking *everything* she had. She didn't want to be fair, didn't want to take responsibility. "I'm just glad this happened to me and I didn't hurt someone else. And—"

This last bit was *really* going to hurt.

"And"—she took a deep breath—"if you need to make peace with *her*, I won't try to stop you. Your life. Just quit with the lectures, okay?"

There. That ought to earn her a place in heaven. Feeling like she'd just completed one of Stan's marathons, she laid her head back.

She heard Dak stand up; then his hand smoothed the hair off her forehead. "Thank you. And I'll try to keep my philosophies to myself."

She sighed. "You're incapable. But I appreciate the thought."

She'd been right. By that evening, he was again channeling Buddha. She'd managed—barely—to refrain from leaping at his throat. It had been a one-car accident with a freakish result. A harsh twist of fate. No rhyme or reason. Nobody to blame.

And nowhere to spill her rage.

She would have ordered Dak out—both Dak and Alcea—except that would have left her with only the drone of the television for company, since

Daniel always seemed to be off ordering someone around. So she bore with their heartiness, wishing instead for Stan's blunt voice telling her things sucked.

They did. With a vengeance.

But the only time she'd seen Stan (*seen* him, what a joke) had been when he'd driven Missouri to Columbia after her ballet lessons Saturday so she could reassure herself that Mommy was indeed still among the living. A faint odor of citrus when they'd visited had told her that Tamara was with them, although her mother hadn't uttered a word. Assuming from her silence that Tamara didn't want a repeat of the scene from Thursday morning, and not wanting one, either—at least not in Missouri's presence—Florida chose to ignore the fact that she knew her mother was there. The memory of that morning filled her with righteous indignation—Tamara could have shown more sensitivity—but it also brushed her with shame. Which she ignored, too.

Along with the strained note she heard in Missouri's voice. She was just too filled with herself to worry about much of anything else. More than understandable, she decided, to leave fretting about the business to Alcea, fretting about doctors to Daniel, and fretting about Missouri to Stan.

At least until the end of the week, when Stan would leave for the Kilauea Marathon. He'd offered to cancel, and she'd almost accepted the gesture, which just showed how incapable she felt of even the teensiest of selfless gestures. But when she'd thrown Stan's offer in Daniel's face when Daniel had mentioned making a brief return to Kansas City, she'd almost heard her fiancé bristle. Daniel hadn't left her side since then, so she'd had no choice except to be noble, although she was feeling far from it. "You've trained so hard for this, Stan. And you have a lot riding on it financially. We'll be fine for the week you're gone."

"But I hate to think of you—"

She'd fumbled out a hand and he'd taken it. "Daniel will take care of me. And Alcea will take care of Missouri." Alcea, not Daniel. She suddenly realized that since Daniel had arrived, her fiancé hadn't once asked about Missouri.

Still Stan had hesitated, until Daniel had blown into the room, muttering about incompetents, glaring at Stan, then stooping to kiss her. When she'd come up for breath, Stan had been gone.

Just as she'd thought, Daniel had descended on the hospital complete with all his weight to throw around. But on the weekend, there were few hospital staff he considered significant enough for him to throw it at. So instead, he addressed the condition like he would a particularly thorny boardroom problem and rousted his minions away from their weekend plans to set them on research, including locating the best vision experts in the region.

And the minions faithfully reported back, although not with anything they didn't already know. As Dr. Treter had indicated, Purtscher's was rare enough that there wasn't much medical documentation. What there was often conflicted. But one thing was clear.

Any which way you looked at it, the prognosis wasn't good.

By Monday, while relieved to be free of the IV drip that had tied her to the hospital all weekend, she felt no more rested than she had when she'd arrived. Daniel's energy and frustration had exhausted her, and the lack of optimistic news from his underlings hadn't helped, either.

That afternoon found her back in Dr. Treter's office. Just as before, the soft-voiced assistant had shown them in. Just as before, the occasional muffled voice in the hall and the hum of the air conditioner were the only sounds she heard while she waited. And just as before, Dr. Treter had taken a place at his desk and delivered the results of her exam in measured, professional tones with a sympathetic undernote. But instead of Stan holding her hand, it was Daniel.

"I'm encouraged by your results. There's some improvement in the look of your retinas."

"I can see some things better, but—" Florida started.

Daniel interrupted as though she hadn't spoken. "What exactly do you mean, *improvement*?"

Florida sighed. Throughout the examination Dr. Treter had just completed, Daniel had fired unceasing questions. The doctor's normally patient replies had taken on an edge, and then he'd started responding only in grunts.

There was a beat of silence. Then, "You were about to say, Florida?"

Daniel grumbled under his breath but shut up.

She tried again. "I actually see sometimes—at least something." There was more brightness in the light patches, more depth to the shadows, some color, and occasionally a shadow moved— or maybe it was only her imagination.

"It wouldn't be uncommon for me to see more pronounced retinal changes than you're detecting visually so far. We'll give it a little more time, but it's likely you'll see there's some immediate improvement. But small improvement, Florida, I must warn you."

The doctor continued, explaining the physiology of the eye more thoroughly. Her Greek Chorus must have brainwashed her over the weekend—she received each word like a challenge. A horrible, awful challenge, but with his affirming at least some improvement, it was one she thought she could shoulder. She listened carefully—knowledge was power—but from the way Daniel was shifting in his seat, apparently he figured he already had enough of that commodity.

She heard a pen scratch on paper. "I'm writing you a prescription for oral steroids."

Her stomach growled in response.

"And I'll want to see you back here in one week. After that, we'll monitor you every three or four weeks for a while, although I'd expect improvement—if it continues—to become only infinitesimal after that." He paused and she heard his chair squeak. She assumed he'd settled back. "While I hate to say it, I need to remind you, again, Florida, that your chances for a *substantial* recovery are very, very small. I wish I could give you better news, but while you may—or may not—gain form perception and/or more clarity over the next few days and weeks, you'll want to start preparing yourself for the future. You won't be able to see like you once did, but there are lots of places and people that can help you learn to regain your independence. On your way out, my assistant will give you a packet of information. It will explain the resources—"

"That's it?" Daniel broke in. "That's all you can do? Just give us a prescription and a *packet of information?*"

One of her hands gripped the armrest; the other squeezed Daniel's. Dr. Treter wasn't to blame. "Daniel . . ."

It was like she hadn't said a thing. His voice rose. "And we're supposed to roll over and play dead?"

"Daniel," Florida said again. "Dr. Treter is just—"

"A quack."

"Daniel!" Her misery increased, now saddled with the additional burdens of embarrassment and anger. "I'm sorry, Dr. Treter. My fiancé—"

Daniel took her elbow while she rose. "Don't apologize for me, Florida. If I gave up at the first sign of an obstacle—or in the face of incompetence—I never would have made it where I am."

Could he hear how unbelievably insulting and pompous he sounded? Florida was actually glad she couldn't see Dr. Treter's face.

Pulling her toward the door, Daniel continued. "We'll beat this thing; you'll see."

She hung back. "Dr. Treter—"

"Emotions are at an understandable high," the doctor said. "It's all right. We can talk more on your next visit."

"There won't be a next visit," Daniel said.

Florida was too appalled to protest. She'd never seen Daniel handle a crisis. She wasn't sure she'd want to again. Trying to convince herself his rudeness stemmed from his distress over her, she gave in to the tug on her arm, stumbled forward, and knocked her elbow against the doorframe.

"God, Florida. Sorry." The right words, but Daniel's voice was terse.

Her temper popped and she mimicked his voice. "God, Daniel. Watch it."

He didn't respond, but she could feel his scowl. She deflated. His anger on top of her anger on top of her misery was just too much. Dr. Treter was right. Emotions were running high and it'd be best to just let this go.

They'd barely left the office—the soft-voiced assistant racing after them to thrust a packet of material into her hands—before Daniel was barking orders into his phone. He told his underlings to jump, and they got to jumping. After an hour that she and Daniel whiled away at a Sonic Drive-In— she ate a corn dog to the tune of Daniel's fingers drumming on the steering wheel—they coughed up the name of a renowned specialist at the Barnes Retina Institute in St. Louis. And the news that the earliest opening Dr. Rosen had was three weeks away.

Cursing, Daniel took matters into his own hands, badgering a poor assistant in the specialist's office until she forked over an appointment for them on Wednesday, two days away. Not content with that success, he hung up, and Florida had to listen to him rant for another half hour: Even Daniel Davenport couldn't get Florida in to see Dr. Rosen tomorrow.

After they checked in to a Columbia Days Inn for the night, behind the scenes, Rita spent her evening rearranging Daniel's schedule and executing arrangements for their trip tomorrow to St. Louis. Daniel spent his catching up on business. And Florida tuned out the drone of the television set he'd flipped on for her, and wondered about Daniel's anger.

Had it blown up out of concern over her? Or because he hated to lose?

Whether Daniel's unwillingness to concede defeat was prompted by love or ego, by the next afternoon when they checked into the Hotel Davenport in St. Louis, one of the more extravagant properties in Daniel's chain, she clearly understood the reason for his success: a never-say-die resolve that roused everyone around him. And damn if it hadn't infected her, too. Despite Dr.

Treter's pessimism, a hum of determination was drowning out the note of despair that ran just under all her thoughts. Surely there was something someone could do. Surely.

As was usual whenever they stayed at one of the hotels in Daniel's chain, their reception was accompanied by great fanfare. From the footsteps that scurried around them, she imagined a half-dozen bellhops were showing the way to their suite, where Daniel assured her a view of the arch soared outside their balcony windows. She stared where she heard their footsteps. Maybe it wasn't her imagination. Maybe she was actually seeing their blue uniforms shifting in the shadows. She started to tell Daniel, then stopped. Somehow she knew nothing less than the full return of her vision would excite him.

After depositing their luggage, the bellhops left them on their own. Daniel guided her to a chair in one bedroom and flipped on the television, then wandered into the other, saying he'd return in a minute. In short order, she heard him back on the phone.

She sighed. The planet wouldn't rotate without Daniel Davenport. Bored, she got up to explore. Hands out, she felt her way around the room, learning where the vase of fresh flowers was by their scent, feeling the fluff of the Egyptian-cotton towels in the bathroom, locating a tray of sandwiches and fruit when her hand landed in the compote.

After wiping her hand off on a napkin she felt stacked beside it, she picked up a half sandwich and carried it to her nose. Smoked turkey. She took a nibble. With thinly sliced tomatoes and a hint of olive oil on Italian. She took a bigger bite. Then practically inhaled the rest of the thing, and picked up another. She could tell from the grip of her pants that she'd already gained a few pounds, but did anyone really expect her to watch her weight on top of all this?

Feeling her way again, she headed to the bed, managing only to graze the luggage rack at its foot and not knock it over. Perching on the edge of the mattress, she devoured her sandwich. Her trip to Perkins with Stan had left her feeling more confident about eating in restaurants and she'd wanted to stop for lunch earlier, but Daniel had demurred, saying they'd get better food at the hotel.

Done, she brushed crumbs off her lips, then felt for the tote bag she'd heard Daniel instruct a bell-hop to leave on the bed. Last night, after she'd called Alcea to let her know their plans, Rita had sent a driver to Cordelia to fetch the things Alcea had packed for her. Her best friend had sounded harried even before Florida had added to her to-do list. Even though Alcea had held the business reins alone for only ten days, her voice was pinched with stress. Her partner was capable of a lot: Give her two carrots and a pound of flour and she'd turn out a culinary masterpiece for forty.

But balance sheets, QuickBooks, and inventory estimates turned her knees to jelly—although they might be the only things that did.

Try as she might, Florida hadn't been able to care about business even for the duration of one phone call, although she'd done her best to answer all the questions Alcea had about orders and statements and marketing plans. She was reassured by Alcea's (surprised) comment that Stan had offered to share his accountant—and even pay for him—for the short term, and business concerns had floated out of her head. Besides, in the World According to Daniel, she'd be back in the saddle soon.

The familiar feel of her tote's rough tapestry was somehow comforting. Groping around the edges, she found the zipper and tugged. She didn't know how she'd be able to tell what was in it, but she could at least try to unpack. It was something to do.

A raspy female voice cut in. "I'll get that for you, honey."

She yelped, holding a hand over her heart. "Good God. Who are you?"

"Sorry I scared you." Footsteps made a heavy tread across the carpet. A hand touched her arm. "Name's Ginger."

Daniel's voice came from the doorway. "She's a maid I hired to help you out. By the way, there's tomato on your shirt."

Ginger sniffed. "Maid? Bah. I'll have you know, I've got my nurse's aide certification."

A hand was suddenly blotting a place under her breastbone. She recoiled, wishing people would *say* something before they touched her. "Nurse's aide?" For crying out loud, she wasn't an invalid. Just like last night, anything she needed, Daniel could do. "I don't think—"

She stopped. *Just like last night.* Maybe that's what Daniel had been thinking of, too?

Negotiating their overnight at the Days Inn hadn't been *too* difficult. Once she'd figured out the room layout, she'd had little trouble getting around. And since the driver had yet to deliver a bag, she'd only had to juggle a few basic toiletries and a robe Daniel had bought at the Target store next door. Makeup hadn't been a problem because she hadn't had any. And when you have only the clothes you arrive in, choosing an outfit is no riddle, either.

She *had* needed him to figure out how to get a toothbrush out of packaging that could have served Fort Knox, and to fiddle with shower faucets as complex as controls on a nuclear reactor, and to negotiate the keyboard of a remote for the television set, and to help her clean up the fruit juice she knocked over on the bed table, as well as—she blushed—helping her extract her panties from the sink. The lace had gotten caught somewhere under the stopper when she'd tried to wash them out.

They'd torn in the process. A situation, she now realized, Daniel hadn't taken advantage of. Instead, he'd tucked her underwearless self into bed, gone back to his work, then crawled in sometime after she'd drifted off to sleep. With nary a straying hand.

Today, breakfast—a sweet roll that she wished was two sweet rolls, and a cup of coffee delivered from a Denny's next door—had gone without incident. And she'd managed to fall short of becoming an embarrassment at rest stops because they'd been equipped with family facilities where they both could enter the same restroom so he could guide her to a stall. . . .

God. There was intimate and then there was *intimate.*

Her skin suddenly crawled. Not only had Daniel spent the day with a rumpled, makeupless, unkempt fiancée whose face was undoubtedly puffed up from all the food she'd been eating; she'd pretty much destroyed any remaining mystery surrounding female allure. Suddenly, her toilette for tonight assumed epic importance.

"Earth to Florida . . ." Daniel said from the doorway. "What don't you think?"

"I don't think I could make do without Ginger. Thank you, Daniel."

The words of gratitude grated. Even though she needed assistance, she didn't want assistance. It wasn't just the unaccustomed feeling of helplessness that vexed her; it was the fact she couldn't return any favors. It was the fact she didn't even want to.

"Then let's get you unpacked." There was the sound of unzipping. Then the bed shifted as Ginger sat down beside her. From the way the mattress sagged, Ginger was a big woman.

"I'll let you girls go at it," Daniel said. "While you're doing that, I'll make a quick visit to the hotel offices. Call me if you need me."

After the door closed behind him, Ginger rummaged in the bag. "*Oo la la.* Nice duds, girl."

"What do you have there?" Despite Ginger's lack of *élan*, she rather liked her—and the fact she had so far treated her blindness as commonplace. Florida reached out and Ginger deposited a dress in her hands. From the texture, it was a cocktail dress she'd bought for travel, made of that scrunchy acetate and spandex combination that never wrinkled and clung to every curve. "Black?"

"Yep."

Bless Alcea, perfect for dinner.

"What else is there?"

"Toothpaste . . . shampoo . . . hair gel . . ." Another sound of a zipper. "A little bag of jewelry. Looks like paste, mostly."

From the tone of disappointment in Ginger's voice, Florida didn't think she'd worry about pilfering.

"There's slippers, fancy sandals with weaving on 'em. . . ."

The Sesto Meucci sandals she'd bought on sale. Only a fraction of her shoes were flats. She thought of the rest, a collection of teetering heels, the kind that created that sexy curve of the calf. She wondered if she'd ever wear them again. Probably not.

"Oh, and here's some jasmine bath oil. Girl, you got it all."

A bath sounded wonderful. Thinking of the confusing stew of knobs and valves last night, she sucked in a breath, blew it out. No place here for stiff upper lips and false modesty. Ginger could earn her keep. "Could you help me with the bathtub?"

"That's what I'm here for."

The mattress shifted as Ginger got up. There was the sound of the bedroom door closing and in short order, the aide had drawn a bath, tossed in some oil, helped her in, and flipped on the Jacuzzi jets before returning to the unpacking. As Florida laid her head back and closed her eyes, she felt the first glimmer of anticipation she'd felt since the accident. This evening would be a brief oasis in a sea of uncertainty and medical exams. Much like that quick lunch at Perkins with Stan. Only this time, in the hotel's lavish Top-of-the-Davenport dining room, she'd dine on sole almondine instead of hamburger, be serenaded by strolling violins, not Muzak, use silver instead of aluminum . . . and grow heady from good wine and the sexual tension that always accompanied her and Daniel's evenings out. After dinner, they'd dance, perhaps, then retire to their suite, where . . .

"Whoa." Ginger's voice came from the bedroom, interrupting her fantasies. She'd left the adjoining door open in case Florida needed anything. "Get a loada this."

Lazily, Florida stretched her limbs, feeling normal for a moment, relishing the feel of the water bubbling around her body. She had a Jacuzzi bath at home, but not on the scale of this one. "What is it?"

"I don't know if they deserve the word *panties*." Ginger's voice was close. Florida turned her head. Yes, she could make out a white blob—a uniform?—within the darker blob of the doorway. "But I think that's what they are. Either that, or a funky-looking headband."

"Are they pink?"

"Hot pink. Some black lace."

Florida smiled. A few months back, she and Alcea had poked through an adult toy store looking for a joke gift for a bachelorette party they'd both been invited to attend. They'd giggled over handcuffs, vibrators, and crotchless panties. Shortly after they'd returned, Florida had found a pair of the latter tucked under her pillow along with a sassy note from her friend. She'd never told Alcea she'd actually worn them; never told her they were a favorite of Daniel's. But Alcea had known that whether she was using them or not, finding them would bring her a smile.

"Is there a silk wrapper?"

"Uh-huh."

Double bless Alcea. The feeling of normalcy increased. "You can bring those in here. I, uh, I'll put them away."

"Sure you will."

Ginger's voice was knowing, but Florida didn't

even blush. It was time for Daniel to find out she was still here underneath her disability. That there were some things that didn't need fixing.

The first inclination she had that more things were broken than she'd previously thought came just before dinner. After her bath, Ginger had applied her makeup—hopefully following Florida's stringent instructions to use a light touch—then made liberal use of a blow-dryer and curling iron before helping her dress. Florida's hands felt her hair; it didn't feel any different from the usual cascade, maybe more wave, but that wouldn't matter. It was so frustrating not to be able to see for herself. But Ginger assured her she looked stunning, then helped her to the sofa in the suite's living room.

When Daniel returned from visiting the hotel offices, to her relief, he seconded Ginger's opinion. "You look fantastic."

She hoped that wasn't a note of surprise in his voice.

After Ginger had departed for her own room, a broad wink in her voice when she'd said, "Guess I don't have to tell you to enjoy your evening," Daniel picked up the phone.

Annoyance replaced anticipation. "Daniel, can't we have one evening where—"

"Just a minute," he said. "I'm ordering room service."

Sharp disappointment stabbed her. And not just because he was ordering a feast laden with lettuce and fit only for a rabbit—which told her he'd noticed the weight she'd gained. But because he'd shattered the image she'd nurtured of dining in elegance, then dancing later, her fiancé leading her across a parquet floor, her cheek resting on his shoulder, her eyes closed. Along with the shaky belief that maybe, in spite of this difficult challenge, life would eventually regain some semblance of normalcy. Granted, she might simply be delusional, but if so, it would've been lovely to stay that way at least through one night.

She could hear him moving behind her, the clink of glassware telling her he was fixing drinks at the fully stocked bar she knew came with each suite. She turned her head toward the sound. "I thought we'd be having supper upstairs."

"I thought you'd be more comfortable here." His voice was nearer. She felt the sofa cushions shift as he sat down beside her.

He'd thought *she'd* be more comfortable? Or that *he* would? She thought of the last twenty-four hours. Sandwiches on a tray. Sonic Drive-In. Takeout from Denny's. Not exactly Daniel's usual fare. A worm of fear crawled up her spine. She'd become more adept at handling mealtime, thanks to a hospital therapist's suggestion that she ask someone to describe the contents of her plate by thinking of it like a clockface, as well as ensuring that utensils and condiments were in the same place each time. Still, there was always the danger she'd stab the table instead of her potato or tip over a wineglass while reaching for her water.

Maybe that wasn't a risk Daniel wanted to take.

Stan's voice suddenly drifted through her mind. *Nothing you do will embarrass me.*

Maybe that wasn't a sentiment Daniel could echo.

She waited for Daniel to hand her a drink. But while she heard him take a sip of his own, nothing happened.

"My drink?"

"Your drink? Of course." The sofa shifted again as he rose. "What'll it be?" She heard the soft vacuum pop of the refrigerator door opening. "Diet soft drink?"

She frowned. "Apple martini."

"Considering your tests tomorrow, you probably shouldn't have alcohol."

Was it the alcohol or the calories he was concerned about? She bristled. "It's one drink. I'm not planning to go on a bender."

There was a moment of silence. "All right. One probably won't hurt."

Like he was her mommy. She started to retort, but like every time that she'd struggled up to wobble on her own two feet since waking up blind, despair suddenly swept them out from under her again. Everything had changed. It was stupid to act like it hadn't.

"You're right. Just bring me . . . anything."

After Daniel had handed her a Diet Coke and sat down again, she asked about his business. He wasn't in the habit of monopolizing the conversation with his own affairs, nor was she in the habit of letting him, but given any encouragement, he could prattle on about them ad nauseam. Which kept him distracted from the topic of her eyesight for the duration of their cocktail hour, such as it was, the delivery of their dinner, and the whole meal. At least he'd ordered sole almondine to accompany the bushels of salad, topped with a low-fat vinaigrette, and vegetables, steamed with no sauce. After they'd finished, the waiter who had hovered while they'd eaten poured decaf coffee into her cup and a dollop of brandy into Daniel's, and then Daniel dismissed him.

Feeling her pulse pick up now that they were alone—and thinking of the panties Alcea had supplied—she was glad when his chatter wound down, then startled to hear him yawn.

"We need to get an early start tomorrow. Do you need Ginger's help, or will I do?" There was no hint of seduction in his voice. His chair scraped back and she heard him move off, probably for more brandy.

She wadded up her napkin and threw it on the table. Enough was enough. "You'll do," she said sweetly. "Ginger laid out my things in the bathroom, so if you can point me there, I'll just need you to tuck me in."

That wasn't all she needed him for. Her blood quickened again. She needed him to make her nerve endings sing. To make her feel alive. And to give her the opportunity to prove to herself—

and him—that there, in the dark, was something she could still do as well as she'd ever done before. Maybe even better.

Daniel led her to the bathroom. She gauged their progress from the way the light shifted— bright in the living room, darker in the bedroom and beyond. She'd been able to see variances in light all along, but she wondered if there wasn't slightly more contrast. The thought gave her hope. When they reached the bathroom, she felt for the switch and flipped the lights on. The glow of the bulbs gave her a benchmark of where the sink and vanity were.

"I'll wait out here," Daniel said. "Call if you need anything."

In the bath, she managed to don her lingerie, spritz on some Carolina Herrera, a mix of floral fantasy, and fluff out her hair without mistaking her perfume for deodorant. She brushed her teeth by transferring the paste by finger to her mouth instead of trying to hit the brush with the tube, another tip from the therapist.

Her hands trembled as she readied herself. Not from fear she'd make a mistake, but from rising excitement. Maybe she was discovering a perk of her situation—making love with no more sight than she had presented an interesting proposition.

Leaving her wrapper untied, almost unbearably eager now to feel his hands on her body, she took a deep breath and opened the door. "Daniel?"

Silence greeted her. The bedroom was dark

against her eyes. She listened and heard Daniel's voice, low, in the living room. She called again.

"Be right in. I'm just taking a call."

Figured. But this time she wasn't annoyed. She took the opportunity to feel her way to the bed and drape herself in what she hoped was an alluring pose, arranging the panels of her silk wrapper so they would tease him with only a filmy view of her breasts but bare a bit of the peekaboo panties she wore underneath.

She heard him enter the room. Her breath hitched. Soon . . . soon . . .

"Turn on the light." Her voice was husky.

There was a snap of a lamp switch and the darkness lifted.

She heard the quick intake of his breath and smiled. "Come over here." She patted the bed.

He approached; she could hear him pause at the bedside, see his shadow, feel his eyes on her. She held her breath, anticipating his touch.

But it never came. Slowly it registered that his breathing was slow and steady, no fire heating it up. Only seconds passed, but they ticked by in agonizing slowness. She grew painfully aware of herself—as though she'd just opened her soul and laid herself out for him to see every last shortcoming—and every last ounce she'd recently gained.

"Daniel?" she whispered.

His voice when he finally found it was almost a croak. "Sorry, Florida. God, sorry . . . I'm just consumed with a problem that's cropped up." His shadow loomed and he finally touched her. Just with his lips: a brief peck on the forehead. "I'm expecting—"

But before he got the words out, she threw pride to the wind and wrapped her arms around his neck, pulling his mouth against hers. After a second's hesitation, he returned the kiss fully. Their tongues tangled. And then he was gently extricating himself from her embrace.

"Not now. I can't. . . . That call . . ."

She swallowed hard, knowing it was more than the phone call. Humiliation crawled over her body; she shifted into a less suggestive position, aiming for nonchalance and wishing fervently that he'd just . . . go.

"It was the Dallas property. There's some problems and I have to . . . It's an emergency."

His shadow was moving away. Away from her. Away from the fiancée he'd treasured and now saw as flawed.

She made it easier on him. "So you need to make more calls."

"Yes. And they may last a while."

"I won't wait up." It had taken every ounce of strength she had, but somehow she'd managed to keep her voice steady.

She heard the snap of a switch. The glow went out. The door shut.

She lay there for a while, rigid, controlled, denying herself any relief in tears. It was an adjustment, she told herself firmly. Not just for her, but for Daniel.

She had to give him time. And be grateful. He was doing everything he could to help her.

Somehow that knowledge didn't give her as much comfort as those few minutes she'd spent scrunched up against Stan in the front seat of his Suburban.

Face it. Daniel was being an asshole.

Holding tight to her pillow, she twisted onto her side. And suddenly she wished Stan were with her now.

Chapter 9

The next morning they ate breakfast solo—and she insisted on pancakes dripping with butter and syrup. Ginger had left shortly after helping Florida dress, and Daniel had dispensed with the ministrations of a waiter. But despite their solitude, neither of them mentioned anything about the night before, although Florida could tell by Daniel's hearty demeanor and effusive compliments— he actually said a bowl of hydrangeas on the table matched her eyes; now, how insensitive was *that*?—that he was trying to make amends.

And while she tried to tell herself yet again that his discomfort around her wasn't his fault, but the situation's, the memory of lying there, exposed and vulnerable to his critical eyes, made her cringe with a shame deeper than any she'd ever known.

And anger. Mentally, she listed painful ways that he could die. But she couldn't find the energy to even verbally take him to task, let alone the strength to drag him to the balcony of their suite and drop him over the rail.

Yesterday had been a day of hope. Today, she wallowed in gloom. Even the idea that the retinal specialist they were about to see might offer some cutting-edge solutions to Purtscher's that Dr. Treter hadn't known about failed to lift her spirits. She hated feeling this way, hated the languor of thought and body that was poised to suck her under. Over the course of her life, she'd had as many knocks as the next person, maybe even a few more than most, and she'd always barreled through them, chin up. But this was different. Unless there was a miracle, her vision loss was immutable. The fact ground with unceasing pressure on her psyche. . . .

Unless this new doctor offered new hope, how could she cope with such limited vision for a lifetime?

She said nothing of any of this to Daniel, no longer trusting his reactions enough to share her thoughts. Instead she sipped her coffee and made noncommittal replies to his comments and hoped she didn't set her cup down on a pat of butter, until it was time to leave for her appointment.

Where, once again, she found herself subjected to tests, most of them the same as she'd been through before, a couple she'd not.

And once again, she found herself ensconced in front of a desk in a chair with too little cushion, holding someone's hand.

And once again, she received the same news, delivered in the same measured, professional tones.

Dr. Rosen had nothing to add that she wanted to hear.

"I'm sorry that I can't offer a miracle," the retinal specialist said. She heard his chair squeak and sigh as he rose. In deference to her dilated eyes, the room was too dim for her to make out much beyond some movement. She had no idea what he looked like, but the husky timbre of his voice combined with his heavy tread as he crossed the office gave rise to images of a bear. When he spoke next, it came from off to her right. "You can't see this, of course, Ms. Jones, but Mr. Davenport, if you'll look here, at these white spots . . . ?"

Beside her, Daniel also got up, she assumed to look at the films of her eyes. When Dr. Treter had joined them, he'd told her he was clipping her test results up to a light box. "Those pale areas on the retina are called ischemia—areas that are scarring. The darker areas on these other black-and-white films indicate an interruption of blood flow."

Dr. Rosen's tread moved around behind her; then a hand gripped her shoulder, long-fingered and strong. "Once that's happened, I'm afraid there's no turning back."

As she was stripped of her last hope, the words fell like a death sentence.

"Goddammit!" Daniel's voice, still off to the right, pierced the heavy silence. "I should have brought her here immediately instead of wasting time on Treter."

I? What was this *I* business? It hadn't been Daniel who'd helped when she'd awakened blind. It had been Stan.

"Mr. Davenport, I understand your severe disappointment, but let me assure you that when I compare her earlier films to today's, I can see Dr. Treter's course of treatment had some beneficial results. Florida is indicating she can see—at a very low level, but there is some return of vision. As much as one could hope for, really. I would have recommended the exact same thing."

Daniel subsided, but tension still filled the room.

The doctor released her shoulder, but instead of moving back around his desk, she heard him pull up the chair Daniel had vacated, close enough that his knee touched hers. Perhaps he understood how much more touch meant to her now that she couldn't see very much.

Unlike Daniel.

"Florida," he said in gentle tones. "You'll want to wait for a few weeks to see how much of your vision returns, as things could still get better. But you need to understand that there won't be much more improvement. Twenty-hundred is possible—and would be an outstanding result—but twenty-two hundred is more likely. That's the upper level of legal blindness as defined by the government—

which gives a tax break in such cases. But, for all practical purposes, the low vision you'd experience at twenty-hundred would still require substantial changes to your lifestyle."

I'm blind. I'm just as good as blind. And that's not going to change.

She could hardly absorb what he was saying, but it was important. And from the way she could hear Daniel pacing, he wasn't listening. So she'd have to.

She straightened her shoulders. Well, since when wasn't it all up to her? She'd handled everything alone all through her life. She could handle this, too. . . . She could because she had to.

"What . . . what do the numbers mean?" she asked.

The doctor paused. "They're a bunch of abstractions, actually. Twenty-twenty is a standard that means at twenty feet, a person with average vision (not perfect, *average*) can see a symbol clearly that's *x* size. With impaired vision, say twenty–two hundred, a person can't see at that same twenty feet what the average eye can see at two hundred feet."

She turned the words over in her head, but they didn't much compute beyond, "That's pretty bad."

"Yes. Pretty damn bad."

She liked that he was giving it to her straight. None of Dak's rah-rah acceptance routine. None of Daniel's "We shall overcome" nonsense. For a

moment, she heard Stan's voice. . . . *This sucks.*
Stan was right.

The doctor was continuing. "There are numerous organizations available to help you with what
we call visual rehabilitation. But you'll want to
wait until Dr. Treter indicates—probably in a few
weeks—that your vision has pretty much stabilized to what it will continue to be. He'll then give
you information for getting a visual assessment.
Although you may not need to avail yourself of
state services"—she knew he was thinking of Daniel's fortune—"there are programs available through
Missouri's Department of Social Services. Sometimes there's a delay in getting scheduled, but you
can't beat it—they're free or provided on a sliding scale."

She noticed Daniel hadn't leaped to assure her
he'd provide whatever she'd need. She swallowed. Her insurance wouldn't extend far; self-
employed, she had a high deductible and only the
bare minimum. At her age, she hadn't been concerned. Until now. "How do those programs
work?"

"You'll be assigned a certified vision rehabilitation
therapist—a CVRT—who will help you with all fac-
ets of acclimating yourself to your disability. You'll
learn how to manage yourself independently as
much as possible; you'll have opportunities—which
I suggest you take—for individual and family counseling. There are support groups throughout the
region. I'd also recommend you look into Hope

House in St. Louis. It's a United Way–funded residential program—it's much more intensive and guarantees you'll function at the highest level possible."

Function.

Daniel spoke up. "What about glasses, contacts?"

"Glasses, lenses—all tools that help the eye focus light on the retina, the nerve layer. Once the nerve layer is damaged, visual aids like those don't help. But numerous other aids are available. In fact, depending on your ultimate acuity, there are video magnifiers that will magnify items up to sixty times—like your mail so you can still read it. There are eyepieces fitted with telescopic lenses to take advantage of what vision you do retain. There are screen readers and a whole host of new gadgets and software; your CVRT will make recommendations. In short, life won't be the same, and I won't make light of what a huge adjustment you have ahead of you. But you *will* have help. Life *will* go on. And it *will* be rewarding."

His words were meant to help her feel better. They didn't.

She felt him rise. "I'll grab my assistant. He can brief you further."

When he'd left the room, quiet fell.

Florida cleared her throat. "I've seen those telescopic glasses. Maybe I have a future as a bit player in the next *Star Wars* movie." Just a little blind-person humor, although she didn't find it funny at all.

Nor did Daniel. Her fiancé stayed silent. And

she wondered just how Dr. Rosen defined *rewarding*.

As they drove home late that afternoon, Daniel was still silent, responding to any stabs she took at conversation with barely a grunt. She desperately wanted to talk to him about her future, even though she knew the conversation would be pure speculation. Her life couldn't really be defined until they knew what kind of vision recovery she'd experience over the next few weeks. Still, reassurance would be nice. Having someone share her fears would be even nicer.

By the time they arrived in Cordelia, the temperatures had soared into searing. It was so hot, the town felt like the gateway to hell. Which was exactly how Florida felt. But as Daniel helped her out of the car, the familiar, earthy smell of the nearby Ozark woodlands hugged her and her heart grew less burdened. Home. She turned her face to the sky and breathed in deep.

"The sun's bright; shut your eyes," Daniel said.

At his peremptory tone, it took some effort to keep a retort off her lips. She already *had* closed her eyes. She wore the sunglasses the doctor had suggested, but knew they wouldn't be effective with a direct, prolonged hit from the sun. She wouldn't get any more vision back and could fry the little she now had. She wasn't a moron.

"You know," he said, guiding her up the walk, "you should wear those inside, too."

Now who was the moron? "That'd be stupid."

She wasn't up to sugarcoating. It had not only been a long day; her patience with Daniel was riding near empty. "I'd lose the piddlin' ability I have to tell where things are by the strength of the light. Besides, sometimes I see forms. Color. Movement."

"Those might be hallucinations."

Dr. Rosen's assistant had said people who lost sight like she had were sometimes subject to vision memories that could exhibit themselves as actual sight. But this was *real*.

She stopped short. How dare he rain on her parade? "Y'all are just a Little Merry Sunshine, aren't you? They're *not* hallucinations. And even if they were, why in the world would I wear sunglasses inside? It doesn't make sense."

"It does. C'mon." He tugged her forward again. "When people talk to each other, they use eye contact. Since you can't, it's awkward for people who can see."

"What *people*? My friends, my family?" *You?* "And why should I care how awkward anybody else feels? That's their problem."

They were moving slowly, her hanging behind, unsure of his guidance. Daniel sometimes got engrossed in his own thoughts or conversation and forgot to announce an impending obstacle.

"Can you pick up the pace?" he asked. "I'd like to reach the house before daybreak tomorrow."

"I don't want to run into the steps to the porch."

"You won't. I'll tell you when we get there."

"Ha. Like you told me about Dr. Treter's door-frame?" From the way darkness loomed in front of her, they must have entered the shadows cast by the house.

"So I make *one* mistake—"

"It hasn't been just one little ol' mistake. Yesterday you—"

A rustling ahead interrupted her. More than the breeze from the trees. At the same time, her foot smacked into a board and she stumbled.

"Dammit, Daniel!" She jerked her hand from his arm and felt for the stair railing to the front porch.

He grabbed her sleeve and she shook him off. Tears welled. Tears were always welling. It was the most annoying thing in the world. "Stop. Leave me alone, I'll do it myself."

"You can't."

"I can! Watch me!"

"Mommy." A thin voice sounded somewhere above and nearby.

She swallowed. "Missouri?"

"Welcome home, Florida!"

"Julius?"

"And me and Dak. And Stan." Alcea's voice sounded, too, shaded by embarrassment. "We're here on the porch. Sorry—we should have said something, but Missouri wanted to surprise you."

She tilted her head up and saw shapes moving above her.

Footsteps rattled down the stairs; then arms wrapped her waist as tight as twine. "I missed you *so much*, Mom. I'm glad you're back."

Her heart had lifted at Missouri's voice. But not enough to completely dispel her annoyance with Daniel. Why hadn't he told her people were watching? God, her fiancé had the understanding of a rock.

Feeling like an idiot, Florida hugged Missouri close. As they rocked together, her ire faded. It was good to be home. Good to be held.

More clattering, and then more arms enfolded her. Vanilla and cinnamon. Alcea. Dak, whose rough cheek bussed hers. She blinked at a flash of silver and something hard bumped her knee. Julius's wheelchair. Stan whispered, "Looking good," into her ear and made her feel unaccountably like she really did, and—she sniffed the air and smelled oranges—her mother.

Florida relaxed in their embrace, these people who loved her. Or—she thought of Tamara—at least claimed to. Trapped in the middle, Missouri giggled. The sound lifted Florida's heart. Warmth struck one side of her face, and turning her head toward it, she thought she might see the bands of color that signaled sunset. For a moment, she thought everything would be okay.

Until she realized none of the flesh that pressed against her belonged to Daniel.

Chapter 10

The morning of the last Thursday in July broke as breathless as the day before it, spilling through the great room windows and heating Florida's lap. Hands clasped, she sat on the sofa, unmoving and waiting for Daniel. While the room was mostly bright light, she could see color, smudged like pastels on canvas, but she was too tense to appreciate it. Daniel was upstairs showering after having spent the night in her bed at her invitation—at her insistence, if you want to know the truth—after Missouri had gone to sleep. Throughout the night, he'd held her. Stiffly. And that was all.

She felt like a fist. Tight. Closed in. Even after a week of trying to absorb what was happening, she still felt she'd fallen into someone else's life.

Well, you haven't, she told herself. *You'll have to*

deal. She thought about everything she'd pondered overnight. *Maybe by yourself.*

This morning, after Missouri and Julius had cobbled together a breakfast of fruit and cereal and juice—hating herself for the fear she'd earn Daniel's contempt, she'd nibbled on a slice of cantaloupe instead of risking a dribble of milk down her front—everyone had scattered. Daniel had made some calls, then had taken himself back upstairs. Julius had retired to his room for a mid-morning nap. Missouri had seen her to the sofa, handed her the television remote, and then headed to Joey's. Florida didn't understand why everyone thought she'd want to "watch" television now—especially since it was just a smear of shifting light and color—when she'd rarely watched it before.

She hefted the remote in her hand. The morning news was over, not that she'd absorbed much of what was said. The world's problems seemed remote and unimportant. She fingered the controls, eventually finding the right button to cycle mindlessly through the channels, keeping the volume low, the talk show babble no match against her thoughts, which circled round and round in an endless loop: Everything was different; nothing was easy. What shape would life take? How much would she be able to do?

Who would help her?

Maybe not Daniel. The words whispered through her head.

Definitely not Tamara. Last night, listening to

the cheerful banter that had sprung up between her daughter and her mother, she'd been incensed to realize that in the short space of time she'd been gone, Tamara, not Alcea, had largely watched Missouri when Stan wasn't there. She'd refused to let reason mollify her; of course neither could play full-time nanny with businesses to run, but it was hard to give a flying fig.

A sentiment she'd expressed in a harshly whispered conversation with her brother and sister-in-law out of Missouri's earshot. She'd overridden Dak's objections and ignored Alcea's aggravation and insisted Tamara, who had continued to board here since the accident, vamoose back to her quarters in their house. She'd used highfalutin arguments like she didn't trust Tamara, she had good reason not to trust Tamara, and better to short-change Missouri of a grandmother than risk heartbreak. She *knew* Tamara was capable of heartbreak.

And she also knew that amid all her incensedness, she'd been experiencing pangs of jealousy. Missouri was receiving attention Tamara had never deigned to bestow on her own daughter. Part of her was aghast she could be so juvenile, but amid everything else, she just couldn't help it. Nor could she let Tamara use her tragedy as an excuse to worm her way into their lives.

She stirred guiltily, knowing her obstinacy burdened Alcea. A fact that also wasn't lost on her best friend. Not long after Missouri had left this morning, Alcea had checked in on her way to work. She'd thrown a load of clothes into the washer, promised to do some grocery shopping on her way back, and, oh, by the way, if Florida had no objections because we wouldn't want *her* inconvenienced, she also needed to go over some business matters later—there were problems with the new menus.

Florida hadn't missed the sarcasm.

She sighed. Alcea would *really* feel overburdened after this weekend. Saturday, Stan would depart for Hawaii. Sunday, Dak would take off for his book-signing trip and research tour, and Daniel . . .

Her mind skittered away from completing her thought.

Still, even shorthanded, with Julius's and Missouri's help, and the occasional look-in from Alcea, they should be fine without anyone else dancing attendance. Especially Tamara. And once she'd gotten past the next few weeks and had started sessions with a vision therapist, Alcea could stop caretaking altogether.

Good thing, since Alcea planned to join Dak in early September for a few weeks before returning for the wedding. She'd made no sounds about changing her plans and Florida wasn't about to ask. Knowing her friend was in perfect sync with Dak on this subject, Florida also knew Alcea would jump on any reason to foist Tamara back on her.

Well, Florida wouldn't give her a one. According to Dr. Rosen's assistant, she'd find ways to adapt to almost everything, except driving.

Along with Jimmy Choo shoes, driving would be consigned to her past.

She thought of her BMW, her memory running a hand over that shiny red finish. Heat built behind her eyes. Oh, crapola. She shook her head to disperse the image. In the last week, she'd cried enough tears to fill an ocean. She was heartily sick of it. Besides, right now she lived within walking distance of all the stores on the square. So someone else had to drive her around everywhere else. No big deal, she told herself, knowing somewhere inside that it was a very big deal, but choosing not to acknowledge the fact.

She'd push for self-sufficiency by the end of August. Just over a month away. She didn't know if it was possible, but she had to try. What other choice did she have? She wouldn't accept Tamara. Couldn't afford paying anyone else. And Daniel hadn't mentioned picking up the cost. And given the way he was behaving right now, she wasn't about to ask.

Upstairs the plumbing fell silent. Her heart in her throat, she fumbled with the remote until the television went off, then sat in silence until he came downstairs.

"I have to leave soon."

Daniel had come downstairs just moments ago. She'd been able to track his movements as he'd taken a stance near the fireplace, where he was toying with the carved figures of her Willow Tree angel collection. Not that she could see in that much detail, but she could guess, clued by the small *ker-chink* of wood against wood. Her imagination filled in other details that remained invisible: his elegant figure leaning against the mahogany surround, one elbow resting on the mantel as he absently picked up first one angel, then another, turning it over in his long fingers before putting it back. His look would be pensive, his blond hair tumbling forward the way it did when he was thinking.

"But you'll be back for tomorrow night's party?"

Alcea was holding a farewell party for Dak. Or so she said. Since she'd never before given Dak this kind of send-off for his annual jaunt— probably because he hated being the center of attention—Florida suspected they'd conspired to put her on exhibit. For her own good, of course. The town's residents could satisfy their curiosity so she'd feel less of a freak show once she ventured outside. And, once curiosity was sated, soft hearts would kick in with offers of help.

Well, she wouldn't need their help.

"I don't know," he answered. "I've been gone. There's a lot of work. . . . Probably not."

She was silent, then patted the sofa. "Come sit by me."

She heard him cross the room. The sofa gave as he sat down, close enough that his knee grazed hers, but not close enough for her to feel the warmth of his body.

"I'm sorry. I know this has all been hard." The apology was dust in her mouth. Why should she be comforting him? Still, maybe he only needed the same reassurance she did. "But by the time the wedding gets here, I'll be self-reliant again. Sure, I'll need some help sometimes, but not all the time. Not like now." She paused. "And I promise not to wear my telescopic glasses during the ceremony. Nobody'll mistake me for something out of *RoboCop*."

She'd hoped for a chuckle. Even a tiny one. But there was nothing.

Instead he stirred; the movement felt uneasy. "About the wedding—"

His cell phone rang. Shifting, he dropped something in her lap. Her hand closed on the object, feeling carved wood and wire. One of her Willow Tree angels.

There was a click as he flipped the phone open. "Speak of the devil. Jenna? Daniel."

The wedding planner. She'd been so caught up in this calamity, she hadn't given much thought to all the wedding plans that must have stalled in Jenna's office. Or to her move to Kansas City. The thought of all that remained to be done seemed overwhelming, but she straightened her shoulders. She'd make the wedding her priority, save the rest for after the honeymoon. Her stuff wasn't going anywhere. And her vision was stronger. Not great. Not great by a long, long shot. But between registering shape and light and dark, she could almost tell what was what . . . as long as she didn't leave these four walls. Still. Taking small bites at a time, she'd manage. Somehow.

She listened to Daniel's side of the conversation. "No . . . yes. That's right. I'm telling her now. I'll call back."

The snap when he closed the phone was emphatic.

"Tell me what?"

There was a heavy pause. "I've told Jenna we want to postpone the wedding."

The words hovered between them.

Initially struck speechless, she recovered her voice. "What? Are you nuts? I know my accident has thrown a wrench into things, but we can pull it off. Jenna's good. And we've—Jenna has already gone to so much work. People have made plans to attend. The church has been booked for months. Photographers . . . that pastry chef Jenna had to have . . . musicians, florists, the hotel . . ."

She couldn't go on. She couldn't go on because from his silence, she knew it was more than a simple postponement, as though there would be anything simple about it. And even though she'd expected it—even though she'd decided during the night, remembering that night at the Davenport St. Louis, that it might be best—now that the moment was here, she fended it off, suddenly wanting to preserve at least a scrap of the future she'd once envisioned. Envisioned . . .

She swallowed and forced her voice into calm. "Daniel . . . we can't. Delaying a wedding like this for a month or two isn't like switching dinner reservations. Even Jenna—and you—can't work that kind of miracle. I'll be fine by the end of September. Well, not fine, but . . . able to handle everything."

He stayed silent. The chasm at her feet grew wider.

And then her mind settled into numb acceptance. "But that's what y'all want, isn't it? You don't just want to postpone the wedding. You want to cancel it."

"Only for a year. By then—"

"By then, nothing will have changed. For all practical purposes, I'm blind, Daniel." She thought of different things Dr. Rosen's assistant had said. "To get around, I'll have to wear contraptions over my eyes and carry a white cane and I won't always hit my mouth when I eat." Her temper bubbled. "And that scares you shitless, doesn't it? Because you wanted a wife as pretty as that Chihuly you gave me. Blindness makes me ugly. It wasn't part of your equation."

"You're twisting things, Florida. I don't want to cancel the wedding. You're—"

"Suddenly seeing things quite clearly. Ironic, isn't it?" She motioned with a hand. "Everything you did this week . . . it wasn't about me, was it?"

"What are you talking about?"

"You just wanted to make me perfect again."

"And that's such a bad thing?"

"No. But you didn't do it for me. You did it for you. Not for me. For you." She turned her head away. "Go."

"It's Addams, isn't it?"

"What are you talking about? Just go." With an effort she held on to her emotions. "Please."

"I thought so."

"This has nothing to do with Stan." But as she said the words, she wondered. "And everything to do with the fact that *you don't deserve me.*"

His footfalls sounded sharp on the floorboards as he gathered things he'd left in the room. She tried to ignore him, sitting stoically, facing ahead, keeping her face carefully blank. He finally crossed to the entry. When she heard the front door slam, she dropped her head back on the sofa. His car fired up. And the crying started. Dragged up from the depths of her soul. She grabbed a pillow and jammed it against her mouth so she wouldn't wake Julius and gave herself to waves of pain and sadness, harbingers of acceptance that things would never be the same. She cried less for Daniel than for the death of her dreams. For the death of her old self. No matter what she did, how her vision turned out, she couldn't go back to what she'd been. Nor did she know what she was now.

As the wave ebbed, she realized something was poking her thigh. Exhausted, laying the pillow aside, she felt beside her until her hand again closed around the Willow Tree angel Daniel had absentmindedly dropped in her lap. She ran her fingers over its arms, uplifted in a V for victory. It had always been her favorite. It stood for triumph.

She held it up to her cheek. It stood for courage.

Chapter 11

By Cordelia standards, Stan thought as he mounted the steps to the porch that sat square in front of Alcea and Dak's house, Dak's going-away party Friday evening didn't set a new record. Judging from the number of cars he'd seen parked along the road as well as the throng visible through the glass of the storm door, instead of the entire town, only half were there. Anyone who had the means to do so had escaped to one of the lakes for the weekend as the heat wave continued. When he'd called Alcea earlier to reverify the time—in the chaos of preparation for his trip tomorrow, he'd managed to erase the message she'd left—she'd told him that included most of her family.

Which was just fine by him. Pausing just outside the door, he rummaged through one of the coolers that lined a bench against the back wall of the front porch. While everyone was now intent on letting bygones be bygones, and his stock had gone up in the O'Malleys' eyes during his marriage to Serena—peaking when they'd seen him suffer over her death—nobody had really forgotten those days when, off the job, he'd been drunk more than sober and intent on sleeping in just about anyone's bed but his wife's. Given that the family was the size of an army, he hadn't been about to try to defend his worthless hide, but he'd always felt a sense of injustice that they'd never looked at Alcea's role in the mess their marriage had been.

Ah, well. Water under the bridge and all that. Besides, you had to admire family that stuck together the way they did, even if you sometimes wanted to throttle their throats.

Choosing a bottle of Evian over a Heineken—he'd hung up his beer stein along with his waywardness, not to mention he was in training—he pushed his way inside, looking for Florida. And Missouri, of course. The house was still a narrow affair, even though some walls had been removed and rearranged. From the front door, he could see straight through to the kitchen. Or he could have if there hadn't been a mass of humanity between here and there.

He caught a glimpse of Alcea, carrying a tray and dressed in a sundress sprinkled with flowers, before she disappeared through the kitchen doorway. Her niece Daisy, a riot of blond curls, pink shorts, and tropical maternity shirt, followed on her heels. Close in age to his daughter Kathleen, she couldn't have been more different from her cousin. His eldest daughter was quiet and sleek; Daisy was . . . well, Daisy. He wondered at Alcea's choice of a new assistant manager for Peg O' My Heart. There was sticking together, and then there was lunacy. Daisy wasn't known for her brains. Daisy's two daughters, Poppy and Fern, bopped along in their mother's wake. Poppy was a few years younger than Missouri; Fern a few years younger than that; and Baby Three was on the way.

Just what the world needed. More O'Malleys.

Stepping farther in, he glanced into the front parlor. Mayor Noflinger and her son, Eldon, tall and eyeglassed and looking not too much different as a high school graduate than he had when he was six, were chatting with Preacher Phelps and his wife, Lynette. Off in the corner, Stan spotted a tuft of Paddy O'Neill's hair, the one on top of his head, which matched the pair over his ears, waving like an antenna as his still-alert bright eyes scanned the room for gossip potential. The man must be ninety by now, but along with Eddie and Freddie Steeplemier, dressed in stripes and overalls and looking like Tweedledee and Tweedledum, plus his cronies Erik Olausson and Julius, he never missed a thing.

As Stan continued toward the back of the house, past the dining room, where Dak was holding court at a Mission-style table, the crowd shifted and he finally glimpsed Florida's bright hair in the kitchen. The room was more packed than the ones before it, crowded with the curious hoping to at least catch sight of the victim so they could chew over their impressions tomorrow.

Squeezing between bodies, murmuring pleasantries, he made his way toward her. She was seated at the oak table that had belonged to Alcea's mother, world-champion busybody. Not his favorite piece of furniture by a long shot. Not his favorite person, for that matter. Some people would live and die by Zinnia O'Malley's word, but he'd been part of far too many family conferences around that table centering on *what to do about Stan and Alcea* and concluding with a sound round of Florida bashing. She'd been the number one problem that had stuck in their craw back then.

As he saw Florida at the table where she'd once been maligned, his heart shifted and he suddenly felt protective. He wondered if it was because of his memories, because she looked more fragile than he'd ever seen her. Or was it because, no matter where they were pretending to direct their attention, everyone within shouting distance was ogling her? She couldn't help but be conscious of the scrutiny.

He studied her expression for any signs of distress, but her face was partly hidden by sunglasses—odd that she'd obscure what vision she had left—and told him nothing. Still, she sat up straight, head high. And he felt proud. Then

wondered why he thought he had a right to feel
proud.

She was talking to Betty Bruell. Which in and of
itself was enough to arouse his protective instincts
and/or make him proud that she was braving the
interrogation she was undoubtedly getting. Com-
pared with Paddy, Betty was a gossip novice, but
as owner of Up-in-the-Hair beauty salon—an appropriate name, since her own teetered as high as
a cell phone tower—the lady wasn't a slouch. She
was pushing seventy-six—he knew this because
the whole town had turned out for her seventy-
fifth birthday party—and becoming deaf as a
brick.

Florida yelled into Betty's ear, "No, they say I
won't get my sight back. At least not entirely."

Well, it wouldn't take long for the boys in the
parlor to pick up on that information, considering
her words had echoed all the way to Montana.
Glancing at Alcea, busying herself at the counter
with a box of Wheat Thins, he noted her satisfied expression.

And, duh, finally realized that was the point to
this whole party. He knew his ex-wife was gaga
over Dakota, but she'd never been overly senti-
mental and Dak had never been overly home-
bound, so he'd wondered at this sudden yen of
Alcea's to bid her husband a public good-bye.
Alcea would know tales were traveling about Tamara's return and Florida's disability and before
the town had either of them sprouting two heads,
she'd decided to disperse the rumors by pre-

senting the reality. Or at least, presenting Florida. He hadn't seen Tamara around.

She'd also know that in Florida's case, despite their relish for gossip, Cordelia would want to rise to the occasion and offer to help. That is, if Florida would let them.

Unlike a lot of Cordelia-ites, Florida had largely kept to herself as she'd grown up. At least as much as one could in a town filled with Paddys and Bettys. Abandonment had made her feel like an outcast. Different. Despite the cheerleader good looks, when he'd first met her . . . or, rather, really *looked* at her . . . she'd been filled with resentment. Their affair had further isolated her as she assumed the role of home wrecker. She'd been a match against Alcea's barbs back then, but not against the combined disapproval of the O'Malley family, who'd had the town's opinion firmly behind them. As always.

Even though fences had been mended, even though Alcea and Florida had become friends and sisters-in-law, he would always regret he'd subjected Florida to the town's derision and the O'Malleys' ire. She'd been a willing and open-eyed participant, true. But she'd also been young. He couldn't claim the same excuse. And he should have known better. But it wasn't until Serena that he'd learned to think with his heart and not his dick. Thank God for that woman. She'd come along before it was too late to make amends with his elder daughter, Kathleen. And so that he could do everything right—or at least try to—with his younger.

He approached the two women and bent down to holler in Betty's ear. "Paddy O'Neill is looking for you."

He lied without a qualm. After all, Paddy *would* be looking for her once he knew she'd gotten all the skinny on Florida there was to get. Besides, chances were, Betty would forget where she was going by the time she hit the parlor.

Betty patted her hair. "That man's always been sweet on me."

Or, considering the gleam in her eye, maybe she wouldn't.

Betty got to her feet and tottered toward the front of the house.

Stan took the seat she'd vacated and patted Florida's knee. "Where's Missouri?"

"I'm not sure. Probably with Tamara. Tamara stuck around only long enough to scoop her up—like an ill wind."

Stan understood the bitterness in her voice. He wasn't sure he was pleased himself. He and Florida hadn't exactly been champions of morality, but they'd mended their ways. He didn't know if the same could be said of Tamara. "I'll go find her. I want to spend some time with her before I leave tomorrow. You still sure you'll get along okay without me?"

"I've managed for a lot of years." Her voice was dry.

"True. But not like this. Still, I guess that schmuck you're marrying . . ." He stood again and looked around, realizing he hadn't seen Florida's fiancé. "Daniel off hiding? Can't say I blame him."

"He couldn't make it tonight. Business . . . you know."

The airiness in her voice was at odds with the sudden strain in her face. Nor had she rebuked him for calling Daniel names. He peered closer. Even with the glasses, he could see telltale puffiness.

"What's with the glasses?"

She shrugged and switched topics. "Thanks for loaning us Abe."

He didn't want to talk accountants. "Just protecting my investment. The glasses?"

"I just . . . they make people feel more comfortable. Eye contact. I can't do that anymore."

Stan snorted. "That sounds like something the schmuck made up."

"Such a way with words."

Again he was struck by her failure to defend Daniel. Plus she was smiling. A wan smile, but a smile. He was glad, even though it puzzled him.

"This morning when I woke up . . . I'm seeing better, Stan. Movement. Shapes. I can tell where things are, and I could see Alcea when she came in, although I couldn't tell it was her until she talked."

"Fantastic."

"Daniel said I'm hallucinating."

He didn't miss the ire in her voice, nor the fact

that it warmed him with satisfaction. "Bullshit. If you were hallucinating, you'd conjure up something more fascinating than my ex-wife."

Florida smiled again. The smile . . . the strain, the puffiness. She *had* been crying. Well, who wouldn't in her situation? Blind and about to marry a schmuck.

"So take off the glasses, for God's sake. Who gives a shit who you might make uncomfortable? Besides, maybe those baby blues of yours aren't as useful as they once were, but they're still beautiful, Florida."

Florida's mouth trembled and he suddenly wanted to take her in his arms. To hold her. Just to hold her. "In fact, *you're* beautiful."

"And y'all are still a liar. I must look like a pig, all this weight I've gained."

About to walk away, he turned back. "You've never looked better." Intending to deliver the comment lightly, he was startled to hear himself sound so serious, but was glad he had when she looked pleased.

Still wondering what had transpired between Florida and Daniel—because he was sure something had—Stan poked his way toward the front of the house, then back, without scaring up his daughter. He paused in the dining room. "Anyone seen Missouri?"

Dak poked a thumb toward Florida's. "They said they'd be right back."

"They?" But Dak had already bent his head toward Mayor Noflinger's and didn't respond.

Leaving the party behind, Stan stepped out on the breezeway. No cool air had arrived with the rose tones staining the western horizon. The evening was heavy with humidity and the rousing chorus of locusts. He'd almost reached Florida's when he heard Missouri's voice coming from Dak's backyard. Reversing course, he stepped out the breezeway door and made his way toward the sound, halting near a clump of forsythia at the corner of the house when he spotted Missouri and Tamara.

They were seated at a picnic table on the back deck Alcea and Dak had erected over the old cracked patio. Tamara's hair gleamed gold and Missouri's ebony in the light cast by the kerosene torches that would soon fend off the descending darkness. As he watched, Tamara picked up one of several model cars arrayed in front of her and turned it sideways. Stan squinted. The model was a 1950 Studebaker Land Cruiser in Aero Blue. He knew because he'd seen the full-scale real deal in the garage when he was a boy. He remembered it well; his father had given it more loving attention than he had his son.

Tamara's breathy laugh carried to him. "Why, when I was sixteen, I lost my"—she broke off and glanced at Missouri—"uh, *watch* in the backseat of a car just like this."

About to step forward, Stan stopped, curious.

"You really rode in one of these once?"

"More than once," Tamara assured Missouri. "It belonged to a boy I . . . dated."

"Cool." Missouri took the Studebaker out of Tamara's hands, put it down, and held out another model: the Chevy she'd picked out from the hobby store. "What about this one?"

Tamara took it, but she was still staring at the Studebaker. Her face was naked with . . .

Christ. She'd really loved his father.

"Gram-Tam?" Missouri asked.

Gram-Tam?

"What, hon?"

"Did you ever ride in a 1955 Chevy?"

"Nope. Never did."

"I'd like to. But *I'd* be really careful not to lose anything in it."

"And I'd make sure of it." Smiling, Tamara reached out and smoothed Missouri's hair, her gaze growing somber.

And Stan started again. In that look was a whole world of regret. Maybe Tamara was telling the truth; maybe she had no ulterior motives for returning to Cordelia. Maybe.

He cleared his throat and moved forward. "Missouri, let's drop off your models at home; your mom is looking for you."

"Okay." Missouri gathered up her models and reluctantly climbed off the picnic bench. She looked at Tamara. "If you want, we can look at all of them tomorrow. Julius has lots of stories."

"I'd like that."

Florida sure wouldn't, but thinking of that look on Tamara's face, he wasn't going to object. Hand on Missouri's shoulder, Stan guided her toward the house. Then, he hesitated and looked back. "Coming?"

A corner of Tamara's mouth quirked. "I don't like crowds."

He gave her a slight smile. "I understand."

She didn't want to subject herself to the gossip mill. He couldn't blame her; he'd never liked it, either.

By the time he brought Missouri back to Florida's side, she'd shed the glasses and was chatting with Seamus Ryan, owner of the Rooster Bar & Grill across the street. Long and lean, the black of his attire and hair relieved by a pair of sharp green eyes, Seamus was ever gallant with the ladies. From her heightened color, it looked like he was testing some of that gallantry on her. Good for him. And good for her. She had guts. She'd been blinded just over a week ago—not to mention she'd just survived an assault by Betty Bruell—and here she was, carrying on a mild flirtation as though she hadn't a care.

Missouri slipped away from Stan to cuddle against her mother. Pulling up a chair, he nodded to Seamus and listened absentmindedly to the conversation, gaze still on Florida. Remembering how adept Serena had been at pasting on a smile to cover her pain, he knew she was suffering despite the smile. The eyes were bright, but red-rimmed. The arm she'd draped around Missouri's waist was holding her too tight. Her voice was bright, but mechanical, as she gave Seamus the

same explanation she'd given him for Daniel's absence.

How in the hell could the schmuck have abandoned her tonight? Empire or no empire, you didn't leave the woman you loved alone at a time like this. Then again, that was exactly what he planned to do, too.

His ramblings faltered. Florida wasn't his to abandon.

Another thought suddenly pierced his brain.

Nor was she Daniel's.

That shithead. He'd thrown her over, hadn't he? Stan'd put money on it.

For the next two hours, he had no opportunity to confirm his conviction. Curiosity finally overcoming the last vestiges of reserve anyone felt around Florida—had anyone really doubted it would?—she was never left alone.

But the inability to have her to himself might be a good thing. He'd been disturbed to find that giddy relief was far—far—outweighing any sorrow he felt at their breakup. And beyond disturbed to discover that the idea of a single Florida had him entertaining a number of fantasies. Good God.

Finally, leaving Alcea and Dak to cleanup duty, he'd escorted Florida and Missouri home to a quiet house. Julius had left earlier to go to bed.

Missouri skipped inside ahead of them and up the stairs. She spoke over her shoulder. "Come up with me, Daddy."

He looked at Florida. The animation in her face had ended with the party. She was pale. If she'd let him, he'd help her upstairs. "Your mom needs me."

Halting halfway up, Missouri turned around. "Mom, Mom, *Mom*. That's all anyone cares about anymore."

Raising an eyebrow, he waited for Florida's retort. But she only turned her face away—and not before he saw her nose had pinked. Frowning, he looked back at Missouri.

She backed up a step when she saw his expression. "Well, it's true."

"No, it's not. But if you behave like this, it soon will be."

Missouri's face twisted. Great, pretty soon he'd have two sobbing females on his hands, but he couldn't let her add to Florida's stress. "We love you. But you can't always be the center of—"

"Run upstairs and get yourself ready for bed, hon." Florida's voice was weary. "Your dad will be up in a minute to tuck you in."

Snuffling, Missouri ran the rest of the way up and disappeared down the hall.

"Florida, don't you think she needs to learn that this situation—"

"Please, not tonight, Stan. She's just tired and feeling ornery. Go on up for a while. I'll be fine down here till you get back."

He grumbled, but gave in after settling Florida with a cup of herb tea. He hated the stuff himself,

but she said it worked to make her drowsy. When he reached Missouri's room, she'd already jumped into her pajamas and into bed. She'd left her bed-side lamp on and scattered her clothes from one end of the room to the other.

He approached the bed and looked down. From the rapid rise and fall of Missouri's chest, he knew she hadn't fallen asleep, even though her eyes were shut tight, her hair a tangle on her pillow, her lashes dark smudges on sweetly pink cheeks. His grumpiness faded. Yes, she was selfish. But what kid wasn't? Missouri was used to being the center of their lives—and for him, a light that had kept him going through some pretty dark days.

"I love you, you know."

One eye peeked open. "I know. I love you, too."

He sat down next to her and smoothed back her hair. "I also know that this past week has been pretty rough on you. But try to hang tough. We all have to work together to help your mom."

"Okay," Missouri finally said with some reluc-tance. "But how long before she's all better?"

He hesitated. Florida had said *not tonight*. Easy enough to just let it go and God knew there was a host of things he'd prefer to handling a little girl's emotions, but he wasn't sure Florida was in any position to call the shots. Besides, Missouri was a smart cookie—she'd figure things out whether they told her or not. If she was left to her imagination, no telling what she might conjure up. Better he be straight with her sooner rather than later, and like it or not, he'd just been handed sooner. Damn, if that protective urge wasn't raising its head all over the place tonight.

"Missouri . . . she's not going to get *all* better. Some better, but not all."

Missouri's eyes went wide. "But she *has* to."

"She wants to. With all her heart. But sometimes you just can't have what you want. Your mom's strong, though. And there are people who will help her learn how to manage without all of her eyesight; then she'll be able to do a lot of the same things she used to do before. You and me . . . we have to do what we can for her. Deal?"

Missouri was chewing her lip. "Deal," she said slowly. She slid farther down on her pillow. "But does this mean she won't be able to see me anymore, not ever again?"

Cripes. How to answer that? He pulled up her covers under her chin, smoothed a hand down her cheek, and thought. Of course. "Sure she can see you. Just not the way she used to. Here. I want you to try something. Close your eyes."

Missouri complied.

"Now give me your hand." She did. He took it and put it on his face. "Your mom will have some of her vision still left, but even if she didn't . . . try to see me with your fingers."

She giggled. He let out a breath of relief at the sound.

"That's silly," she said. "My fingers don't have *eyes*."

"Try anyway."

Her fingers roamed over his face. "Cool. I *can* kind of see you." Her eyes opened. "And you need to shave."

He smiled. "And you need to sleep."

He pecked her forehead and stood up.

Just as he reached the door and flipped off the light, she spoke again. "I don't want to move. I still want to see you all the time."

He stopped in the doorway. He couldn't make out her face in the dark. "I wish you weren't leaving, either, but we'll still be together a lot." In fact, just as much as they were now, if what he thought about Daniel was true. But just in case he was wrong: "And you and Mom will be happy with Daniel."

"I guess. He's okay. Kind of fakey, though."

You got that nailed. Stan couldn't help feeling satisfied at her remark, but he kept his opinions to himself. "*And* his house has a swimming pool."

"So does yours. An indoor one, too," Missouri pointed out.

"But you'll have Daniel's all to yourself. I have to share mine with the other people in the condos."

"I wouldn't care," Missouri murmured sleepily. "If we moved in with you, Julius, too, we could be a *real* family because you're my *real* dad. And I have a real grandmother now, too."

As he headed back downstairs, her sentiments swept him with bittersweet longing. Once upon a time, he'd had the opportunity to choose her and Florida over Serena. He had no regrets, but couldn't help wondering if life was bringing him full circle, presenting him with another opportunity. And was it one that he wanted? He didn't know. Strength of will in a woman—and both Alcea and Florida had it in abundance—wasn't something he'd ever handled well. Actually, handled at all. Yet . . . yet . . .

In the great room, Florida had curled up on the sofa, head propped on the armrest, hand curled under her cheek, eyes closed. She looked lovely lying there, like Sleeping Beauty. Sleeping Beauty without a will. Would that a kiss on the lips would make her all better.

He shook himself, realizing he'd gotten caught up in Missouri's fantasy, realizing it was appealing to him more than it should. Even if Daniel had dropped the ball here, it didn't mean Florida wanted him to pick it up. Been there, done that.

Although he tried to keep quiet, his footsteps roused her. Yawning, she sat up. There were tear tracks drying on her cheeks.

"She didn't mean it, you know," he said.

"Who doesn't mean . . . ? Oh, Missouri. I know she doesn't. She's just confused. And upset. We all are."

"Especially you. You've got a right to be." Stan sat down next to her and, natural as breathing, put an arm around Florida's shoulders and pulled her close. Unresisting, she let her head rest on his chest. He wouldn't have wished what happened to her on anybody, but he rather liked the way the tragedy had softened her edges. In the past, she'd always been so . . . certain. "So the prick dumped you?"

Florida gave a watery gurgle. "You're so sensitive, Stan. But, actually, I kind of dumped him. How did you know?"

"Your behavior. And that big glass paperweight is gone."

Florida jerked upright, face pointed toward the stand where the expensive sculpture had once rested. "The Chihuly is gone? Why, that jerk. He could have at least asked."

"Good ol' Daniel. All about money."

She frowned at him. "I kinda recall another fella who was like that."

He frowned back, even though he knew she couldn't see him. "And I kinda recall a woman who liked things that way."

Florida relaxed back again. "Okay, okay. I admit it: I rather enjoy money. What a sin. But I love— *loved*—Daniel for more than that. At least, I thought I did. But . . ."

"But?"

"Well, things were bothering me even before all this happened. I just didn't want to see them. I'd caught the brass ring, you know. I wanted to hang on to it. And . . ." She sighed. "I've got some wonderful friends. Alcea. You. Julius. Even the O'Malleys have been kind. But it's not the same as having someone special. Being married. I've been alone a long time. I was tired of being alone."

Guilt stirred. After their affair, after he'd married Serena, and until she and Alcea had become tight enough that the town decided to forgive her, she'd been a near pariah, someone mothers warned their sons against. She hadn't had many prospects. Until now, he hadn't realized she'd wanted them. She'd always seemed so independent.

"I'm sorry, Florida."

"Oh, don't be. Better it happened now than after the vows."

He hadn't been talking about her breakup, but he decided it was wiser not to tell her. In fact, maybe it was time to lighten this up. "Or you might be accused of reliving your gold-digging past."

"I loved you for more than that. You know that." Her voice was sharp.

"Sorry. Bad joke." Very bad. Especially considering the twinge he'd felt when she'd referred to her love for him in the past tense. It was time to move away from this subject. Far away. "I know you did. Then Missouri changed you. Serena changed me. Dakota changed Alcea. . . ."

He stopped and considered. "Well, at least as much as it's possible to change Alcea."

Florida huffed a laugh.

He was still considering. "Or maybe we just draw the right people into our lives when we realize our old ways aren't working anymore and we need something different."

"My, you're profound."

"Or as nuts as your brother."

"Y'all share some genes, too."

"Don't remind me." All that considering had

made his head hurt. "But I do have my moments. Occasionally even a deep thought slips in. Now. Back then, of course, I was an immature asshole."

"Yes, you were."

"Hey." He poked her. "You don't have to agree so fast. And cut me some slack. Most men do act like morons when they're running scared."

"Scared? Is that what you call it? You had more women dangling on a string than there's laundry on a line. I call that a lot of things, but not scared."

"Scared," he repeated emphatically. "You and Alcea were damn scary. Still are. And Missouri's getting that way. She's smart as hell. Determined to get what she wants. Just like you. And back then—"

"It was you."

"Huh?"

"Back then. Alcea and I both wanted you. And your money. We're kind of competitive."

"No kidding? And spendthrifts. Alcea threw money around like there was no tomorrow. She didn't care about much besides that, our daughter, and maybe our country-club membership. So I glommed on to you."

"*Glommed*? You sweet talker, you."

"And then *you* wanted to spend it right and left."

"Yeah. Everything was all our fault." Now Florida poked him.

"Let me finish, already. Didn't I *say* I was an asshole? I didn't know how to fix my marriage, so I made it worse. Then my noble solution when both of you started squabbling was to go find another woman or two. But then, Serena . . ."

"Got her claws into you."

"Nah. Serena didn't have claws."

He thought of his late wife. She'd breezed into town, a recent widow, to check out a condo development—the one he still lived in—left to her in her husband's estate. Serena hadn't been overly bright, but she'd *been* bright. Brightest ray of sun in the room, with a smile that lit his life and eyes that danced with a child's delight. She'd made him feel like he was the most important man in the world.

"But," he said, "she did have her own fortune and by some miracle, she loved me. At first, I didn't trust our happiness. I didn't believe in that kind of—God help me as I'm about to sound like Dak again—purity of heart."

"I know. I'm the one you slept with in your confusion."

"Running scared again."

"Glad I could help y'all surmount your fears." She paused and her voice turned serious. "And then came Missouri. And Serena not only forgave you but *welcomed* her once she knew. I'll never get over that. She was quite a woman."

"She was the real deal. . . . I cherished her, Florida. She taught me to love."

Florida's hand went to his shoulder, down his arm to his hand. She linked their fingers together. "And now life's fucked us both."

He smiled. "Guess it has."

For a few long minutes, they sat in silence.

"You sure it's okay for me to leave tomorrow?" Although he'd trained for months and had a wad of money on the line, he'd cancel the trip in a minute at her say-so. He suddenly realized he *wanted* her to say so. "I mean, with Daniel—"

"No, you go do your thing. You've worked long and hard—and it's important to your business. It'd make me feel even worse if you gave it up because of this. Besides, I have to learn to get along without help."

He didn't agree, but knew that tone of voice. An argument would be lost before it even started.

"As for Daniel," she continued, "the way I'm feeling . . . well, it hurts. Of course it does. But not for the reasons you'd think. I mean, I thought the man was made of deeper stuff. And my ego is punctured—really punctured—maybe more than my heart. But it's not like when you—" She stopped. "I mean, there were things wrong between Daniel and me before all this. I just didn't want to see them." She snorted. "*See them.* Guess I'm smarter blind than sighted."

"You're smart any which way. Don't forget it."

"Maybe. Whatever. But I think I'm hurt less by his—his—"

"Complete lack of character?"

There was a smile in her voice. "Possibly. I'm hurt less by that than I am by—" Her breath hitched, all trace of humor gone. "By having the last trace of what I thought would be my future erased. Through the last week, I knew he wasn't who I thought he was, and I knew I couldn't—shouldn't—marry him. But I couldn't admit it to myself because then *everything* would be different."

He shifted, about to take her in his arms, when he heard the back door open and close in the kitchen. Damn. He settled back again.

Florida turned her head toward the sound. "Must be Alcea."

"Does she know about Daniel?"

"No. I didn't want to spoil her party."

Alcea and Dak wandered into the room, Alcea hesitating at the doorway as she took in the two of them on the sofa. An hour of KP hadn't dampened her looks any. The light sheen of perspiration (his ex-wife had never done *sweat*) simply brushed her forehead like gold.

"Touching," she said, eyebrows raised.

Florida sat up, finger-combed her hair. "We were just talking."

Dak kicked off his sandals and lowered himself into a coral-covered easy chair, putting his feet up on the ottoman. "Ahh." He looked at Alcea. "And that's the last farewell party you ever give me."

Perching near Dak's feet, Alcea was still looking from Stan to Florida. "Where was Daniel tonight? I don't remember you telling me he wasn't coming."

"He . . . I mean, I . . . ," Florida fumbled.

Stan jumped in. "Business emergency."

So he lied. Florida obviously didn't want to talk

about it tonight and it wasn't like this was the first time he'd told Alcea a whopper.

Nor was it the first time Alcea had given him that measured look that said, *Yeah, right, bub.* But glancing again at her friend—maybe seeing the remnants of tear tracks—she didn't push. "Well, then. Florida, if you're ready, I can help get you to bed."

"You don't need to bother."

"No bother," Dak said. Stan saw Alcea roll her eyes at the comment—it wasn't her husband that had made the offer. "We're family. Until after the wedding, when you've moved in with Daniel—"

Florida stirred again, looking uneasy.

Alcea was still watching her. Closely. "Until then, though, if you'd let Tamara—"

"No!" Florida took a deep breath, let it out. "No," she repeated more calmly. "I'm sorry, but no."

Dak held up a hand, obviously forgetting Florida couldn't see it. "Understood. We'll just have to agree to disagree. We'll keep her away as much as we can both now and on your future visits."

"Future visits?"

Dak looked puzzled. "You do plan to come back here occasionally after you move, don't you?"

"Oh, that. Yes, of course. When you and Alcea are gone in September . . . will she still be here?"

Alcea and Dak exchanged a look that told Stan they were hoping that by their return, everyone would be playing nice. Looking at the set to Florida's chin, he thought they were pitching a lost cause.

"Yes, but we'll ask her to stay away from your house."

Florida chewed her lip. "That won't keep Missouri from running over there. Tamara needs to leave."

Dak sighed. "Florida, if you're determined to continue letting the past rule the present—"

Stan's eyes crossed.

"—I won't try to stop you. But trying to impose your feelings on everyone else, including your daughter, won't work. At the hospital you said—"

"I know what I said." Florida crossed her arms.

Dak had a point. Still, "Florida just wants—I want—to protect Missouri from getting hurt. Her grandmother doesn't exactly have a reputation for dependability."

Florida looked happy to have Stan championing her fears. Despite himself, he felt his chest puff. Just a little puff.

"C'mon. Missouri's security is with you and Florida, even with us, but not Tamara. If her grandmother packed up tomorrow, she might ask questions, but she wouldn't be hurt."

"That's tomorrow. What about in a month, two months?" Stan said.

Dak smiled. "There's nothing constant about life except change. We may live with the illusion of permanence, but there's really not much that's within our control."

This time, Stan's eyes crossed so hard they almost disappeared behind his nose. But he kept quiet. Actually, thinking of Serena, he'd have to admit there was something to all that airy-fairy BS.

Florida still looked disgruntled. Her situation obviously proved Dak's words, but apparently she didn't like having it pointed out.

"Speaking of when we're gone," Alcea said. "I don't think Julius and Missouri can do everything you need. I know a lot of people will pitch in if you ask"—she emphasized the last few words—"but we're assuming that if you need more than that, you'll ask Daniel?"

"What am I?" Stan asked. "Dog meat?"

Alcea gave him a cool look that said, to wit, yes.

"Uh, yeah. Daniel," Florida said.

Alcea's gaze traveled from Florida's face to Stan's. Stan tried to look dense, usually not an expression he had a lot of trouble with, but Alcea's expression only grew more suspicious. He'd never been able to fool her.

She looked at Florida again. "So, are you ready to go upstairs?" Her voice was bright. Too bright. He knew her. She'd get Florida out of here and interrogate the hell out of her.

He stood up. "I told Florida I'd help her."

"You?"

"Me," he said firmly.

Touching Florida's arm, glad—and moved—to see relief on her face and not annoyance over a high-handedness he'd never taken with her before, he waited till she rose, then took her hand and placed it on top of his forearm like he'd seen Daniel do (only he'd be careful not to run her into a wall). They mounted the stairs, leaving Dak still looking clueless and Alcea looking like she'd swallowed sour fish. He was glad Florida hadn't been able to see that expression—it had been entirely too reminiscent of the time when she and Alcea had been rivals.

Once at Florida's room, she turned and put her hands on his chest. "I can take it from here."

"You sure?"

"I have to learn to be independent." She opened the door, felt for the light switch. Light flooded into the hallway. "I can see you. Well, the shadow of you. And colors."

"Great . . . but, Florida?"

"Yes?" She tilted her face toward him.

"It's okay to need people. Everyone does." He paused. Images of Hawaii, of jagged lava fields and vistas filled with rain forests, ocean, sand, and a finish line all got lost in the blue of her eyes. "I'll cancel the trip; Jess can go in my place."

"Stan, you'll be gone a week, not an eternity. The worst has already happened. Go. If you want to help me, go." She leaned in to brush his cheek with her lips, then gently closed the door.

Touching the spot where she'd kissed him, he lingered a few seconds, then turned toward the stairs. Okay, he'd go. She was probably right.

What more could happen in the space of a week?

Chapter 12

"I don't need help."

In her bedroom the next evening, Florida felt around and pulled a clean blouse out of the laundry basket. She held it close to her face. Black. Ruffles. It was the cap-sleeved blouse she'd been wearing when Daniel had walked out the door two days ago.

Fumbling around, she separated one hanger from the others, then slipped the blouse over it. Her mouth tightened. That was okay. She didn't need him. She didn't need anyone. At least for a lot of things.

Putting her face nearly in her plate let her figure out what she was eating. Holding a mirror up to her eyeballs let her see, well, her eyeballs, although she hadn't been tempted to try mascara. She could even read if the print was big and only an inch from her nose. Eventually, with whatever the vision therapist taught her and some fancy tools, she'd be able—maybe differently, slowly, or awkwardly—to manage independently.

"Oh, c'mon. Don't send me away. Dak's out running errands, and I don't want to go home to an empty house." Alcea grabbed something else out of the basket and set to work. "And I don't want to look at another income statement, either." They'd spent several hours going over business matters Florida could have taken care of in half the time. Alcea had a true mental block over All Things Math. "My brain matter is already permanently melted."

Florida didn't really want her to go away. But she didn't want her to stay, either. Alcea's determined attempts to master QuickBooks had only highlighted how much her friend was doing for her. Florida was getting deeper and deeper into her debt—without the ability to return the favors. And it wasn't just Alcea; it was other people, too.

Just today—prodded, she'd bet, by Alcea— Seamus Ryan had offered to run her around on any errands she needed. Rosemary Butz, Betty Bruell's manager at Up-in-the-Hair since Betty had retired, had told her—amid dozens of exclamation points and *oh mys*—that she'd stop by "any old time you want" and cut her hair. And Ernie Burcham, town bigot and loudmouth and owner of the largest local grocery, had reminded her that his Piggly Wiggly had delivery service for the disabled. And, sheesh, even *his* solicitousness had touched her.

Almost as much as it had annoyed her. She felt like a stereotype. *The Disabled.*

"So . . . you and Stan looked cozy last night." Alcea's voice was casual. Maybe too casual.

Florida pulled out another garment and held it an inch from her face. Denim shorts. She laid them on the bed and smoothed them out. At first, figuring out these small things had been a kind of game, but any entertainment factor had long faded. This wasn't a game. No blindman's bluff, where she could yank off her blindfold when she tired of it. How long would it take for her to learn to live independently? And exactly how independent could she really be?

"You know, I need to get a few new clothes. Shorts and pants, anyway. These are too tight." She sighed. "I need to diet."

"I think you look good. Less scrawny. About Stan—"

"I wasn't scrawny. I was modelesque. Like Klum or Moss or—"

"Gandhi," Alcea inserted. "You're avoiding the topic."

"What topic?"

"You know what topic."

"Oh, Stan. He was just . . . commiserating."

"Okay, God knows you've got a lot to commiserate with, but—"

"Y'all don't know the half of it. . . . Daniel's not coming back."

There was a pause. "You mean, this weekend?"

"I mean, ever. It's over. He doesn't . . ." Her

lips quivered and she clenched her teeth. She was tired of all this moaning and weeping. "The man doesn't want a near-blind bride."

Alcea was silent. "Then he's a Grade A shit-bucket." Alcea rounded the bed.

"I didn't know the FDA rated shit-buckets."

"They do." Alcea gathered her into a hug. "And Daniel Davenport has an unusually high crap content. I'm so sorry, Florida."

"Don't be. I decided I don't want him, either." The *Reader's Digest* version of what she'd said to Stan. It felt good being held, but she didn't want to rehash it again. At least not now. She pulled away and gave a huge sigh. "Really. I'm better off without him."

"That goes without saying."

"Although," she continued, picking up a—shirt to face—pink blouse, "I do have one big regret."

"What's that, sweetie?"

"The world will never see a four-foot-tall ice sculpture of Daniel and me."

There was a beat of silence.

"You *are* kidding, right?"

"Nope."

Suddenly they were laughing. Alcea grabbed her again. She dropped the shirt and they clung to each other. Laughter turned to tears, then back to laughter. Finally, Florida pushed Alcea away.

"Okay, enough waterworks for a while." Wiping her face with the back of her hand, Florida grabbed another garment.

Alcea did likewise. "So Stan was *commiserating.*" Her tone was suggestive.

"He was being a friend. Like you. God, Alcea. I don't know what I'd do without you."

Or Stan. The thought took her by surprise. She'd grown accustomed to his dependability where Missouri was concerned, but who would have guessed that the man would become such a stand-up guy for her?

"You know I love you." Not a big sucker for sentiment—Alcea's voice was brisk. "God, who would have thought I'd ever say that? But Stan . . . Be careful, Florida. Stan tends to think of Stan first. And since Serena died, he's lonely."

"So you think he'll hit on me?" Florida realized her laugh sounded bitter. "I'm flawed, Alcea. Pretty soon I'll be wearing some kind of headgear to read the newspaper, for God's sake. You think anyone wants to look at *that* across the breakfast table?"

"Yes, I do."

She thought of Daniel. The memory of that night in St. Louis was still raw; maybe someday she'd share it with Alcea, but not now. "I don't."

"Serena managed a miracle with Stan," Alcea continued. "But without her . . . Just be careful is all." She moved to the closet to hang up some clothes.

Feeling a niggle of irritation at her friend's ill opinion of Stan, Florida bit her lip. Of course, Alcea had reason to have a jaundiced view of her ex-husband, but Florida had looked at both sides. Okay, granted, her perspective might have been just a tad prejudiced, but . . .

Well. She hated being disloyal, but Alcea's viewpoint wasn't entirely objective, either. Alcea viewed her lavish spending during her marriage and her near-slavish devotion to their daughter, Kathleen, as excusable—a way she'd filled the emptiness. Only natural during the years of Stan's serial adultery.

Florida, though, had seen, not only dollar signs when she'd looked at Stan, but a man torn between his mother's strict moral code—and the certainty she'd disinherit him if he ever divorced Alcea—and a grasping wife who was most interested in how much of a splash she could make in Cordelia's small pond.

When Stan's mother had died, and he'd finally divested himself of his unhappy marriage, Alcea had gone through the settlement like wildfire, then leaned on him some more. It was no wonder he'd shied away from marriage with Florida. At that time, Florida knew, she'd appeared to him as no less mercenary and scheming than his ex-wife.

Which, admittedly, she had been. But she'd also been lonely. Loneliness—the inheritance from a mother she'd never known. And, more than that, she'd been in love. Really and truly in love.

Still, chances were, any marriage between them wouldn't have flourished. Even though her love had been real, when Serena had come along, it should have been obvious that had they wedded, their marriage would have fallen into the same pattern as his first one. She'd been as strong-willed as Alcea, and at the time, he'd been just as proportionately weak. Now . . . ?

Stan had changed. And so had she. For that matter, so had Alcea. Even before Alcea had met Dakota, she'd begun the process of reinvention, worn by near destitution and a burning desire to make more of herself than arm candy. And she'd succeeded. But that didn't mean she knew everything.

"I don't need to be careful of Stan, Alcea. We get along just fine now."

"I know you do, but just remember, Stan doesn't give more than he gets. Less, actually."

A decade ago, Florida would have agreed. Except, since Missouri had been born, she'd daily seen the love he lavished on their daughter. And not just on Missouri. Hadn't he dropped everything to cart her to Columbia on the day she'd woken up blind? And then sat through the appointments and shouldered her emotions. The situation must have had eerie—and painful—similarities to his experiences with Serena. Yet he'd gone willingly and never murmured a selfish word. Doing something like that . . . it took courage. A quiet kind, maybe, but courage. And last night . . . last night, she realized, he hadn't let her get maudlin. He'd sympathized, but steadied her.

She repeated his words. "He has his moments."

"See?" Alcea shook out a shirt with more vigor than necessary. "You're already dewy-eyed. You *know* Stan. He can be sweet, yes. But he's a selfish—"

"Hush." Irritation finally spiked. She didn't want to argue with Alcea, but she sounded so . . . know-it-all. So certain. *Nothing* was certain. She tried for an even tone. "Isn't he paying for Abe to help us?"

"His accountant protects his investment."

Same words he'd used, but thinking of how sincere he'd sounded about canceling the marathon he'd worked so hard to ready for, she knew he wasn't totally propelled by self-interest. "Look, I know your marriage was seven kinds of hell. I know all of us were to blame. And I know Stan found it impossible to keep his pants zipped back then. But he did try to help out when—"

"How did he try? He held the purse strings, but when my family needed help—"

Florida stifled a snort of exasperation. Help? The O'Malleys had always relied on one another, watched one another's backs. Alcea didn't know what it was like to *really* need help. She hadn't had a cobbled-together family like Florida had grown up in. She hadn't lived in a mansion of silent rooms with a grieving widowed mother like Stan had. She'd had noise and laughter and siblings and squabbling. . . .

She still did. If Alcea had gone blind, both of her younger sisters would be dancing attendance, and her mother would be camped on her doorstep. Her nieces and nephews would rally around. Dakota would be relentless in his efforts to help.

Alcea shouldn't complain. She had no right to complain. Not about that. Not about Stan. At least not in that way.

She couldn't refrain. "Hold on. If I remember right, Stan gave your brother a job even though everyone knew Henry couldn't handle it."

"Okay, granted," Alcea said, "my brother was a deadbeat, but—"

Florida knew she was bringing up old hurts; she didn't want to dredge up the past, but her tongue had a mind of its own. "And then when Henry died, Stan extended deadlines and re-worked mortgages for his widow, so she could make ends meet. He also gave her a job that she had some trouble with—I know because she was my assistant, remember? He also helped Lil"—the middle O'Malley sister—"get a loan to buy Henry's business."

"But he could have done so much more!"

"How?" Florida burst out, feeling suddenly intolerant of anything even approaching injustice. *Let's say it like it is, not like we want it to be.* "You threw money around like it was grass seed. And when you divorced, Stan even carried your mortgage when your settlement didn't demand it. Your whole family—which I might point out is the size of a village—was needy back then, even though y'all didn't realize you had more riches than most. The ones that really count. You all kept turning to Stan for help—yet at the same time, I've never seen a man so despised by his in-laws."

"For good reason." Alcea's voice was stiff with

anger. "He was having an affair. A long-standing affair. With *you*."

Florida deflated as quickly as she'd blown up. Exhaustion crept up to smother her anger. "You're right. What I did was unforgivable. I share the blame. A lot of it."

"Well . . . we all do," Alcea said grudgingly.

"I shouldn't have brought it all up; it was a long time ago. Forgive me . . . again?"

Alcea paused and for a moment, Florida thought she might not. "Of course. The past is past."

That wasn't the old Alcea talking; it was the one that had been born under her brother's influence. *Live and let live.*

"And right now," Alcea continued, "we have to figure out what to do for the present."

Be present in the moment.

"You mean about me."

"About you."

Florida swallowed. What if you didn't like *the moment*? "Dr. Rosen told us—me—about a residential program in St. Louis. Hope House." In the wake of Daniel's desertion, driven by the need to do something for herself, she'd had Julius help her call them yesterday. She was eligible—or would be once someone helped her complete the paperwork they were sending. "They teach you how to handle things in more depth than the vision therapist will."

"Things?"

"You know, *things*." Everything that she used to take for granted. Everything that once was so easy. "Doing laundry. Crossing the street. Shopping. Cooking." Using a white cane. Learning Braille. Even though she wasn't totally blind, Dr. Rosen's assistant had said that sometimes it was easier to learn how to handle things sightless than to struggle trying to accomplish a task using low-level vision. As for the cane, along with helping her maneuver in dim light, it signaled to people who saw her that she might need assistance. She found the idea repulsive.

"Sounds ideal. When do you start?"

No, it didn't sound *ideal*. It sounded God-damned unfair. "They think they can get me in in early October, so I can finish by Christmas."

Christmas . . . with storefronts dressed in wreaths and lights, and gaily colored gifts, and Missouri's shining face . . . it'd all be one big kaleidoscopic blur.

Alcea must have heard the note of desolation in her voice. "We'll get through it, Florida. It'll all work out."

We? Anger spurted again and she tamped it down. Alcea was just trying to support her. "But it's a twelve-week program, a residential program. That's impossible. Who would take care of everything here?"

Alcea didn't say anything.

Belatedly, Florida realized how ridiculous she'd sounded. In her present condition, her absence would actually make her household easier to handle, not more difficult. "Sorry. I forget I'm part of the burden. The biggest part."

"Don't talk like that," Alcea said. "Negativity will only hurt, not help."

Anger flared again. Her brother's influence again. Alcea sounded like a New Age idiot. "And don't you talk like *that*. I won't put a positive spin on this; don't ask me to."

"I'm sorry." Alcea's voice was stiff. "But we *will* need to think of some alternative for when you're gone. You know I'll do what I can, but between two households, Missouri, Julius, and our business . . ."

. . . and coping with having her addlebrained niece Daisy operating as second-in-command— Alcea was right. Alcea was putting Daisy in charge of Peg's while she was gone in September, a rather slow month with the tourist season subsiding after Labor Day. Florida would supervise somewhat—at least issue instructions for the accountant and their attorney, Mel Murphy. They should be able to muddle through—even though they'd have a legal bill as long as a country mile— while still giving Alcea the time she treasured each year with Dak. But leaving Daisy in charge for longer than that would be a disaster.

Which served Alcea right for hiring Daisy in the first place, but Florida wished her point didn't have to be proved.

"So maybe you'd consider letting Tam—"

Before she could get Tamara's name out, Florida interrupted. "After my next appointment with Dr. Treter in eleven days"—yes, she was counting, as she wanted to get *going*, for God's sake—"I'll have a vision assessment. Then a CVRT—a certified vision rehabilitation therapist—will come in to teach me how to cope with the basics, probably a few times a week at first for a few hours each time. Julius is here; he can help me. And then there's Missouri. . . . Where is she, anyway?"

"At Joey's. She's been there since ballet this morning. I think Barb Norsworthy thinks they're better off with her than . . ." Alcea trailed off.

Another country heard from. Florida sighed. "Barb Norsworthy is the world's biggest fussbudget." Still, her spirits took another hit. Was there anyone who didn't doubt her capabilities? "Anyway . . . ," she continued. "That'll take care of August. So by the time you leave to join Dak after Labor Day, I should be doing fine for the short term. And after you return, there will be only a little over a week before I'll head off to that school. By then, I'll have something figured out for those months."

"I've already figured them out."

From Alcea's tone, Florida knew her chin had jutted out in that mulish way she had. And she also knew exactly what she'd figured out. "Not Tamara."

"Florida, listen—"

"No! Missouri can go live with Stan."

"Stan has a business to run; what's Missouri supposed to do with herself when he's at Strides? Sit in the condo by herself?"

"No. She can come over here until Stan picks her up. Julius can watch her like he always has."

"Not like he always has. You've always been upstairs in your office."

"Not always. I leave them alone sometimes."

"When I'm next door. And not for very long."

"Dak will be back by then."

There was silence as both pictured Dakota supervising Missouri. He got so absorbed in his writing, he wouldn't hear a nuclear missile explode in the backyard.

"Okay," Florida conceded. "Maybe not Dak. But Julius—"

"You *know* putting an old man in a wheelchair in charge of a little girl who has a penchant for rope swings over rocky creeks is a stupid idea."

She should never have told Alcea about Missouri's escapade near Memorial Park. "Are you calling me stupid?"

"I'm calling you *stubborn*."

"I am not. I'm willing to look at other options. I know: Instead of coming home after school, she can go to Peg's and hang out with you until—"

Alcea sucked in a breath. "Sit down and let me explain a few truths to you."

Florida flushed. But sat.

"For the rest of August, we'll juggle however we can. Hopefully that therapist will help make you more self-sufficient and I won't be needed as much once she's done her thing. For the last two weeks in September, after Dak and I return, we'll manage the same way."

"Wait," Florida said. "I thought you'd be gone for three weeks."

"I'm cutting the trip short by a week. I didn't see any way around it." *And*, her tone said, *I hope you appreciate it.*

Shamed, Florida bit her lip.

Alcea continued. "For the twelve weeks when you're at Hope House, unless you've won a lottery you didn't mention and can now afford to hire full-time, live-in help to care for your daughter and Julius and/or a business manager for the franchise, we *will* use Tamara. And Missouri won't come to Peg's after school. Because as much as I love her and as truly fabulous as I am, I can't do it all, Florida. Tamara is able and willing. *I* need her help."

"Able?" Florida muttered. "She's almost as rickety as Julius."

"It's just a little arthritis. And she's free," Alcea added.

"Maybe Dak could pay for . . ."

Sensing Alcea's outrage before she completed her (what really was a stupid) thought, she trailed off. She squirmed, suddenly feeling like a worm for even suggesting Alcea and Dak bear that kind of expense on her behalf.

"And you think *I* threw money around? Tamara's the perfect solution. Missouri likes her. Julius has known her since her childhood. She wants to do it. Yet we should hire a stranger?"

Hell, yes. The idea of having her mother presiding over her house, over her daughter, made her want to retch. But she kept still, knowing Dak would completely support Alcea. Not because of the money, but because he'd think it was serendipity that Tamara would be thrown into his half sister's life up close and personal. She was sure that with his cockeyed optimism, he thought they'd end up best friends forever.

When she didn't respond, Alcea continued. "Didn't think so. So that takes care of now till Christmas. Except for the two weeks in September when I'll be with Dak. During those two weeks, Tamara could also—"

"We don't need her then. I'll be here." Offhand, she couldn't come up with any more flippin' arguments against using Tamara while she was in Hope House—although, give her a little time and she would, she *would*—but she couldn't tolerate having her underfoot while she was still under the same roof.

"Listen, Florida. . . ." Alcea's voice turned cajoling. "You can't expect Julius and Missouri to handle your needs and their own, no matter what that therapist teaches you. Julius has a heart condition. He's forgetful. And he's not exactly safe, not with that habit of rocketing through the house at ninety miles an hour. Do I need to mention, too, that he can't get upstairs? Do I really need to tell you it'd be too much to ask of him?"

Alcea paused. For a long time.

"Well? Do I?"

"No." Florida knew she was being as mulish as Alcea probably looked.

"And," Alcea continued, "while I know Missouri will help you, you can't very well ask her to babysit Julius, become your personal handmaiden and your household's chief cook, laundress, accountant, and bottle washer, until you're up to speed. She's *nine*—she can drive only as far as her bicycle can take her. Not to mention, there's a little matter of school come September."

Abruptly, Florida stood up. "I *get* it."

"Good." Alcea stood up, too. "Then Tamara will stay here while you're at Hope House. And she'll help out during those two weeks while I'm off with Dak."

Florida picked up another garment and snapped it out. Over her dead body. Maybe she couldn't come up with another solution for the months she'd be at the school for the blind—although she'd ransack her brain trying—but there were still four weeks between now and when Alcea was scheduled to leave in September.

Four weeks was plenty of time to prove they didn't need Tamara.

Chapter 13

Knowing it was a highly unrealistic ambition, but deciding to aim for the stars anyway, Florida woke on Sunday determined not to bother Alcea ever again—and thus stave off the specter of her mother becoming a full-fledged member of the household.

To that end, when Alcea phoned shortly after she'd opened her eyes to see what she would need today, Florida told her—after knocking the receiver off the bed stand to the floor, then fumbling around to find it—an emphatic, *"Nothing."*

After a pause, Alcea said, "Okay," in a way that sounded suspiciously like, *You're out of your cotton-pickin' mind,* then hung up, leaving Florida to meet her own challenge.

Setting her mind firmly on each task, she got herself up, showered, and dressed without even bothering Missouri. Wielding a blow-dryer on her own wasn't hard, even though she suspected the style she managed was reminiscent of a broom. She applied mascara with the mirror pressed up to her nose and thanked God for a complexion that didn't need much makeup—and could tolerate none at all until she felt more confident her blush application wouldn't look like she'd used an aerosol can to spot each cheek. Dressing, like folding laundry, proved only a matter of holding garments up to her face until she hit a shirt whose blurred color was a match with the shorts she'd tugged from a drawer.

See, Alcea? she thought as she stepped into the bathroom for one more swipe at her hair. *I can get myself presentable for a day at home, even if I probably can't master a toilette fit for . . . for a wedding.*

Lowering her hairbrush, she stared at the blurred blob of her image in the mirror, caught up again in all of the coulda-shoulda-been thoughts that had been playing an endless refrain in accompaniment to everything she'd done since the accident.

But it wasn't really Daniel that was uppermost in her mind. It was . . .

Okay, since truth was hitting her square between (in?) the eyes these days, she might as well admit she was mourning the loss of the life Daniel had offered more than she was pining for the man himself. Long ago, when she'd latched on to Stan, she'd entertained vaulted visions of herself, the bank president's wife, sipping Cristal on the deck of some yacht (never mind that Stan had owned only a powerboat). But love had also entered into the mix. Maybe not a mature last-forever kind of love, but she'd been head over heels. By the time Missouri was conceived, the money had no longer mattered.

With Daniel—*admit it*—it always had. Right now, she'd still sell her soul to get her sight back. But on some level, she was relieved her loss of vision had prevented her from living to regret her choice.

Squaring her shoulders, she gave her hair a last whack, then slapped the hairbrush down on the vanity. Forcing bounce into her steps—determined to face the day with courage and make all the right choices from now on—she headed through her room and down the hallway toward the stairs. The idea of regaining some control over her life filled her with zeal. Which took a hit as she tripped over what she hoped was one of Missouri's stray slippers and not a dead rabbit.

Steadying herself with a hand on the wall, she pushed it aside with her foot. Optimism. Pessimism. Too much of either one was dangerous. She straightened and gave herself a talking-to. She needed to balance on a line between hope and reality. Needed to be careful not to slip into fantasy or fall off into denial.

Needed to be careful not to fall, period.

She put less bounce in her step and took the stairs with caution. There was no past—no dwelling on her sighted life. And no future—no more thoughts of what might have been. She'd take things one day, one moment, at a time. She grimaced. She hated being so . . . inert. Like her brother . . . like Stan . . .

Or, rather, like Stan had once been, she corrected herself, feeling with her toe for the next step. When she'd first met him, he'd lived in a constant state of reaction, buffeted by the wills of the strong women in his life. Including his mistress . . .

She'd loved him, all righty, but she'd been such a youngster, glorying in the heady power she'd had to crook a finger and make him come running. She'd exercised it often. Although not all the way to the altar. Stan had possessed an uncanny sense of self-survival. He'd rebelled against them all—in often unattractive and instinctual ways. Like a reptile.

His experiences with Serena had changed him, though. She liked to think she'd softened the clay, although it had taken Serena to mold it, and Stan's own choices to fire it. And, wow . . . cheesy metaphors galore . . . had she overheard too much Oprah recently or what?

But still . . . cheesy metaphors or not, Stan had changed shape. She hadn't realized how much until lately . . . when he'd willingly put her needs ahead of his own. The old Stan wouldn't have done that. The old Stan wouldn't have done a lot of things. Like run marathons. She smiled. Or offer not to, just for her.

Yesterday afternoon their time, he'd arrived on Oahu. He'd phoned last night to give Missouri a rundown. His group was spending a few days training, resting, and sightseeing before moving on to the Big Island for the marathon Saturday. He'd told Missouri he was beat from the long flight. Now she pictured him well rested and sipping a mai tai under a palm tree while admiring a thong or two. . . .

No, that was the old Stan. The new Stan took his training seriously. He was more likely running on the beach after nothing stronger than Gatorade, his feet kicking up white sand while a tropical breeze riffled his dark hair . . . and he admired a thong or two. He hadn't changed *completely*. Sighing, she reached the bottom step. She wished she could be there.

In the thong he was admiring.

That last thought startled her so much, she would have toppled down the stairs if she hadn't reached the bottom. Whoa. From what dark, twisted place in her psyche had that sprung from? Good God. Was she still carrying a torch for Stan? All through her engagement with Daniel? She examined the possibility, then rejected it. Maybe she hadn't been in love with Daniel as much as she'd been in love with the idea of Daniel. But she'd gotten over Stan a long time ago. Way, *way* over.

But, a little voice said, *weren't you just saying that the person he'd been then wasn't the person he was now? . . . .*

Slapping that little voice silly—like she needed that kind of complication now?—she'd just put

out a foot to step onto the tile of the entry floor
when there was a sudden clamor of bells. Her
stomach leaped into her throat. Julius whizzed
around the corner. She yanked her foot back just
before he flattened it.

" '*O most wicked speed*'!" The blur halted. "I'm
gol-darned sorry. Didn't mean to about knock you
off your feet. Ain't this the sweetest thing?" The
chimes sounded again.

Sweet? More like heart-stopping. "What are
they?"

"Bicycle bells. Dak put 'em on for me before he
left. Should help us out."

"Slowing down might help out more."

"Yep, that's what I told Missouri. We need milk
from the store." He rang his bell. "I'm on my way
there now." He fussed with the doorknob.

She didn't normally let Julius go anywhere un-
accompanied, given his need for speed, but until
she was trained with the cane, she couldn't con-
nive to go with him. "Julius, I don't think—"

"Now, Florida." There was an old man's pride
in his voice. "The Piggly's just around the corner.
What's gonna happen?"

There was a ramp from one side of the porch
to the driveway and—he was right—the grocery
was less than a block away and smack on the
square. Everyone around here knew him. . . . She
was struck by a sudden thought. His ability to
grab an item or two from the store when they
needed it would negate at least one reason to have
Tamara here. He'd be fine. Still . . .

"Maybe Missouri could go with—" She sniffed. Something was burning. "What's that?"

He rolled out the door, calling over his shoulder. "Can't have cereal till I get back, but I've got toast going."

Going, all right. Up in smoke. Trailing a hand along the wall, she hurried as fast as she dared to the kitchen, the smell of burned bread growing stronger. Movement and Missouri's voice came from the counter. "Mom! Julius must have set the toaster on high or something."

There was a clattering noise.

Florida moved toward her daughter. "What are you doing?"

"Bread's stuck. I'm trying to get it out."

"With what?" She'd reached Missouri. Feeling for her daughter's arm, she pulled it back. Something gleamed in Missouri's fist. "With a knife? Missouri! You know better than to stick something like that in the toaster."

"*Gol*, Mom." Florida couldn't see Missouri's expression, but her mind inserted an eye roll. "I wasn't letting it touch the sides or anything."

Florida closed her eyes, got her adrenaline slowed. She'd thank Julius for fixing breakfast, then tell him from now on, he was to cook nothing that required heat. "It's okay. Just leave it." The challenge of cleaning the toaster blind would probably fill an afternoon. She sniffed again, smelled coffee. "Could you pour me a cup of coffee?"

That was something she hadn't been able to

figure out. With cold drinks, she could hook a finger over the rim and feel when the liquid hit her hand. But coffee? Well, how did you do that without scalding a finger?

After she'd seated herself at the table, Missouri not only fetched coffee but brought her a banana and a granola bar. They sat munching together, Missouri humming tunelessly under her breath. Florida swallowed the last of her banana and considered how best to tell Missouri about the broken engagement. While there hadn't appeared to be much love lost between Missouri and Daniel, she wasn't sure how her daughter would take the news. To make the move easier for Missouri to swallow, she'd admit, she'd played up the perks— the housekeeper, the swimming pool, the travel, the private school. . . . Florida hadn't been the only one dreaming about pie in the sky. Hell's bells. Nothing like teaching her daughter how to think shallow.

Picking up the napkin Missouri had put next to her plate, Florida wiped her mouth and dived on in. "I need to tell you something."

The humming stopped. "Okay."

"The other day, Daniel and I . . . we had this discussion—"

"You mean you fought?"

"No, we didn't fight; we kind of disagreed about—"

"You fought."

Florida paused. "Okay, we fought."

"And you broke up."

Florida nodded. "And we broke up." Gee, that was hard.

"So you're not getting married anymore?"

"No, honey bun, we're not. We decided that we just didn't love each other enough for marriage."

"But you're okay? I mean, you're not too very, very sad?"

"No, I'm not. Sometimes making the right choice hurts, but breaking our engagement is for the best. I'm sorry. I know you were looking forward to living in Kansas City."

Missouri was silent. Florida could make out the pale oval of her face, but not her eyes or expression.

"I know it's hard to switch gears this fast," she continued. "And Daniel's been a part of your life for quite a while. I'm sure he'll get in touch with you to say good-bye." Because she'd call Rita and make certain of it. "He'd probably like to see you again, too. Just because I won't, doesn't mean—"

Missouri's chair scraped back and from the agitated movements as she flung herself off it, Florida thought she was extremely upset. Then she realized her daughter was dancing around the kitchen.

"Yippee!"

Florida sat back, stunned. She'd hoped Missouri wouldn't mind too much, but hadn't expected her to act like she'd won the lottery.

Hopping back to her chair, Missouri scrambled up onto her knees and, forearms providing support, leaned across the table until her face was close to her mother's. So close, Florida could make out her dark eyes, sober now. "I liked him okay, Mom, but . . . I didn't really want to move."

"You didn't?"

"No, and Julius didn't, either. We talked about it when we were doing the hobby cars."

"Why didn't you say something?"

"Because Julius said you deserved to be happy and we shouldn't make problems. But we did decide he'd stay here, because he said he was too old to change stripes or something like that, and Uncle Dak had said Tamara could take care of him after we left, and then whenever we came back to visit, it could still be the same. Except Gram-Tam would be here, too. I decided that would be okay, especially if I had a swimming pool and a big room with my own bathroom when I wasn't here." She paused. "Why don't you like Gram-Tam?"

Gram-Tam? Puh-lease. Florida skipped over the question. "You had things all figured out, didn't you?"

"Uh-huh."

Florida leaned in and touched her forehead to Missouri's. "I love you."

"I love you, too. Can you see me—I mean, my eyes and nose and stuff—when we're this close?"

"Yes, I can see all your *stuff*. Can you see me?"

"Yeah, but you look like you have one big eyeball."

Florida laughed. It felt so good to laugh.

Missouri sat back. "Can I go tell Joey we're not moving anymore?"

Florida had wanted Missouri to help her do some laundry and clean the kitchen floor. But they could do it later. "Sure. Go on with you, but be back for lunch."

Probably something enticing along the lines of PB and J, so Julius didn't burn down the house. But that was okay for now. Once she'd returned from Hope House, she should be able to cook. Which would be interesting, since she'd never been much good at it before.

After Missouri left, Florida shunned more coffee in favor of a can of Diet Coke, which she knocked onto the floor while getting down a glass. She fumbled around on hands and knees with a roll of paper towels, only to scatter a tray of ice cubes not fifteen seconds later, turning the kitchen into a minefield. Again, the hands and knees routine, before she tackled the toaster, getting as many crumbs on the floor as she did in the sink. Once more . . . well, it was one way to get the floor washed.

Having created as much chaos as she could in the kitchen, she headed into other regions of the house, managing within a single hour to misplace the television remote, a comb, her cell phone, and the receiver of the cordless after she'd picked the latter up to call her cell and so retrieve it. Somewhere amid all this frivolity, she realized Julius had been gone too long.

Putting her face nearly into the clock hanging on the kitchen wall, she read the time. Half past eleven. More than two hours. Far too long. She wouldn't worry, though, not yet. Julius was a chatterbox and a gossip hound. He would have had to go only about six feet off the front walk before running into a kindred spirit. Between here and the grocer's, he'd likely encountered two dozen kindred spirits. And then had stopped to browse through the models at Harvey's Hobby House. All that took time.

Still.

Biting her lip, she considered her options. Summon Missouri to look for him. Since there was no phone within shouting distance that she could find down here, she could use the extension upstairs to call her. But there weren't any guarantees that once Missouri fetched him, the two of them would come directly home. They were better at finding distractions—especially in Harvey's Hobby House—than following directions.

She could feel her way next door, easy enough using the breezeway, and see if Alcea could help. She was probably home. Probably sitting right next to the phone. Maybe with Tamara. Both of them just biding their time, chuckling over stubborn ol' Florida and waiting for her to ask for help.

Which Florida just wasn't going to do. So Missouri it would be. She moved to the stairs, then hesitated.

No, not Missouri. She'd look for Julius herself.

I mean, really. How hard could it be? She'd made the walk hundreds of times. People knew she was legally blind. If she had any trouble, there would be somebody nearby to help her. In fact, she'd take her wallet (if she could find her purse) and do a little shopping. The clerk would help. *That* would show Alcea how really independent she was.

Before she could change her mind, she felt her way around the house, finally locating her purse upstairs. Tucking her wallet into her shorts pocket, she picked her way back down, wondering if Julius would glide back through the door before she got going. When he didn't appear before she reached the front door, she didn't know whether to be glad or not.

She managed to traverse the front porch and steps without a concussion. She kicked a flowerpot but didn't fall over it. The walkway was a little trickier, but not too bad, since it followed a straight line between a tall red oak and the dogwood trees that took partial refuge in its dappled shade. If she strayed, the grass, stiff as straw after all the hot weather, provided a toe bumper. Reaching the sidewalk, she unlatched the gate by touch, shut it behind her, then turned right and stopped to orient herself.

She'd learned squinting didn't do a thing, so she just let her gaze—such as it was—wander and absorbed as much information as she could from the shapes and colors in front of her. The sun was reaching its zenith. She followed her intended route in her mind's eye. Right after her house, she'd encounter a curb with a step down to a narrow alley screened by trees that ran alongside the edge of Cowboy's property and behind the stores that fronted one side of the square. Dumpsters, sometimes spilling over with cardboard boxes, lined the backs of the stores, and the alley ended in a turnaround amid a copse of trees with a scraggly path that led to the square's sidewalk, just to one corner of the Piggly Wiggly. Even on a midday in summer, the light would be dim. She'd stick to the sidewalk.

Straight ahead, about twenty feet after the alley, the Stationery Stop sat on the corner of Main and Maple Woods Drive. She could see its reddish brown bulk from here. She'd turn right there, head past Parsons Sound Arcade and Sandwich Shoppe (proprietor Stella Parsons believed in multitasking), then Harvey's, then the pocket park with the copse of trees, and—voilà!—she'd be at the store.

Sounded easy. Didn't look like it, though. She took a deep breath and moved forward.

At first she didn't hold out even one hand, more afraid of looking like an idiot than she was of falling. She figured if she walked with her arms at her sides, she'd look pretty normal except for the fact she was moving at the rate of a turtle on Valium. But after she had an up-close encounter with the newspaper dispenser that sat against the side of the Stationery Stop—she hadn't remembered it was there until she'd banged into it and scraped her knee—she stuck out her right hand. Stitches on her forehead wouldn't do much to ac-

cessorize the telescopic glasses she'd eventually
wear.

When she finally made it just beyond the brick
corner of the Stationery Stop and turned right
toward the grocery, she felt like cheering. She was
halfway there. Still keeping her arm out in front
of her, she took baby steps, looking down much
of the time, able to discern the blurry black lines
that indicated breaks in the sidewalk. She congrat-
ulated herself on good progress, not just because
it was a point of pride, but because, unlike what
she'd thought, there was nobody about to help
her if she needed it.

Probably because everyone else was smart. The
heat from the sidewalk burned through her shoes.
Even though it was just closing in on noon, the
day had already turned into a scorcher. Across the
street, she could make out the wash of lawn
around St. Andrew's. It had faded to olive from
the summer heat. The church itself was nestled in
the dim shadows of oaks and sycamores, its rough
stone discernible to normal vision, but not to hers.
She did think, though, she could make out a hint
of the spire against the brilliant blue of the sky.
She could also hear the choir *Hallelujah*ing at full
throttle.

What a dummy. Of course there weren't any
people around. It was Sunday. The late service
was still in session. All the stores on the square
were closed: tradition, and one their proprietors
were loath to break, even though the strip malls

and the Wal-Mart farther west weren't so fastidious.

She stopped. Which meant the corner grocery—where she'd imagined Julius jawing to his heart's content next to a cool breeze from the dairy case—was closed, too. Julius, in his eagerness to be of help, must have forgotten just like she had. Of course, Julius forgot most things anymore. He'd grown to rely on her to be his memory. Anxiety caused a sudden rush of heartburn. So where was he?

Not knowing what else to do, she continued on, hoping the store had changed its Sunday policy and had opened today. Hoping to find Julius just as she'd pictured him. But when she finally, finally reached the store, she could tell it was closed by the gray that pressed against her eyes when she put her face up to the storefront, even before she tried the door handle.

Turning, she looked around. Or tried to. Straining her eyes, she sought movement. Straining her ears, she listened for a car. For footsteps. For someone that might help. But the only thing catching her attention was a blur dashing across the street. A dog. Or a bear. Or a dinosaur. She wouldn't know, she thought bitterly, unless it came up and bit her.

Slowly she made her way back the way she'd come, trying for a quicker pace, but afraid to speed up too much. She was the only person who knew Julius might be in trouble. She had to get back and find Alcea. Pride no longer mattered. She should have never, ever, *ever* launched this expedition without at least her cell phone. She'd just *had* to show them, hadn't she? And in the process, she'd risked her dear friend.

With each step, she said a prayer: *Make Julius be safe at home. Make Julius be safe at home.* By the time she hit the copse of trees, she'd probably uttered the chant a hundred times. She stopped in the shade and let her heartbeat settle. The combination of heat and anxiety was making her light-headed. A squabbling cacophony rose to her left and she started. Just starlings, she thought, trying to peer down the path that led through the trees to the alley.

The path to the alley. That was it. Julius knew the shortcut, of course. And that would have been his most likely route. While the path wasn't concrete, it was flat and packed hard after a dry July. He'd consider it an adventure akin to dirt bike racing.

She veered toward the trees. In what seemed like hours, she emerged into the alley. She bore another scraped knee from a tumble over a tree root, and after getting tangled up in a low-hanging branch, her hair probably looked more like a shrub than a broom. Stumbling forward, she called Julius's name.

And was almost immediately rewarded by the feeble ring of a bicycle bell off to her right in the shadows of the buildings.

"Julius?"

The bell sounded again.

Feeling her way forward, she made out a lump where there shouldn't be one. "Julius!"

Kneeling, she ran her hands over everything she could touch. The wheelchair was on its side, Julius, too. His good arm was trapped beneath him. His breathing was labored, the laboring that accompanied his angina attacks. The ones that could lead to heart failure if he didn't get to his nitro and oxygen.

"I . . . hit a . . . helluva . . . pothole." Julius's voice came in gasps.

"Don't talk," she said, mind racing, and felt for his pockets. "Do you have your pills?"

"My will? Is this . . . the . . . end?"

"Pills! *Pills!*"

"Uh. Front . . . pants pocket. Right . . . no, left."

Her hand closed on the small vial of nitro. Pulling it out, she untwisted the top and, working mostly by feel, knocked some into her palm. Holding it close to her face, she picked out one, dropped the rest back, then felt for Julius's face. His mouth was already open. Carefully, she put the tablet on his tongue, then the bottle into his fist.

She didn't think she should try to move him. What if something was broken? What if further exertion killed him? Even though he'd grown thin, he was still a big man. Too big for her to get him into a righted wheelchair without his help—or someone else's. She hated stirring him up any more than he already was, but she saw no help for it.

Gathering air into her lungs, keeping a steadying hand on his shoulder, she yelled. "Hell-oo! Help!"

Minutes passed; she yelled and nobody came. She heard the bells toll noon and the end of church services, heard engines fire from cars parked around the church green on the other side of the row of buildings. But nobody heard her. Julius's breathing had grown easier, but that wouldn't last long. Even though they were shadowed by Parsons, the heat was still searing, the humidity a blanket.

"I've got to go for help," she finally said.

"I'm sorry . . . to be so . . . much . . . trouble."

Tears sprang to her eyes. "It's not your fault, Julius. It's mine." Standing, she set her chin. "I'll be back as soon as I can. You hang on, you hear?"

"Yes. I'll stay here." He rang the bell.

An agony of time and four falls later, she finally fumbled up the steps to her half brother's house. She tried the front door; unlike the back or side would be, it was locked. She leaned on the doorbell, then leaned on it some more, panting from fear and exertion. After anxious seconds, the door flew open.

"What the hell? Are you all right?" Alcea reached for her.

Florida shook her head. "Not me. Julius! In the alley. He's fallen. Go fast."

Alcea grasped the situation immediately. She pushed past her. Florida heard her clatter down the steps, and turned to the other figure that had appeared in the doorway, knowing it had to be Tamara. "Call nine-one-one. I'm not sure. . . . He might have had a heart attack."

The shape disappeared into the house. Seconds later, she heard Alcea's car fire up and a blur raced down the driveway. Wearily Florida felt for the door and made her way inside, where she collapsed into a chair, praying hard.

And hating herself.

By evening, Tamara was ensconced in the bedroom down the hall from hers. Florida didn't object.

Chapter 14

Julius didn't die. Nor had he experienced a heart attack. Alcea had paused long enough to grab the oxygen tank, so by the time the paramedics arrived, Julius was already righted and breathing easy. They'd pronounced him fit enough to go home (not in the least because he stubbornly refused to go anywhere else).

By the next day, he'd bounced completely back—well, as much as you could with congestive heart failure. The only evidence of his misadventures was scrapes on his arm, a bump on the noggin, and a spirited tale for the regulars at Peg's, which got better each time he told it.

But Florida's bounce was gone. Although her own scrapes would heal, her psyche was scarred. She was haunted by ifs: If she hadn't found him. If she hadn't gotten to Alcea in time. If Alcea hadn't been home. She cursed herself for letting him go. Cursed herself for not noticing how long he'd been gone. And condemned herself for being too proud to ask for help before trying to find him herself.

He might have died.

More than anyone now, she knew how thin the line was between normalcy and disaster. It was one thing to take chances with herself. Another to mess with someone else's life. So she'd made not one murmur of protest when she'd heard Alcea depositing Tamara's luggage in the bedroom next door. Had done nothing but nod when Alcea informed her it was the only solution.

But having Tamara planted in her household and knowing it needed to be that way didn't mean she had to make nice with the woman. Over the course of the next five days, when Alcea was conspicuously absent and claiming work as an excuse (which was probably the truth, although not the whole truth and anything but), Florida did her best to avoid her mother.

Which wasn't difficult, since Tamara was apparently taking similar pains. While she was undoubtedly gloating over the circumstances that had gotten her much more than a toe in the door, she was probably afraid if she made too much of her presence, Florida would pitch her out. She couldn't know Julius's brush with disaster had punctured all the air in Florida's tires. Satisfied with a don't-ask-don't-tell policy, Florida didn't plan to enlighten her, glad she stayed out of the way, running the house, but leaving Missouri or Julius or Florida herself to fill Florida's needs.

Not that there were many, since she spent most of the next five days hugged by the arms of the club chair in the great room. Feet up on the ottoman, she laid her head back against the leather, closed her eyes, and listened to the drone of the television, sometimes the radio, or occasionally a book on audiotape. Midweek Alcea had dropped off a package of shorts and pants, but Florida couldn't get excited over the designer labels considering they were a size larger than what she'd once worn, and probably could stand being a size larger than *that*. When evening approached, she obediently shuffled to the kitchen for supper, then took the stairs to her room, where she closeted herself for the rest of the night. Each morning, she rose to the same routine. And each morning, it got harder to force herself out of bed.

Weary of the puzzles posed by everyday living, and cringing at the idea of letting Tamara get too close, she relied increasingly on Missouri's help, even for those things she could handle herself. Her daughter carried in trays for breakfast and lunch, dried her hair, picked out her clothes, worked remote controls, fetched and carried . . . and chafed. A whine increasingly tightened her voice.

Undoubtedly Stan would take exception to how she was ill-using their daughter. If he were here to see it. But he wasn't. Like everyone else, he was

off living his life. While he gallivanted in
Hawaii . . . while Dak chatted up Oprah . . . while
Alcea baked muffins and Missouri played with
Joey, and Julius spouted Shakespeare, and Tamara
took over her house . . . she stayed stuck in place,
caught in a netherworld where she could neither
go back nor move forward. So who cared what
Stan thought? Who cared what anyone thought?
The world still turned, but it had left her behind.

In her saner moments, she was ashamed at her
thoughts. Shame and guilt made inroads into her
bitterness, but lost the battle against the surge of
lethargy that even hostility increasingly couldn't
penetrate. She ended each day more tired than the
one before. And feeling more useless.

With Tamara at the helm, the household assumed an organizational gloss. Mealtimes became
orderly affairs: The food on Florida's plate was
arranged in neat sections so she could see a space
between each. Utensils and glassware and gar-
nishes were set in the same place every time so
she could unerringly reach for what she needed.
Missouri and Julius provided the table talk; Tamara and Florida stayed quiet. Tamara so quiet,
Florida could have forgotten her mother was there
except for the faint scent of oranges mingling with
the smells of meat loaf and mashed potatoes.

No longer did she trip over slippers or throw
rugs. Everything found a place and stayed there.
No chair remained pulled out from the table; no
ottoman strayed far from its mate. Drawers and

closets marched into order and a basket of audio-tapes appeared on an end table next to the sofa. Megawatt lightbulbs replaced anything dim.

For three days, she managed to ignore Tamara's contributions, until on Wednesday afternoon, while Tamara was out and Missouri at Joey's, Julius had made it impossible.

She was nesting again in the club chair when he called to her from the kitchen. "I want to show you something."

She didn't feel like getting up, but because it was Julius, she did. Even in her state, it was impossible to ignore that while she might have lost her sight, he spent his days in a wheelchair. Peas in a pod, she thought bitterly.

When she reached him, he told her to put her hands on the wheelchair handles, then led her into the laundry room. "Feel the knob."

She did. A few raised bumps met her fingers.

" 'Was not that nobly done?' "

"What are they?"

"LocDots. You see, if you twist the knob so they match . . ." He hoisted himself up and demonstrated with his good hand on top of hers. "One dot means wash; two dots mean rinse. If you line them up with the others, you can pull the knob and start the laundry. Dryer's done up the same way." He sounded as proud as if he'd just given birth. He sat back down.

For his sake, she drummed up some enthusiasm. "Great. Best thing since chocolate." She wondered if they had any.

His voice was puzzled. "Chocolate? You hungry?"

"No, I—never mind. Tell me about these. LocDots?"

"Yeah. They're self-adhesive, so you can put them anyplace you want. Dishwasher. Oven. Thermostat. Clocks."

Her interest was piqued, despite herself. Pretty clever, really.

"Follow me." He was gone.

"Julius!"

He rang the bell and she followed the sound to the kitchen table.

"Sit down," he instructed.

She did. Something was scattered on the table-top. Reaching out, she picked up a piece of paper and held it to her eyes. "Money. What's all this for?"

"Look. I mean, feel."

She did. Some bills were folded one way, others another.

"If you hold the money to your face, you can see what it is, but if you don't want to do that when you're shopping—"

She didn't.

"—then when you get bills, you leave them dollar bills flat, fold the fives widthwise, tens lengthwise, twenties in fourths . . . or any which way you want." Some change rattled in his hand. "And you can tell these by size, thickness, ridges, or lack of 'em. I know, I tried. Got pretty good at it, too."

A glimmer of interest flickered. She fingered a quarter. "Where'd you learn about this? And where did you get the LocDots?"

He hesitated. "Tamara ordered 'em. Called some store and had them sent express."

She dropped the quarter and put her hand back in her lap.

"Now, Florida, don't go acting like that. She found that information you got from that eye-doctor fella and went through it. Pretty interesting stuff. At that school, you'll have O-and-M lessons. Know what that stands for?"

She shook her head, not wanting her irritation at Tamara to rub onto Julius, but finding it difficult not to storm out of the room. She didn't want Tamara intruding on everything in her life. She didn't want her help.

"Orientation and movement. You'll learn to get around outside, use public transportation. And household management. Cooking. Plus there's all this newfangled techno-gadget stuff that does things like read bar codes, special cell phones, stencils you can use to write a letter or sign a check. Measuring cups and remote controls you can use by feel. She also read me about this organization—Federation of the Blind? They have a newspaper-reading service, and this big federal library has bunches of talking books that are different than those audiotapes because somehow or other, you can look through the books for things without actually, well, looking, don't you know. And they deliver them right to the door."

"Wonderful." Her voice was flat.

Julius stayed silent, but only for a few seconds. " *'How sharper than a serpent's tooth it is to have a thankless—'* "

—*child*. "Stop!"

But of course he didn't. "She just wants to help, Florida. I knew your mama when she was a little girl. Do you remember that her mama ran off, too? Abandoned her, left Cowboy, when Tamara was just a little girl. You should know that'd leave some scars."

"That just makes it worse. She knew how much it hurt."

"Not sure she did. Your granddaddy—he tried to make it up to Tamara. Spoilt her good, he did. And she grew up wild and rambunctious. Loose, although I hate to say it. I'm not so sure she had much compassion in her by the time she was growed. When she left you here, he'd learned his lesson by her, though. Was hell-bent not to make the same mistakes with you, although his heart bled for you—you were such a clingy little mite. And you grew up . . ."

"Almost just as selfish," she said slowly.

"Don't know what shellfish got to do with it."

"*Sel*-fish."

"Ah. Yes, that's it. Your mama didn't care about nobody but herself back then, but seems to me that life's taught her some. At least she's trying to make amends. Let her, Florida."

Her mind resisted the idea. But as Julius rolled off to his room for a nap, she turned his words over in her head and remembered her youth. The torrid affair with Stan. The way she'd tried to entrap him after he'd met Serena. Her grandmother . . . her mother . . . now her. Maybe selfishness was part of her genes.

Except . . .

Except that she had never abandoned Missouri, nor would she ever. Just the thought of her own child left in someone else's care brought tears to her eyes. No real mother could do that. Nobody with a scrap of humanity could do that. The momentary kinship she'd felt with Tamara fled. She was not like Tamara. She didn't care about the apology she sensed underneath everything Tamara was doing for her. Nothing she did would ever be enough.

Following Julius's example, she felt her way upstairs for a nap, leaving the money lying on the table. Blood money.

She'd awakened late in the afternoon, and lain there listening to the voices downstairs. Since Tamara had arrived, when they were out of Florida's orbit, there was a lilt to Missouri's voice and a heartiness to Julius's. Hearing comments about a "sweet little T-bird," she surmised they were working on another model, huddled together and laughing like they had before her accident. She rolled onto her side, her feelings of isolation weighing more heavily. Then when she heard, "Look at this, Gram-Tam," she thought she'd scream with frustration. That evening, she snapped at Alcea, cursed her brother over the phone (God help him if he said one more word about positive thinking), and reamed out Missouri when she tripped over the gym bag her daughter had left next to the door.

Then the next morning, when she entered the great room and was greeted by the scent of oranges and tobacco, a smell that followed Tamara back inside whenever she'd stepped out on the porch to smoke, and saw her blurred form dressed in red sitting on the corner of the sofa, she unleashed her anger. Invectives. Poison. It all poured out. When she stopped, sides heaving, the shape was still, undoubtedly stunned by her attack.

With a whir of bells, Julius swerved around a corner. "You call? Tamara and Missouri just left for the store."

"Then who in the hell—"

She stalked to the sofa, reached out—and ended up with a handful of pillow. She'd napped there yesterday morning, under a red blanket. She threw the pillow to the floor in disgust. She didn't need to see Julius's face to sense his bewilderment as she burst into tears.

By Friday evening, life had become unbearable and she'd become invisible, absorbed by the household that hummed around her. Each hour ticked by filled with the same dreary sameness as the one before. The challenges would never cease, but she'd lost interest in trying to meet them. Her mood was so sour that despite the compassion she knew surrounded her, she'd managed to drive the people who loved her away. Dak hadn't called since Wednesday. Alcea had become as elusive as Tamara except when she had a question about Peg's. Julius now tried to slide by without speaking and the bicycle bell had fallen silent. And, worst of all, Missouri had stopped bouncing into her room, her hair smelling of the Powerpuff Girls Shampoo that *Gram-Tam* bought her now.

And Florida couldn't blame them. She was an ingrate. And an embarrassment—spilling, stumbling, talking to people who weren't there.

If she could escape from herself, she'd certainly do it, too. Her misery increased until she was ready to hurl herself off a cliff. But since, she thought bitterly, it was impossible for her to drive anywhere to find one, she'd do the next best thing.

She'd get in her bed and stay there.

Chapter 15

Although the second week of August blew in with a searing wind and an ocean of humidity, on the Monday evening of his return to Cordelia, Stan headed out for a run. He wouldn't push too hard—the marathon had left him with about as much stamina as Paddy O'Neill had hair. Plus it was hot enough to melt his Nikes. He'd take the three miles from the condo to the square at a lope, lap the square a couple of times, and call it a day. It would be enough to ease the ache the marathon had left in his muscles.

After that, he'd catch a shower and check up on things at Strides before he stopped by Florida's. Thinking of her—of *them*—his pulse accelerated. And it wasn't because he'd just picked up the pace, but because he wanted to see Missouri, he told himself. Because he was concerned about

Florida, he added. His appearance would be a surprise; they weren't expecting him back till tomorrow.

Following the race Saturday, he'd partied (much heavier on the water than on the scotch) and dined (ravenous enough to eat the whole roasted pig) before collapsing in a solid twelve hours of shut-eye. With nothing for the group planned for Sunday, and his cohorts more than capable of finding the airport after conquering the volcano rim, he'd surrendered to his growing conviction— all the stranger because he'd never grown a sixth sense in his life—he should return to Cordelia. He'd left Honolulu yesterday morning. With the time difference, he'd arrived in KC this morning, Cordelia by noon.

Focusing on the Ozark hills on the horizon, blurred in a blue haze of humidity, he lengthened his stride, releasing the pain and tension his muscles had stored during the long plane ride. Once he'd arrived at the condo, he'd crawled between the sheets, too weary to check on either Strides or his women. His women? He gave himself a shake so Florida wouldn't need to. . . . How prehistoric. Besides, make that singular. Missouri was the only person he could lay any claim to.

Something he increasingly seemed to forget. Even after his week away, the trip he and Florida had taken down memory lane on the night before he'd left, coupled with the knowledge—okay, glee—that Daniel was gone, still retained the same disturbing impact it had held before he'd left.

Since his marriage to Serena, and even after her death, he'd been faithful. First to her, then to her memory. Simple enough explanation: He'd loved his wife. And he'd grown up. He was no longer interested in one-night wonders or even passionate affairs. He'd learned to like marriage. His marriage. And he'd met nobody since Serena that he'd even fantasized over sharing his life with. In fact, he'd thought maybe you only got one shot and he'd had his.

Certainly he'd never considered Florida in the role of his wife, no matter what lies he'd fed her during their affair. Even in the testosterone-driven insanity of those years, he'd held on to some instinct for survival: Somewhere inside he'd known they wouldn't work. Florida had been far too much like Alcea.

But for the last week, his ex-mistress's face had hovered in his dreams. Not the vision of youthful physical perfection he carried in his memory, nor the elegant, confident woman that had emerged in her thirties, but the one he'd seen last Friday night. Reeling from twin blows: blindness and Daniel's asshole-edness. Yet, in public, she cloaked herself in dignity. The same courage Serena had worn as she'd faced her death.

Main Street was quiet at this hour. Although traffic picked up during Cordelia's rush hour (more like a five-minute sprint), it was mostly confined to the newer developments that sprawled on all sides of town except east of Florida and Alcea's. (A problem with septic tanks that refused to perc and a city council that had run out of the dough to extend sewer lines east while they argued over the plan.) On the old square, some stores bucked tradition and stayed open late, but most, including Peg O' My Heart, didn't.

Starting his second lap, he cut the corner at Oak Haven Road, angling toward the restaurant and flapping a hand at Clueless Joe, a relic from the sixties who'd blown most of his mind following the Grateful Dead. Since the Dead were, well, dead, Joe now spent most of his days on a bench outside Up-in-the-Hair. He didn't wave back. Stan hadn't expected him to, poor fella.

Starting down Main, he passed under the orange-and-red-striped awning of Peg's. The lights were off inside, but the interior was bright from the early-evening light slanting in through the plate glass windows. Sorting receipts, Alcea was seated at an orange Formica table on a checkerboard of tile. She looked up as he passed. He saluted and continued on.

Then, as he reached the corner and Sin-Sational Ice Cream—neon already glowing for another night of lines that would snake down the square—he stopped. Jogging in place, he considered a moment, then turned around to double back.

During the past week, he'd called Florida's several times. The first time, Missouri had relayed a disjointed account of Julius's alley misadventure, fear in her voice. Florida hadn't elaborated much more, guilt in hers. And when he'd followed up with a call next door, Alcea hadn't been much more enlightening, becoming incensed enough as she'd told the story that he'd invented a reason to hang up before she really got rolling.

Something he regretted because on his next call, he learned that since Julius's . . . fall or whatever it was . . . Tamara had been charged with taking care of the household and Missouri had told him she was having a really *good* time with Gram-Tam. And then Florida had refused to come to the phone.

Another call next door hadn't resulted in anything beyond Alcea's acerbic, "If you don't like the situation, then you come back and fix it."

Thinking about that brief conversation—if you could call it a conversation—he picked up the pace. Even though he wasn't so sure that Tamara was as bad a sort as Florida would have her, he couldn't say he was keen on the fact Tamara had been installed under the same roof as his daughter. He should have said something then. And maybe, by God, he *would* fix it. If Dak was balking at forking over the money, even though his own cash flow was tight, he could dig up enough to hire a caregiver, housekeeper, whatever Florida needed. For Missouri's sake, of course.

Reaching the diner, he steeled himself against whatever mood Alcea might be in and tried the door. It was still unlocked.

As he stepped inside, she looked up, expression torn between surprise and the unstated wish that she had locked the door earlier. "Look what the cat dragged in."

Ignoring the barb—he had a mission here—he leaned back against the doorjamb. Better to make a hasty retreat. "Burning the evening oil?"

She looked disappointed he hadn't risen to her bait, but dropped the attitude. "I should be happy we had such a great day." She motioned at receipts and cash register tapes littering the tabletop. "But at this rate, I'll be here all night. And I've still got some franchise business to take care of once I get home."

"Isn't Abe taking care of a lot of it?"

"Yes, but there's some things I have to do myself. Florida is so much faster with the books than I am."

"You use bookkeeping software?"

"*Florida* uses bookkeeping software." She leaned back and stretched. "So, how went the marathon?"

He thought of what it had felt like, up against some of the world's top runners. Well, not *up against*, exactly. More like trailing behind—and by several football fields—but still . . . it had been something, testing himself on the rough terrain surrounding an active volcano, the park spread out in breathtaking glory around him, clear, sweet air filling his lungs. "Nothing that'll make the Marathon Hall of Fame, but I finished. Somewhere in the ranks of the triple digits, I believe."

Alcea was watching his face, and he suddenly felt embarrassed. But it was Alcea who reddened. Fiddling with her pencil, she looked down. "You know, most people wouldn't have even tried. Give yourself some credit—I can hardly believe it, but you've turned into a man who goes the distance. And, thanks, by the way, for paying for Abe."

He studied her. Yep, it was Alcea, not a nun in disguise. "Well, thanks. But maybe I shouldn't have gone."

"Shouldn't have . . . ? Oh, you mean Florida." She looked back up. Eyes hard. Yep, definitely Alcea. "Are you again implying you could have managed better than I have?"

"No." God forbid he might be more efficient than Alcea. "But"—he gathered his courage—"I wouldn't have put someone in charge that she hated."

"Do you want to tell me what else I was supposed to do? Dak's gone. You're gone. I have a business to run—one, may I remind you, that is also supporting your ex-mistress, who, in turn, provides for your daughter?"

Her reference to Florida as his ex-mistress surprised him. Since she and Florida had become buds, she hadn't rubbed their noses in their past sins in a long time.

She continued. "Julius is too old to take care of things. Tamara is both willing and able."

"But maybe not the best guardian."

Alcea looked surprised that he was bucking her. She should be, since it had happened only a handful of times—at least outright. During their marriage, he'd become the Grand Master of passive resistance. Letting her rage, he wouldn't give in as much as refuse to defend himself—at least for his defensible acts. Then he'd go find another blanket to crawl under. Of course, that strategy sometimes backfired. On one notable occasion, she'd driven his new Lexus into a fishpond. On another, she'd barricaded him and Florida into an upstairs bedroom—after absconding with their clothing—and he'd been forced to call the rescue squad. Any wonder she scared him?

"Missouri and Tamara get along great," she said.

He urged his spine into attention. "From what I understand, so did Tamara and Dak and Tamara and Florida. Before she dumped them onto her father. Tomorrow, I'll call a home-health-care agency and—"

"No."

"This isn't your call, Alcea."

She continued to look surprised. "It isn't yours, either."

Now he was getting riled. "Missouri *is* my daughter."

"And Florida is my husband's sister. Dak wants Tamara there."

"Dak thinks he's Dr. Phil." He moved to the table and she drew back. Not in fear—more's the pity— but in astonishment. Ignoring the look, he rested his fists on the table and leaned toward her. "He thinks if he throws them all together, they'll experience spontaneous healing."

Her eyes narrowed. "Maybe they will."

"Don't be an idiot."

She stared at him. "Don't *you* be an idiot."

"I'll be an idiot if I want to be an idiot." He suddenly straightened. Rubbing his hand over his face, he sat down across from her. "Oh, for Christ's sake. Let's stop this shit."

Although, if he was honest about it, he'd found the whole interchange rather exhilarating. He'd stood up to Alcea—actually, he thought, for the second time in the same month, remembering when he'd snatched Florida out of her grasp before he'd left—and he hadn't died. He could get used to this stuff.

Alcea looked like she was more than ready to continue arguing, but instead she took a deep breath. Make that two. "Listen, Stan. Tamara's okay."

He rolled his eyes.

"No, I mean it. You have to remember that Dak was talking with her long before she showed up on our doorstep, and she's been living with us since then. We've gotten to know her. Maybe she was a witch when Florida was young, but she's not now. Dak should know. He had as much reason as Florida to hate her, and for a while he did. But, Stan . . . hate destroys. Florida needs to let it go. Especially now."

This time he rolled his eyes so far he thought he'd have trouble getting them back.

"Okay," Alcea conceded. "Dak can be a little—"

"Goofy?"

She glared. "*Easygoing*. But he's also a pretty good judge of people. Tamara deserves a chance." She gave him a pointed look. "Or are you going to tell me people can't change their stripes? If that's the case, Missouri should have been offered up for adoption a long time ago."

Touché. "But Missouri—"

"Is happier than she's been since Florida's accident." Alcea frowned. "Or at least until a few days ago, she was."

"Why? What happened a few days ago?"

"Florida got into her bed. And hasn't gotten back out."

"What do you mean?"

Now Alcea rolled her eyes. "Just what I said. Since Friday, she's laid there like she's dead."

That strange conviction he'd felt in Hawaii returned and he finally recognized the sixth sense for just what it was: dread.

Stan skipped the last lap around the square, Strides, and a shower in favor of heading directly to Florida's, letting himself in when nobody answered his knock—and making a mental note to give Tamara a few terse words on leaving a defenseless woman alone in her bed.

Although Florida wasn't alone. Julius was dozing in the great room, his hair aflame and the chrome of his chair glinting from the squares of light falling through the windows. The cordless phone was cradled in his lap.

He touched Julius's shoulder and the old man awoke with a snort. "Wha—? *'Bloody will be thy end'!'*"

Stan stepped back. From the way Julius was

brandishing the phone, Florida hadn't been left so defenseless after all. "Uh, *Julius Caesar*."

Julius's eyes focused. "No, ninny. *Richard III*." His eyes lit up. "Hey, you come to spell me?"

"Spell you? I came to see Florida. And Missouri," he added, feeling ashamed his daughter was almost an afterthought. "How are you doing? They told me you took a tumble?"

"Nope, *I* don't look for trouble. It finds me." He nodded emphatically. "Didya hear about that spill I took? Wasn't a big deal, although the way Florida went on about it, you'd think she pushed me off St. Andrew's bell tower. She rescued me from my own foolishness, but keeps calling it her fault. Or at least she did. Haven't been able t'get up there to see her. And she hasn't come down. *'All's cheerless, dark, and deadly.'*"

When Stan didn't answer, Julius shook his head sadly and rang his bell with all the mercy of a game show buzzer. "*King Lear*. Well, do you wanna spell me? Tamara and Missouri went over to Sin-Sational for hot dogs; then it's on to feed the ducks." Memorial Park and its duck pond was just down Maple Woods Drive from the ice cream parlor. "Tamara tries to get Missouri outta here every evening, even if just for a bit, since Florida's taken to laying up there all day like the world's stopped turning."

"Maybe it has, for her. I remember Serena experienced some bad days. It's stupid for everyone to think Florida won't. Or shouldn't."

"Well, my heart breaks for her, it truly does,

but it's downright grim around here. Tamara doesn't think Florida should be left alone, so I'm charged with staying within hollerin' distance while they're out. But if you'll spell me until Alcea gets in from Peg's, I'll call ol' Erik and tell him to pick me up. Beadler's Feed and the Rooster are having a showdown tonight at the Bowl-o-Rama. Sure would like to see that." He'd already picked up the phone.

"Sure, I'll spell you." The urgency he felt to help Florida had only increased with Julius's words and since he'd planned to be here later anyway, it was just a slight shift in his plans. But he suddenly felt self-conscious about seeing her in all his dirt. "Mind if I borrow a shirt and take a quick shower? If I'm staying, I'd like to clean up."

"Take what you want." Julius was punching in a number. "But can you shower upstairs where you can hear her? If I'm gonna catch the start, I'll need to get goin'." Julius spoke into the phone. "Hey, you no-goodnik, can you swing by . . . ?"

As Julius finalized his plans, Stan headed back to his rooms and picked out a tan checkered shirt (as opposed to a red, a green, or a blue one) and borrowed a spray can of deodorant. This'd have to do. On Stan's way out, Julius zoomed in. Only by pressing himself against the wall did Stan avoid being flattened. He held out the shirt, so Julius could see what he'd taken.

Julius nodded, then went to his dresser, where he rummaged in the bottom drawer. "Need some boxers, too?" He pulled a pair out of a wrapper.

"These're new. Asked Tamara to pick them up for me at the Wal-Mart yesterday. Three-fer-one sale. You're welcome to 'em."

Looking at the wildly striped pair of satin shorts, Stan blinked. Three-fer-one. Bet even that deal wasn't moving them much.

Julius followed his gaze. "Right nice, aren't they?"

"Um, right nice. Thanks." Beggars couldn't be choosers.

After parking Julius safely near a flowerpot on the front porch to wait for Erik, Stan climbed the stairs, feeling the silence thicken around him as he went. On the landing, everything was dead quiet. For a moment, he hesitated, suddenly transported back to Serena's last days, the sense of déjà vu so overwhelming, he almost turned back. Then he squared his shoulders and headed down the hall to Florida's room.

He pushed open the door and leaned in. "Florida?"

Cool air wafted out, fortunately without the sour note he'd learned to associate in Serena's with loss of hope. When she didn't answer, he stepped inside. The light was dim, but he could make out her figure in the middle of the king-sized bed. He approached on soft feet. She was sleeping. Eyes closed, her chest rising and falling in even rhythm, a puff of air escaping her lips with each breath. Even with tangled hair and rumpled nightclothes, she was beautiful.

He touched her shoulder. It was cold. "Florida?" he repeated, alarmed.

"Mmph." Then her eyes popped open, filled with fear. "Who's there?"

"Shh. S'okay. Me. Stan." He pulled the sheet up over her shoulder and perched on the edge of the bed.

The fear faded. "You're back." She turned to her side, snuggling into the covers. "I'm glad you're back."

Even uttered in a half sleep, the words gave him more pleasure than they should have.

"Except"—she yawned—"y'all stink."

And those snapped his ego back to size. "I know. Everyone's flown the coop for a while. I'm going to use your shower to get cleaned up. I'll leave the door ajar, so yell if you need me."

"M'kay." Her eyelids were fluttering shut again.

He watched her a moment, his heart seeming to slow into the same cadence as her breathing. The dread he'd felt climbing the stairs dissipated. Unlike Serena, Florida wasn't dying. She was still right here with him, still vibrantly alive, with the future spread out before her. She just needed to adjust to a new situation. She just needed help.

Help, he thought fiercely, that he was more than willing to give her. He stroked back her hair and then headed for the bath.

Stan's gentle touch on her hair roused her again from the edge of sleep. She opened her eyes. A light flickered on in the bathroom and he was briefly silhouetted before the door mostly closed.

She could see a glow that indicated he'd left it ajar. After a brief lull, the shower started up.

Rolling onto her back, she stared up at the ceiling, consciousness bringing with it the same numbing darkness that had tugged at the corners of her mind all last week and finally blackened it entirely on Friday night. She hated this. Hated being near blind. Hated how the realization nothing could be done about it had sunk in and turned her limbs leaden. She needed to stop it. For Missouri's sake, if not for her own, she needed to find a reason to get out of this bed.

Under cover of the blankets, she ran her hands down over her nightgown, feeling its wrinkles. When was the last time she'd bathed? Changed? Washed her hair? Briefly she was ashamed, thinking of what she must have looked like to Stan as he'd sat here beside her. And she'd had the nerve to tell him *he* smelled? Her hands skimmed back up her body, slowing just over her breasts, finally lingering there as her nipples tightened. A tingle passed through her groin, piercing her torpor, reminding her she was still alive.

One hand crept over the softness of her abdomen toward the V of her legs, but stopped short. She turned her head toward the light glimmering around the bathroom door. Then she shook herself. She was depressed, not crazy.

Still . . . she stared at the door some more, thinking of the man—the naked man—right on the other side. They'd had problems, serious problems, in their relationship. But sex hadn't been one of them. Before she could talk sense to herself, she flung back the covers and made her way to the bathroom.

Stan was encased behind the frosted doors of the shower stall. Moving on autopilot, not letting herself think too much, she stripped off her nightgown, letting it drop on the floor, and, feeling carefully, stepped into the Jacuzzi tub before he could see movement. A short wall separated the tub from the shower, but of course, the moment she turned on the taps, he knew she was there.

"Yow!"

Because the water in his shower went from warm to freezing cold.

"Sorry," she said over the rush of water. "I just needed a bath. Hope you don't mind sharing."

She'd intended a throaty, seductive voice, but it came out more like a hoarse whine. Now that she was here, she felt foolish. And scared.

There was silence on the other side of the partition. Then, "Uh, no. You do what you need to."

The water in the shower continued to run. He had to be freezing, but it hadn't driven him out.

Maybe because he saw her exactly as Daniel had. Flawed, incomplete. Fat. What an idiot she was. She should have thought this through. Feeling despair creeping up on her again, but not knowing how to extricate herself from what was becoming a really embarrassing situation, she fumbled among some bottles sitting in the corner, and finally located some foaming bath oil, emphasis on the foaming. She could hide herself under the bubbles. Hurriedly, she dumped some under the spigot and lowered herself into the bath. When the water neared her shoulders, she shut off the taps, then flipped on the jets. She dunked her hair, then let her head sink back against the plushness of a vinyl pillow, the froth tickling her chin.

And still the shower ran. She wondered if he intended for them both to stay put until they were pickled. She was about to call out, to tell him he needn't fear an attack, when the water abruptly stopped. And then the shower door opened. And then Stan stepped out.

She couldn't see him clearly, but could tell from the uninterrupted sweep of flesh tone that he hadn't bothered to wrap himself in a towel. Why should he? she thought bitterly. It wasn't as though she could see any details. She turned her head toward the wall.

The only sound in the bathroom was now the whoosh of the Jacuzzi jets.

"Florida?"

His voice was near. He undoubtedly wanted to know what in the hell she was doing. Well, she'd be glad to let him in on it if she could only come up with an answer herself. Instead, she'd stumble around making some stupid excuses about why she'd had to crawl into the tub this very second and then he'd stumble around trying to avoid the obvious fact that she was lying.

"What?" Being blind was bad. But she was learning humiliation was worse.

"Do you—are you—?" He cleared his throat. "I want to make love to you. Quite a lot, in fact."

She almost wept with relief. "Then what are you waiting for?"

Expecting him to drop straight into the depths with her and have at it, she was surprised when instead he lowered himself onto his knees outside the tub. He was near enough that she could make out more details—the dark sheen of wet hair, the bulk of his shoulders—but she couldn't read his expression. She reached and found a forearm resting on the side of the tub. She skimmed her hand along it, then up his shoulder to his neck. His muscles were more defined than she remembered. Her hand came to rest on the side of his face.

"Do you want help out?" he asked.

"Um, no. Here."

He was quiet. "You're lovely, you know."

She turned her head away from him. "Am I?"

In answer, he caught her hand as it slid from his face, put it to his lips, and kissed her palm. Then gave it a flick of his tongue. Unexpectedly, under the water, she felt his hand cup her foot. She started, then relaxed as his thumb massaged the arch.

"You are."

His words were a balm.

Anticipating what would come next, wanting what would come next, she drew her legs apart. But instead of his hand skimming up the inside of her thigh, he withdrew it completely, then jolted her anew as she suddenly felt his caress along her upper hip. His fingers were spread, his thumb gently, suggestively, tracing her pelvic bone, nearing that ache in her groin, but never touching it.

His touch abandoned her again. Then landed on the tender area between her breasts. Twisting, arching, she exposed one to the air, nipple immediately hardening, and heard above the jetting water the sharp intake of his breath. But he withheld his touch. Instead, he skimmed his fingers along her collarbone; then once more, contact ceased.

She moaned with frustration, then felt his fingers along the base of her ribs, at the soft junction where waist flared into hip. They dipped into her belly button and she moved, trying to tempt his hand where she wanted it, then finally trying to capture it with her own, but it had already left her.

Only to close around her calf and then stroke the back of her knee. Removed again, it lit on the soft rise of her abdomen, then slipped tantalizingly closer to the junction of her legs. But then his touch vanished again, leaving her panting, wanting more. Far more.

Each time he withdrew his hand, teasing her with a diabolical, delectable design, her nerve endings stood on high alert, waiting to feel his stroke again, as she wondered where it would light. She couldn't see; she could only guess. And it was unbelievably erotic.

Her senses strained, increasingly losing their

ability to tell what caused sensation to ripple through her body: him or the foaming caress from the water jets. She writhed, trying to move where either had access to tender skin, feeling as though she was under some kind of sneak attack, never knowing where his hand would touch next. Finally . . . finally . . . as her head arched back, his hand landed on her breast. A pang shot through her so fast, she cried out, and felt the first wave of orgasm.

Then a second as he rolled a nipple between his thumb and forefinger, pressure increasing, bringing an exquisite agony. He leaned in, his other hand easing behind her head, his lips traveling the curve of her exposed neck until he swept her lips with his tongue and covered her mouth. Kissing her hard and deep, he eased into the water beside her at the same time his hand dipped between her thighs. She cried out against his mouth. Without releasing the grip he had on her core, he pulled her on top, then down on his penis, his hand still stroking. Hands, water, mouth, sucked her into a mindless vortex of feeling.

Heart still pounding, Stan drew Florida in against him. They were lying in her bed. After that mind-blowing experience in the Jacuzzi, he'd bathed her, washed her hair, his touch growing increasingly seductive until he'd dried her off and led her to the bed, where he'd made love to her again. This time slowly, tenderly, reveling in the feel of her, more softness than the angles he remembered. He liked her body this way. She'd flowered under his endearments, under his hands, as though he were bestowing a benediction.

But he was about as far from a saint as anyone could get.

Maybe she'd made a mistake.

Maybe he had.

He hoped not. He also hoped . . .

Ah, hell. He didn't know what he hoped. He just didn't want to be the rebound guy. Nor a Band-Aid for her self-esteem. And he was afraid maybe he was both.

Pulling her closer, he breathed in the jasmine scent of her hair. She was pliable, soft. Maybe being the rebound guy or a Band-Aid wasn't so bad.

She yawned. "What time is it?"

He twisted to look at the bedside clock. "Time to get up. We only have about fifteen minutes, give or take a few."

They weren't total idiots. When they'd left the Jacuzzi, she'd had him call Sin-Sational to check on Missouri and Tamara's whereabouts. They'd tried the cell first, but Tamara never seemed to be able to remember to take it with her, so it had echoed back from downstairs. They'd been in luck. The clerk had called Missouri to the phone just as they were leaving. "Don't make us come back yet, Daddy. We have hot dog buns for the ducks and everything." He'd assured her that he really didn't need her home yet. Really.

Florida raised her face for a kiss. "Y'all sure we

can't linger a while longer?" she murmured against his mouth.

"I'm sure." He'd spoken with Missouri about forty minutes ago. "It's a fifteen-minute walk to Memorial Park from Sin-Sational. I can't see anyone wanting to commune with waterfowl more than twenty. Then it's twenty minutes back here." He dipped his head to kiss her again. "So, much as I'd like—"

"Florida?" Alcea's voice floated up from downstairs.

They froze.

"I thought you said Alcea wouldn't be home for hours," Florida hissed, scrambling up with the sheet hitched to her chin.

"She said she'd be at Peg's all—"

"I need help with this!" Footsteps sounded on the stairs.

Franchise business. She'd said *franchise business* when she got home. Stan threw back the covers. "Shit." He thought better of the covers and pulled them back up.

"Not again!" Florida's expression was pure panic.

Despite the fact his pulse had hit the heart attack zone, Stan had to laugh. "We're acting like idiots. I'm no longer married to her, you know."

"Florida?" Alcea was outside the door. "I can't figure out this damn spreadsheet. I need your—"

The door flew open. The years fell away. Stan experienced a transcendental moment he was sure Dak would envy. They'd all featured in this same tableau before. The one that had been the final straw on an already-feeble camel's back.

He thought it might take a crane to hoist Alcea's jaw off the floor.

"Alcea?" Florida spoke into the sudden quiet.

Alcea's face had gone from white to red. "More commiserating, I see."

Before either of them could respond, she'd backed from the room and slammed the door.

Chapter 16

The next morning, the phone woke her. Florida opened her eyes, facing the side of the bed where Stan had lain last night, and saw only a play of light over a blur of white pillow and sheets.

The phone rang six times, then stopped. Either somebody had answered it or nobody was home. Since she'd taken to sleeping in, she'd heard Tamara's dusty Focus engine rattle to a start most mornings, and Missouri's chatter as she climbed into the car. She assumed they ran errands, trying to get done whatever needed to get done before she was awake, but she didn't know for sure. She hadn't asked. She'd been too tired to ask.

Until last evening. In Stan's arms, she'd felt alive for the first time in the three weeks since she'd opened her eyes unable to see. She wrapped her arms around herself, thinking of the way his body had felt pressed up to hers. All his training had sculpted him into long muscles and quiet strength. He didn't have the feel she remembered, but—she smiled to herself—he still had the touch.

She snuggled down into the covers, still smiling. She wondered if he might be able to escape sometime today and join her again. Of course, with Tamara hovering around the house, Julius using it as a racetrack, and Missouri running in and out, last night's breath of privacy had been nothing short of miraculous.

She could go to his condo, she supposed. But that would require getting up, getting dressed, getting out. . . .

The first two she could manage, but she wasn't so sure about the third. Although Cordelia would rally around her, and eventually accept the sight of her stumbling along the sidewalk much as they did Clueless Joe roosting on a park bench—a quirk of the town, nothing to get all het up about—she hated the stares she'd felt between her shoulder blades the night of Alcea's party. She closed her eyes. She'd get up before Stan came for lunch—he said he'd come for lunch—and then maybe she'd be up to venturing out after her afternoon nap. She smiled again. To his place.

The phone resumed its ringing. Six times. Seven . . . eight . . .

"Damn!" Apparently Tamara had (again) forgotten to turn on the answering machine. Her mother was hopeless when it came to anything smacking of technology. Too many years in communes. She fumbled for the receiver on her bedside table. "Hello, already!"

There was a beat of silence. "Florida. It's Alcea. Tamara there?"

From her clipped voice, last night had not been forgiven. Florida frowned. What was to forgive? She wouldn't have chosen to have Alcea find out so soon and the way she had, but was it her fault her friend hadn't knocked? Besides, Stan no longer belonged to Alcea.

"I don't know. I haven't . . . seen her."

"Haven't seen her, or haven't been up to notice?" Alcea's voice held no patience.

Since Friday, she'd been hounding Florida to get out of bed. Florida didn't have the energy to fight her, but she could damn well ignore her.

When she stayed silent, Alcea's sigh whistled through the line. "I wanted to ask her to drive you into Columbia this afternoon; I can't take you."

"Columbia?"

"For your appointment with Dr. Treter. Did you forget?" The impatience was back.

"Um, no. Yes. Why can't you take me?" she asked, even though she knew. Stan wasn't mentioned, but he was right there between them.

"A problem here at Peg's. The produce truck broke down on I-70 and I need to get supplies in from somewhere else. Daisy can't handle it alone."

"There's a big surprise."

"Don't you dare start, Florida."

Florida bit her tongue. Actually, she hadn't been referring to her opinion on Alcea's hiring of her bubble-brained niece. She'd meant it wasn't a wonder Alcea didn't feel inclined to do her favors today.

"Okay, I'll change the appointment."

"You can't!"

"Why ever not?"

Florida could feel the steam escaping from the phone.

"Because," Alcea said. "Isn't he giving you all the info for your vision assessment?"

"So? Another week won't matter."

"Another week won't . . ." There was an outraged silence. "Yes, it *will* matter. It's another week where the rest of us—no, where *I* am turning my life upside down to try to accommodate you."

"I can't help it."

"You can help it more than you have."

"And if you'd hired that woman you interviewed from that restaurant in St. Louis instead of Daisy, then—"

"Daisy's skills or lack of them have nothing to do with this. She at least tries to pull her weight. That's more than you do, laying in bed all day. Oh, excuse me, except when you bring in the service stud."

Now it was Florida's turn to be outraged. "That was crude."

There was a pause. "Yes, it was. I'm sorry." Alcea sounded near tears now. "No, actually I'm not sorry. You need to *get up*. Nobody can help you if you won't help yourself."

"Just get over it? Is that it? Well, I'm sorry, but I can't just put my chin up and march on like a good little soldier. I've lost my *sight*, Alcea. And if I want to sleep late and take some naps, I will. I'm just givin' myself a chance to *adjust*."

"And that's exactly what Dr. Treter can help you do. Adjust. Go, Florida. Please go."

"I can't drive!"

"Oh, for God's sake, grow up! If you won't ask your mother to take you, then ask Stan." Alcea banged down the phone.

Stan. Florida rolled over to replace the phone, then flopped onto her back, now near tears herself, and so excessively sick of crying she refused to let them escape. Stan was the real reason Alcea wouldn't take her to Dr. Treter's. Also the reason she was as grouchy as an old badger. She'd read in Oprah's magazine once that relationships always started with some given or other. Like, "I talk; you listen." Or "I'm strong; you're weak." In her and Alcea's case, they'd been drawn together by mutual financial need, yes. But more than that, they'd been connected over their given: "I hate Stan and so do you."

While time and events had dampened the volatile emotions of the past, obviously, like trace memory, or knee-jerk reactions, they weren't completely gone.

Florida ran her hands down her body again, becoming aware of the gentle ache between thighs that had cradled Stan last evening.

No, the feelings certainly weren't dead. Far from it.

But what exactly had they transformed into? His touch, his words, had been a blessing, a healing relief for the wounds Daniel had left behind. Stan had made her, at least for a short while, feel whole again.

Much as he had when they'd launched their affair years ago. By then, at twenty-five—after four years of male attention in college, as well as enough passes during her first entry-level job in the tax department of a midsized accounting firm weighted with men that she could have filled a courtroom with sexual harassment cases—she was well aware that her combination of looks, ambition, and smarts was a turn-on. She was also self-aware enough to know she used men to prove her desirability. Over and over and over. Trying to fill an emptiness that her mother had left.

When a need for the familiar had finally driven her back to Cordelia, and her business degree had landed her a job as Stan's assistant (and, later, the bank's managing assistant), Stan's attractiveness had been especially potent. At first because he'd belonged to Alcea.

When Florida was growing up in Cordelia, nobody had represented normalcy to her more than Alcea's family. While not the wealthiest or most influential or even the largest family in town, the O'Malleys, in Florida's view, were as close as it got to perfection. They'd lived around the corner and down the street on Maple Woods Drive in a rambling bungalow with a front porch as wide as her grandfather's had been narrow.

Plump and never still, Alcea's mother, Zinnia O'Malley, had bustled through church socials, PTA events, and homerooms bearing plates of cookies, friendly curiosity, and a lap broad enough to hold all four of her children. Pop O'Malley, a familiar fixture in a faded fishing cap and wild plaid shirts, had been the genial father, the quiet anchor for the family swirling around him.

The youngest O'Malley daughter had trailed Florida by a few years. The middle daughter had babysat her on several occasions. But it had been Alcea who had captured her awe. Seven years older than Florida, Alcea had been unaware of Florida's worship—and, come to think of it, probably far too arrogant then to have paid her any attention if she hadn't. As a braid-bearing kid, Florida had watched Alcea shake her pom-poms at the Cordelia High School football games, speed through town in the passenger seat of football star Stanley Addams's Corvette convertible, and walk across the bandstand in Memorial Park to accept the crown of Miss Cordelia. Not long after, Alcea had won Stanley Addams's wedding ring and a huge house on a hill.

But when Florida had returned to Cordelia, she'd found the crown tarnished by an unhappy marriage, and Stan more than a solicitous boss.

Given her past adulation of Alcea, his attentions had not only overwhelmed her.

They'd validated her.

Florida tucked her hands under her head and stared toward the ceiling, a pearly wash of light and shadow. Had that been what had happened yesterday? Had validation been the sum total of the interlude she'd shared with Stan? Or had the love she'd once felt for him been rekindled?

Because after their affair had been ignited by mutual passion and her unconscious desire to prove she was as worthy as Alcea O'Malley, their relationship had grown into something more than fevered coupling.

Understandable. Despite Stan's popularity, his wealth, and the position awaiting him at the bank his father had once run, he'd been a lonely only child coping with his father's early death and his mother's increasing moralizing. Stan's marriage to Alcea had been not just his desire to win the town's most coveted marital prize, but also an attempt to join the exalted realm of the O'Malleys. The bid had failed spectacularly.

In Stan, Florida found an unlikely kindred spirit. They'd shared a sense of separation and worshipped the same idols.

But what were they to each other now? A cure for what ails? For her, compassion; for him, relief from loneliness?

Or something more?

She reached for the phone again. She didn't feel

much like leaving the safe womb of her bedroom, but she suddenly wanted, needed to hear Stan. And she had the perfect excuse. Before she could change her mind, she held the phone up to her face and punched in the number for Strides.

He picked up on the third ring and when she relayed her request for a chauffeur, he didn't hesitate. "Don't worry about it; I can juggle things around—one of the perks of running the joint."

He sounded unconcerned, but Florida knew he was serious about making Strides more than a local success. Another absence so soon after his trip was probably hard to swallow. Something, she thought bitterly, that Alcea obviously didn't care about. "You know, never mind. It's no big deal—I can just reschedule."

"No." His response was so swift, she wondered if his feelings mirrored Alcea's. "Jess can mind the store another day; the business won't tank. And I'd rather you asked me than anyone else."

The husky undertone in his voice made her swallow a sudden lump. "I'm sorry. If there *was* anyone else to ask—"

She stopped. They both knew there *was* someone else. But, bless him, he didn't mention Tamara.

"I'll be there at twelve thirty."

Shortly after she hung up, Missouri and Tamara returned. Judging from the tone of Tamara's cautious greeting, she'd lifted an eyebrow at seeing Florida out of bed. When Florida didn't respond, Tamara took herself off to the kitchen, apparently deciding, like Florida already had, that continuing silence was the best way to maintain an uneasy truce.

When Missouri would have followed her, Florida called her back. "Hey, kiddo, help me get dressed." She could manage something by herself, but she wanted to look good.

"I want to help Gram-Tam bake cookies."

Florida felt her temper spark. Sheer bribery. *Gram-Tam* had never been the cookie-baking type. "Right now, *I* need you."

"But she said we'd need to do it right away so she could get lunch on."

Quite the domestic goddess, that Gram-Tam. "Missouri."

"Oh, all *right*."

They went upstairs, Missouri dragging her feet. As she pulled out various outfits for her mother's approval, Missouri maintained a sullen silence. Fuming over misplaced loyalties, Florida didn't try to break it.

After her shower, Florida shrugged into the cropped pants and lacy top she'd finally decided on. Smoothing down the blouse, she realized it was warm. She turned her gaze where Missouri was slouched in a chair. "Thanks for ironing these."

"I didn't. Gram-Tam did it while you were in the bathroom."

Gram-Tam again. In a knee-jerk response, Florida unzipped the pants. "If I have to accept even one more favor from—" She realized Missouri had snapped to her feet, and stopped.

"I *asked* her to!"

"Oh, Missouri. I'm sorry. I know you're doing the best you—"

"You are such a . . . a . . . *baby*."

Florida followed the blur as Missouri stomped to the door. Mentally kicking herself for her impulsive reaction, Florida held out a hand. "Missouri, I—"

"Don't ask me to help you again!" The door slammed behind her.

Florida pressed her lips together, then pulled the zipper back up. If Dak and Alcea had possessed any idea what forcing Tamara into her household would do to her relationship with Missouri, maybe they would have thought twice.

When Stan arrived, she was leaning against the vanity, about an inch behind the mirror, trying to use an eyebrow pencil. She'd shrugged off the squabble, deciding further apologies were useless until Missouri calmed down. Sensing him even before she noticed the movement in the doorway, she turned and was folded into his arms. Her disgruntlement vanished. After a thorough kiss, he reached around her to pick up a cotton ball, then gently removed a swipe of makeup she'd left on her cheek.

"You don't need this stuff," he murmured, leaving a trail of kisses along the spot he'd just cleaned. He reached the corner of her mouth. "Not any of it."

She relaxed into his embrace. "It makes me feel more . . . female."

"There's nothing wrong with your femaleness."

Maybe there wasn't. She no longer fretted over her weight gain. There was too much else she could fret about if she wanted to. She accepted a long kiss, then sighed as she leaned her head against the hardness of his shoulder. She inhaled the clean smell of him. "No, only my eyesight. Let's go get this over with."

She hadn't yet pulled out any sandals (partially because it required crawling around on her hands and knees to locate a pair that went with her pants, partly because it reminded her she'd eventually have to give her beloved heels away), so he rummaged around to find some he deemed appropriate, then helped her strap them on. His hands on her feet were tender. She wondered at how naturally he seemed to fall into this role. She supposed it shouldn't surprise her. He'd cared for Serena all through her illness; he had the experience to be patient.

Suddenly she frowned.

Except she wasn't sick. Not in the same way Serena had been.

Late that afternoon, just after her appointment with Dr. Treter, she felt as much an invalid as Serena, and a bigger baby than Missouri had ever thought of being. Once again her tears were flowing. Once again she was sick of being such a leaky mess, but she didn't seem able to stem the flood.

"I'm sor-sorry."

She wept against Stan's shoulder. She'd known what to expect. Dr. Treter had only confirmed what he'd told her at their last meeting: From now on, any improvement to her vision would be infinitesimal. It was time for her to accept her fate and learn to live with the vision she had.

"I—I guess I was just hoping for a miracle."

"Shhh. No need to be sorry—the reality is still a blow." He held her tight. "It's okay. It'll be okay."

"No, it won't."

"It'll be a big adjustment. But I'll help."

"I don't want to adjust. I want to see again!"

She knew she was behaving like a brat, but the stark reality of her situation had sunk in like it never had before. Easy for Alcea to say she should get her act together. She should try this sometime.

"You don't have to start this minute. Not even this day or even this week. But when you're ready, we'll tackle this together. Maybe life won't be quite the same as it once was, but you'll create a new one."

She sniffled and pushed away. "But what if I don't want the life I can have?"

"Then you don't want any life at all?"

A pause. "No." Her voice was truculent.

Stan was quiet, but she could sense a tender smile. Then he pulled her close again and tilted her face up to his. "I hope you don't mean that," he murmured against her mouth. "Because I hope we can create a new life together."

Her breath left her and she sagged against him, glad to let him be strong. With Stan to care for her, cherish her, maybe everything *would* be okay.

She pushed aside a small voice of rebellion that suddenly clamored for her attention. It said she'd lost sight of more than her vision.

Chapter 17

"Stan!"

On Friday evening, halfway down Main, Stan reluctantly stopped his jog at the sound of Alcea's voice. Over the ten days since he'd taken Florida to Dr. Treter's, the temperatures had escalated to a sizzling 106 in the shade, making running outside sheer hell and sheer idiocy.

The heat had finally broken last night in a fit of thunderstorms, leaving the air clean and now dipping into the seventies as the sun reached the horizon. Before he joined Florida this evening just like he had every night since they'd made love, at the top of his wish list was a long run around Memorial Park instead of on the treadmill he'd been using at Strides through the heat wave.

Talking with his ex-wife, especially considering her continuing crankiness over him and Florida, lay somewhere around the bottom. Since walking in on them, Florida had told him, Alcea had made only perfunctory daily visits, which consisted of a curt inquiry into Florida's health and an immediate segue into whatever business issues needed addressing.

Expression stern, Alcea walked toward him. She wore one of Peg's signature orange uniforms. On her, it looked like haute couture. And even though, he knew, she was working long hours, she looked about as haggard as Heidi Klum.

She halted in front of him. "I saw you pass by."

He hadn't even glanced into Peg's.

"You've got to stop," she said.

"Running?"

"No, idiot. You've got to stop this nonsense with Florida."

He was surprised she'd be so bald, especially since she was quite happy with Dak. "Alcea," he started, voice gentle. "What's past is past. I know it must be hard to see—"

"Don't be a dope. I'm not talking about your . . . love affair or whatever it is. I'm talking about the way you've both been acting like she's on her last legs."

"I'm not acting like . . . look, it's only been four weeks since she woke up blind. She needs some space."

"Maybe. But she doesn't need to be enshrined. What's with all that hokum you dragged into her bedroom?"

"Hokum? Oh, you mean the fountain?" For a

minute, he'd thought she was referring to something else.

"And the scented thingamabob and the CD
player and—"

"I'm just trying to give her a peaceful place to
get things together." He'd found one of those little
tabletop fountains at O'Neill's Emporium and installed it in Florida's room along with a plug-in
scent dispenser and a CD player.

"She lays up there like she's stoned. Enya and
patchouli oil? Come *on*, Stan. At this rate, she'll
never get out of that bed. Why should she?"

"She'll get out. I completed her paperwork and
her vision assessment has been scheduled, but
they couldn't get her in right away. They'll send
out a rehab therapist after that. And she'll—we'll
all, Missouri and me, too—start counseling soon.
Then there's Hope House. Before all that, though,
I'll—"

"Enable her."

"Enable? She doesn't need a twelve-step program."

"No, she needs a kick in the butt."

His anger stirred. "Stop it. Your attitude hurts
her."

A shadow passed over Alcea's face. "I'm sorry
about that. I really am, but I'm so frustrated with
her. This isn't the Florida I know. The Florida I
know is a fighter." She gave him an appraising
look. "You'd do well to remember that."

"What's that supposed to mean? Maybe the
green-eyed monster has got you by the—"

"The *what*? You've *got* to be kidding. Believe it or not, I could care less about what you and Florida are doing behind closed doors." She turned on her heel and stalked off.

"You do too care," he muttered.

Shrugging her off, he continued down Main. Okay, maybe the whole New Age atmosphere in Florida's room was a bit much, especially since Florida had never leaned toward, uh, *hokum* like her brother did. But it had seemed to calm her, much as listening to opera had once soothed Serena.

They'd fallen into a peaceful routine. Daily, he stopped by over the noon hour, usually bringing her soup or a fresh salad from Peg's, which alleviated the need for either one of them to see Tamara, who seemed to wear the same sour look on her face that he saw on Alcea's. He always invited Missouri to join them, but she usually scampered off to share PB and J with her friend Joey, something he encouraged, since he figured she needed as much normalcy as possible right now.

In the evenings, he left Strides as early as he could or at least took a long break, leaving the gym in Jess's hands. Again, they'd dine on trays he brought to Florida's room, since the few times they'd gathered around the kitchen table had been awkward affairs. Even though Florida couldn't see Tamara glowering with disapproval (which seemed to him to be mighty like the pot calling the kettle black), he could.

Not only that, Missouri seemed infected with the same attitude, even though, while not trying to keep things totally secret, he and Florida had taken some pains not to reveal the full extent of their closeness. By some unspoken agreement, he and Florida weren't risking Missouri's heart until they were sure of their own. The *l* word had yet to come up. Somehow, he hadn't been able to let it trip off his tongue. But then . . . neither had she. He hadn't stopped to examine why. From the murmurs at the back of his brain as well as the looks he got around the supper table, he'd found himself afraid to discover the answers.

The last time they'd attempted to dine *en famille*, Julius, who could usually be counted on for a steady stream of gossip, had turned traitor, too, muttering, " '*Unquiet meals make ill digestions,*' " appending that with, "*Comedy of Errors*" when nobody even bothered to guess at the reference.

Stan had wondered at his selection, since the meal could hardly have been more quiet, and there certainly hadn't been anything comic about it.

Afterward, Julius had pulled him aside. "You need to get matters in hand here. Little Missouri just picks at her food."

"I know. I know. Having Tamara here is wearing everyone down."

"What's Tamara going to town got to do with it? It's Florida I want to talk about. She's wearing everyone down."

Stan looked heavenward, then tuned his voice up. "Florida's upset, working through things. Can you blame her? Things will get better once she gets the specialized help she needs."

"Can't happen soon enough, I say. I feel for her, but the gal needs to crawl out of herself and take a look around." He trilled his bell for emphasis.

Swallowing his disagreement, Stan had started to walk off, but Julius had grabbed his arm. "Even though you don't know your Shakespeare from squat, you're not such a bad sort, Stan."

Faint praise, but it warmed him. "I try."

"Know you do. Know you're juggling things best you can, too. But don't you coddle her too much, son. A body gets used to it and won't do for themselves." He tapped the arm of his chair. "I know."

Thinking of that conversation as well as Alcea's remarks, Stan headed toward the green awnings of Sin-Sational Ice Cream. Even though Julius's remarks had made him feel good, he remained disgruntled. Seemed everyone thought Florida could just snap her fingers and perk right on up. It made him more determined to protect her. To comfort her. To . . .

Well, you know. He thought of their lovemaking and his blood warmed. They'd had no further opportunity for sex, but he'd been satisfied watching how her smile lit her face when she heard his voice, the way she reached to touch him as if for reassurance whenever he was nearby, and how she snuggled against him when they reclined on her bed after supper, TV on, or talking, or simply listening to Enya. . . .

Enya. He really should pick up something new. Alcea was right about that—her room was getting reminiscent of an opium den. Maybe some flute music or something . . .

While it had been only a few weeks since Daniel had left, he seldom worried anymore about being the Rebound Guy. His coming together with Florida felt as natural as breathing, as inevitable as sunrise. As if their feelings had only been waiting to catch them up again, lying quiet while they learned the life lessons that would make their relationship prosper this time and . . .

Christ. He really *had* spent too much time listening to Enya. Maybe he should just get out some Black Sabbath.

Last night, they'd sat on the front porch's wicker settee, enjoying the fresh breezes that had wafted in on the heels of the storm, listening to the slowing patters of rain on the rooftop as bolts of lightning sparred in the east. He'd angled himself with his feet up, pulling Florida against his side. One hand played with her hair.

"This feels so right," she'd whispered. "Familiar . . . yet different. Don't you think it's different?"

"It should be. We're not the same people we were."

"You're . . . steadier. Reliable. Y'all didn't used to be dependable."

"You make me sound like a pair of trusty old slippers."

She laughed. "Well, you are, kind of. Which is pretty amazing when you think about it."

This conversation was just great for the ego. "How so?"

"Think of all the situations you've righted. You mended your relationship with Kathleen, switched careers, became a wonderful dad to Missouri, and cared for Serena. And now me."

"You make it easy," he said. "You're more—" He stopped.

"More what?" Her hand slid up his chest, stopped at the back of his neck, her fingers twining into his hair.

"More beautiful than you've ever been." That hadn't been what he'd planned to say, but thank God he'd stifled *manageable* before he'd blurted *that* out. She would have beaned him. Or at least, the old Florida would have. He felt a moment's unease, realizing he truly didn't know what the new one would do. But before he had time to ponder it, she was pulling his head down to hers.

Just as their lips met, the screen door slapped. He pulled back to see Missouri and cleared his throat to warn Florida.

"Who is it?" Florida asked.

"Me. Remember? Your daughter?"

"Don't be sassy. C'mere, daughter." Florida patted the wedge of space remaining on the settee.

Missouri didn't move. "Gram-Tam says it's bedtime. Read me a story, Daddy." Stan noted that she didn't even look at her mother.

Florida was frowning, but unable to see Missouri's expression (which, now that he thought of it, mirrored Tamara's, which mirrored Alcea's, which mirrored Julius's), she didn't react beyond giving him a little push. "Go on. Skedaddle. I'll wait here."

He followed Missouri inside. From the back of the house, he could hear a murmur of voices. Tamara had taken to joining Julius in his quarters after supper. Sometimes they watched television; sometimes they talked. Tamara seemed easy in Julius's presence. Perhaps because he'd been so close to her father.

Upstairs, he looked through Missouri's bookshelf while she prepared for bed in the bathroom down the hall. Odd that she wasn't protesting bedtime. Even odder that she'd asked for a bedtime story. Once she'd learned to read, she'd stubbornly insisted on doing it herself. She was just like her mother used to be. The thought stuttered. *Used to be.*

Ignoring a twinge of uneasiness, his gaze skipped over *Chilton's Chevrolet Engine Overhaul Manual* and landed on the collection of Winnie-the-Pooh books Serena had bought Missouri when she was—what? Four? Five? Not long, anyway, after Serena had first gotten sick, but before she'd become bedridden. His fingers traced the spines. His concentration on his wife had been so complete back then, he couldn't remember much that had happened around them.

He was still lingering over Winnie-the-Pooh when Missouri came in wearing a pair of pink pajamas scattered with butterflies.

Her gaze followed his fingers and she shook her

head, pulled out a Harry Potter book, and handed it off. "In case you haven't noticed, I'm too old for Winnie-the-Pooh." She climbed into bed, crunching a pillow under her head.

He settled next to her, crossed his ankles, and opened the book. "You've also outgrown bedtime stories and you've read this one before. What gives?"

"Nothing." She plucked at the blanket.

"No, something." He closed the book and waited.

"It's just . . . Mom's changed."

"That's to be expected, Missouri. She—"

"And so have you," she blurted.

"Me? How?"

"I don't know. You're just all . . . well, goo-goo eyes over Mom and she's acting like that Feelie in *Hamlet* that Julius read me. All boohoo, poor me. You know. It's disgusting."

Feelie? He racked his brain and dredged up a memory from English 12. Ophelia? Hadn't she gone nuts? "Missouri, that's not fair. Your mother's gone through a lot. She needs our love and understanding."

"I need those things, too!"

"You know we love you," he said gently.

"I know, but . . ." Missouri bit her lip. "It's like I'm not even here."

Like she's not even . . . ? Damn. Of course, she'd feel like that. He'd thought the new relationship growing between him and Florida would thrill their daughter, but he'd forgotten how much she'd been through herself. Granted, Florida had told him Missouri was glad they weren't moving, but she'd been buffeted around as much as rest of them since Florida's accident. And now—well, he and Florida had been so wrapped up in each other. . . .

Feeling ashamed that he hadn't paid more attention, he set the book aside and gathered her against him. "I'm sorry. You're right. You do know I love you, right?"

"Mmph." Missouri had buried her head in his chest.

"And your mom does, too."

She was silent.

"Missouri?"

Another "Mmph."

"With everything that's happened, we haven't been much of a mom and dad lately. How about we change that tomorrow? I'll come by at noon and take you and your mom to lunch. How about it?"

"At Sin-Sational?"

He gave a mental sigh. Maybe someday she'd outgrow hot dogs and ice cream. "Sure, if that's what you want."

He held her until her breathing deepened, then tucked the covers under her chin and returned to Florida, thinking the appointment he'd made for family counseling at Dr. Treter's suggestion couldn't come too soon. Downstairs, he relayed their conversation to Florida.

Her face had worn an expression of pretty concern while he'd talked; then she'd taken his hand

and held it to her cheek. "You're doing the best you can. Missouri will adjust eventually, just like we all will." She'd pulled him toward her and he'd forgotten his concerns about Missouri as the scent of jasmine filled his head.

"You know," she'd murmured, "it's as though my tragedy somehow led us to our destiny."

Struck now by the memory, he halted midjog in front of Sin-Sational Ice Cream.

She'd been listening to far too much Enya, too.

He looked up at the ruffles of the awning rippling in the light wind. Maybe even paying more attention to herself than was healthy. He felt disloyal at the thought, but then his mouth tightened as he remembered the way Missouri's face had fallen when Florida had begged off from lunch today. "Y'all just go on ahead and bring me back a hot dog. I'm just not up to facing people today."

They'd gone on, but for the first time since her accident, he felt a twinge of annoyance at Florida. He'd done his best by Missouri today, showering her with attention, extending his lunch hour to take her by Up-in-the-Hair so she could pick out fingernail polish—Burpin' Purple or something like that. She'd liked it because it had matched the rubber shoes she wore all the time. Mocks? Crocks? Whatever. It still hadn't been enough to raise her spirits. She'd been smiling when he'd returned her to Tamara, but her eyes had been sad.

He dragged a hand over his face. Was everyone right? Was he helping create some kind of monster glossed with Southern-belle helplessness? He shook his head and resumed his jog. In minutes, he'd reached Memorial Park and the trail that extended about a mile around the duck pond. Stretching his gait, he breathed in the rain-cleansed air. The fluff of clouds foaming across the blue sky eased his mind as the usual feeling of peace that accompanied his runs washed over him.

It'd take time, that's all. Just like Florida had said.

But when he got to the wooded side of the park, he suddenly veered onto the longer trail that surged up beside Navajo Creek. He'd run a short distance into the woods, past the island with its broken-down duck blind, past the footbridge, past the infamous rope swing, site of Joey and Missouri's exploits, before he finally stopped to turn around.

This time, he wouldn't run away.

Less than an hour later, he turned the corner to Florida's house. He'd dropped some clean clothes off at lunchtime so he could shower before they ate—at the table this time, he'd determined. They'd brave all those sour looks for Missouri's sake.

He'd just unlatched the front gate when he again heard his name.

"Woo-hoo? Mr. Addams!"

Turning, he saw Florida's neighbor crossing the street. She had cropped brown hair, Capri pants, and a concerned expression. "Barb Norsworthy. My son, Joey, is a friend of your daughter's," she said as she reached him, saving him further need to rack his brain for her name.

He shook the hand Barb extended. "Great kid, Joey." Anyone who thought Missouri walked on water was all right in his book.

"I hope everything is going okay? We were so sorry to hear of Florida's difficulties. We trust you'll let us know if there's anything we can do."

"Sure, sure. Thank you." He reached for the gate.

"Mr. Addams? There's a matter concerning our children I wanted to discuss with you."

"Stan." He turned back around. "Something wrong?" He hoped not. Florida usually handled this stuff.

Barb Norsworthy took a breath. "I'm afraid so. As you know, I work part time at H&R Block, so I'm gone in the afternoons."

He didn't, but, "Uh-huh."

"And I've always allowed Joey to come here when I'm at work. But . . ."

He was surprised to see her face redden. She didn't seem the blushing type. "But?"

"When I looked for him in the backyard today, I found them behind the copse of trees at the rear of your property. And"—her face looked like a beet about to burst—"they were both nearly naked!"

"*What?* If your son touched my daughter—"

"This was *not* Joey's doing, Mr. Addams."

"Well, it certainly wasn't Missouri's."

"Then tell me why your daughter's shirt was off and she was yanking down my son's pants!"

He sputtered to a stop. "You're kidding. *My* Missouri?"

"Yes, *your* Missouri." The color in her face had faded, but her mouth stayed pinched. "Sexual curiosity is perfectly normal for children. But this type of behavior usually occurs at a much younger age."

Who did she think she was? Dr. Brazelton? *His Missouri had stripped in front of a boy?*

"This aberrance is probably indicative of the stress your daughter is experiencing since her mother's accident. She's acting out. I've noticed she's been allowed to run wild lately. Her lack of supervision may be placing her in harm's way."

Oh, for Chrissakes, let's not go overboard. He opened his mouth. "Let's not go over—"

She didn't let him finish. "I don't want to prohibit Joey from associating with your daughter, but until better supervision is provided at your house, the kids should only play at mine and only when I'm home to supervise."

He straightened. Missouri adored Joey. And Joey worshipped her. He was no psychologist (not like Barb Norsworthy), but Joey's adulation was probably exactly what she needed right now. Just as long as they stayed fully clothed. "Missouri's grandmother could—"

Barb's color heightened again. "She's not the best person to put in charge of children. She's not spry enough. And . . . I've heard things."

Of course she had. This was Cordelia. "Mrs. Norsworthy, that was all a long time ago."

Sheesh, he was defending Tamara. But the words rang true. Florida and Tamara had issues to address. As did Dak and his mother. But for the rest of them, the past belonged to his parents and Tamara. Whatever had happened then should stay there. Missouri mattered now. And for better or worse, she loved Tamara.

"I know, but I'm sure you understand that I need to do what is best for Joey. Missouri is welcome at our house anytime, provided I'm home, and Joey is certainly permitted to be at yours if *you* are there to monitor them." She started back across the street.

He watched her go, thinking she walked as though she had an eggbeater up her butt, then looked back at Florida's house, his gaze moving up to the windows of her bedroom, where he knew she lay in the half-light of approaching dusk. Of course, she'd need to rejoin life. But eventually. There was no reason to rush.

He glanced over his shoulder to see Barb Norsworthy disappear inside and sighed.

Except there was.

He let himself in the gate and headed up the walk, wondering where Missouri was now. Cowering in her room, embarrassed at getting caught?

Well, she should be. Thinking of her bare-chested in front of a boy made him grind his teeth.

He stopped outside the front door, giving himself time to stop steaming before he went inside. He'd only make the situation worse if he came down on her hard. Barb Norsworthy, much as he hated to admit it, was probably on target: Missouri was—what had she called it?—acting out. He needed to address this situation with sensitivity.

Not something he'd ever been accused of having in an overly abundant supply. He almost turned around to seek out Alcea's counsel. Almost. But thinking of their earlier conversation, he knew he'd simply fuel her frustration with Florida.

A frustration he was beginning to feel himself, even though he harbored more than a suspicion he was partially responsible.

Stepping inside, he heard voices in the kitchen. Julius's low rumble and Missouri's high pipe, accompanied by the occasional chime of the bicycle bell. They were probably working on a model—he'd brought over a '66 Dodge Charger the other day that had gotten a vote of approval. Missouri didn't sound upset. Maybe she'd forgotten the incident by now. Or maybe she didn't think it was all that important. Was that good or bad? He sighed. He needed advice. Or—forget advice—maybe her mother would feel up to handling it altogether. Surely it needed a woman's touch. He headed upstairs.

When he opened Florida's door, the smell of patchouli oil almost knocked him over. Okay, maybe Alcea had a point. He stepped into the room and closed the door behind him. At least Enya was mute. Florida lay on her side, asleep. This was an odd twist. Although she was usually still asleep when he arrived midday, by evening she'd normally risen and dressed. Sometimes, he suddenly realized, it was her only accomplishment of the day.

Frowning, he approached the bed, hoping she wasn't sliding further into despair. But her face was serene, unpinched by the worry and exhaustion he noticed when she was awake. Her hair fanned out over the pillow. Awake, asleep, blind, sighted, thin, fat—although she wasn't, she just thought she was—she was beautiful.

Sitting on the edge of the mattress, he touched her shoulder. "Hey, you," he said softly.

Without opening her eyes, she smiled sleepily. "Hey, you." She twisted around so she could blink up at him, although he knew she could see only what she described as a watercolor wash. "I'm sorry; I meant to get up, but I guess I dropped off again."

She looked so vulnerable, his concern over Missouri died in his throat as an upswelling of emotion suddenly overwhelmed him.

He loved her. Completely. Self-absorption, blindness, warts and all. Maybe he'd never stopped. Maybe the lessons he'd learned first from Alcea and then from Serena had just been preludes. Maybe they'd stripped him of all the artifice and left him with only the core of what he'd originally felt for Florida. He wanted to care for her. Protect her. Cherish her.

But all he said was, "I guess you did."

She yawned. "I'm hungry."

"I'll get you a tray in a minute, but . . . listen, there's a situation that's come up with Missouri."

"Is something wrong?"

"No. Yes. She's fine. Except . . . Barb Norsworthy came over to talk with me when I got here. She was upset."

"She's always upset."

"Well, this time I think she had a good reason. It seems our daughter . . ." As he relayed the incident, he felt Florida's attention start to wander.

"Is that all?" she said when he'd finished. "Sounds like Barb Norsworthy got all worked up over nothing much."

"Nothing? According to her, Missouri was practically attacking the kid."

"Barb Norsworthy always needs something to grump about. She'd complain if Jesus came down and handed her a twenty-dollar bill." She snuggled against him. "I don't think we should do anything. I'm sure they both got an earful from Barb. If we add to it, we'll blow it all out of proportion. Missouri's not a sinner; she's curious, that's all. Kids are, you know."

He was surprised she'd dismiss it so easily. "But she'll be in fourth grade. Isn't this kind of thing more like, I don't know, kindergarten?"

She smiled. "I've never outgrown it. If you think you need to talk with her, Stan, then talk to her. Just be gentle."

He stared at her. She'd never relegated anything like this to him before.

Her hand crept up his thigh and under the leg of his gym shorts. "I'll show you mine if you'll show me yours." Her face softened. "I love you, you know."

"I love you, too."

A frown creased between her eyebrows, and he gave himself a mental thunk. Here he'd waited to hear those words from her, and he'd blurted them back with about as much feeling as "Have a nice day." But, jeez, they should be discussing Missouri right now, not—

"Whoa." He jumped. Her hand had found its destination. Abruptly, he stood up, warmth fading. "Now isn't the time."

"What's wrong?"

He knew she could make him out, but not his expression. Her own was bewildered. Hurt. His anger died in his throat. "Nothing. Nothing's wrong. . . . I do love you, Florida."

Yet he suddenly realized that just like Alcea and Julius had tried to tell him, a lot was wrong.

Chapter 18

He spent Friday night in Florida's bed, like he had several times in the past week. And like each of those times, he was up and out the door early—this morning very early—before Missouri rose for ballet lessons. And before anyone was stirring in the Norsworthy household. He'd wager Barb Norsworthy didn't approve of sleepovers. He didn't want to give Florida's neighbor another excuse to keep the children apart.

So for both Missouri's sake and the sake of the family reputation, he didn't linger like he'd like to. Instead, he headed directly for Strides, his mind churning with the same thoughts that had kept him awake for most of the night. The love that had swept him yesterday as he'd watched Florida sleep had been startling, not in its depth, but in his realization that it had been part of him for years. An emotion that had lain dormant, but had provided the foundation Serena had built on.

All very romantic, of course, very . . . *karmic*—Dak would be proud. But this morning, he was wondering where, exactly, that love could take him. Julius . . . Alcea . . . they'd both tried to tell him . . . and now it was obvious. Obvious that he'd done his part to turn Florida into an invalid. And equally obvious that she'd accepted the role. He didn't know if he meant anything more to her than salve for her wounds. The Rebound Guy. The Band-Aid.

Even if that was enough for him—and he was no longer certain it was—he couldn't let the situation continue. It wasn't fair to her. Or to Missouri. He had to get Florida back on her feet. Even if she rejected him once she recovered her independence. Even if he felt, like he had instinctually known a decade ago, that he'd drown under her tide. He couldn't let her settle for less than she was.

He sighed. No wonder he'd never been much into self-sacrifice.

Not the least because he was completely clueless how to accomplish loftly goals.

After putting in a morning at Strides, he headed back to Florida's for lunch; then, letting her think he was returning to work, he sought out Tamara. He'd decided to start with her rather than suffer through any of Alcea's *I told you so*s. As usual, Florida's mother had headed outside for a post-meal smoke. When he let himself out on the porch, the humidity wrapped him like a blanket. He glanced at the thunderheads bubbling up in the west. Looked like they'd have a show later on.

Hair, earrings, and blouse all the same brassy gold, Tamara was seated on the settee. When she saw him, she nodded a greeting. When he didn't trot down the steps to his car, but instead turned and settled his hips against the railing, her brows rose.

Of course, she'd be surprised. He hadn't exactly tried to be her best friend since she'd come to town. But he didn't really despise her, at least not for having an affair with his father. Leaving Florida on somebody's doorstep, though . . . that was another matter.

He decided she wouldn't mind if he just launched in. From what he'd seen of her, she wasn't too big on the niceties. "I want to talk to you about Florida. I'd like to see her up and around."

"Interesting." She blew out a stream of smoke. "Why?"

"Seems to me you've made it your business to keep her down. Part of your gene pool. The Addams men like their women weak."

Maybe he did despise her. "What's that supposed to mean?"

"How well did you know your daddy?" She squinted at him. "Not well, I'd guess. He died when you were pretty young."

He shrugged. Growing up without a father, but with the ghost of one who had been a paragon of strength, as his mother had constantly reminded him, hadn't precisely endeared S.R. Addams to him.

"He was a big man in town." Tamara was still watching him. "Bank president. Wealthy. Larger than life and liked to throw his weight around. Remind you of anyone?"

He looked away. Not entirely. He'd had the weight-throwing thing down pretty cold, but he'd never had the same spine of steel as his father. Something his mother hadn't been reluctant to point out.

"It took a strong woman to match him. I was that strong." She paused. "Your mother wasn't. She worshipped the ground S.R. walked on, but that's not love. But I . . ." Face softening, she gazed out over the yard.

In the shadows of the porch, he could see the beauty she'd once been. He remembered the look on her face the night of Dak's farewell party when she'd gazed at the model of the Studebaker his father had once owned. "But you loved him."

The softness hardened and she looked back at him again. "But S.R. decided he wanted adoration more than he wanted an equal partnership. More than he wanted love. He betrayed me. Told me he wanted me. Wanted our child. Sent me north to a relative of his to bear Dak. Then behind my back, he confessed all to Ellen, who, of course, would have slit her throat if he'd asked her to."

Stan squirmed, uncomfortably reminded of Serena's reaction to Florida's pregnancy. She'd been almost as excited as Florida, had doted on Missouri from the day she was born. Of course, he hadn't asked her to accept his love child. At the time, it would have suited him if she'd never known at all. So there *was* a difference. Although his initial reluctance to accept Missouri into his life didn't exactly make him feel better.

"So your mother rolled over, played dead, and agreed to raise his son. *My* son. And they gave me money. And I pretended to be oh-so-grateful. Then I ran away with it and Dak. And that somehow made S.R. and Ellen heroes and me a pariah." She shrugged. "Fuck 'em."

"I don't think anyone blamed you for running off. They blamed you because you knew Dak could have found a good home with my parents, and instead you stayed a step ahead of my father's detectives, gave Dak a life no better than a nomad—"

"He loved it!"

True, but that was beside the point. "And finally abandoned him on his granddad's doorstep, along with your six-year-old daughter, once my father was dead. You didn't love your children. You just wanted to keep them from him. You just wanted revenge."

She sighed. "Yeah, yeah. I've heard that story."

"What *story*? It's the truth." He'd heard it from his mother and he'd heard it from Florida. And when Dak had discovered the truth before marrying Alcea, it had nearly destroyed him.

"*Part* of the truth. I'll admit I didn't feel a qualm

at causing S.R. Addams any pain. Or Ellen for that matter. You've got the basics straight. I did run off with your parents' money. I didn't honor our agreement to let them adopt Dak. And I did leave both Dakota and Florida with my father . . . someone, by the way, that I knew would love them." Again, she looked away. "Like he loved me. Although I never thanked him for it. But you have one fact wrong."

"Which is?"

"I *did* love my children."

"Right. Then why'd you leave them?"

She hesitated. "They needed more than I could give them, especially Florida."

He snorted. "Why didn't you even send them a note, a birthday present, call them at Christmas?"

She squashed out her cigarette; her bracelets clanked together. "Enough. This should be about you and my daughter, not me. She's laying upstairs like she's dying. And it's you that's encouraging her to do it. And that's hurting Missouri."

That was about it in a nutshell. But he was surprised she was that perceptive.

Her voice turned dry. "Yes, not only does Missouri talk to me—mostly because nobody else listens to her anymore—but Barb Norsworthy made it quite clear that she thinks Missouri's perversion is the result of my evil ways."

"I didn't know she'd talked to you."

"Probably because she wishes she hadn't. Oh, don't look so worried. I just told her to go suck an egg, nothing worse. Although I should have

said worse. Calling my granddaughter perverted."
She shook her head. "Stupid woman. So what do
you intend to do about it?"

"Contract killing?" he suggested, wishing he'd
told Barb Norsworthy to go suck an egg.

"Not a bad idea, but I wasn't talking about Saint
Barb. I meant Florida."

He rubbed a hand over his face. Tamara would
love this. "Have you talk to her."

"Me?" She barked a laugh that stopped with a
cough. "You think she'd listen to me?"

Wait till she heard the best part. "She would if
you told her she reminded you of, well, you."

"How do you figure that, Sherlock?"

"You abandoned your kids—"

"*Abandon* is such a harsh word."

"—and that's essentially what she's doing to
Missouri right now."

Tamara laughed again. "Gotta hand it to you.
It just might work."

He smiled. "That's what I thought."

"And isn't it great that you get out of doing
any dirty work? It's like playing good cop, bad
cop; you get to keep her goodwill. While I—"

"She already hates you."

"Gee, that makes me feel better. But I'll do it."
Tamara pushed herself up, straining the last little
way. Her mind was so sharp, sometimes he forgot
that years and tobacco had started to take a toll
on her body.

She looked at him. "You know, if you want this
relationship to work—and maybe you won't once

Florida is back to being Florida—you'll need to learn to stand up to her someday."

Before he had a chance to ask exactly what she meant, Missouri skipped outside. She didn't look like a pervert; she looked like his sweet little girl. Maybe Florida was right. Maybe it was all just a fury over nothing. Still . . . true tempest or not, it didn't lessen the need to stir Florida out of her growing apathy. Counseling would help, but maybe Tamara could be a shot in the arm first.

Missouri grabbed up Tamara's hand. "You said we could go to the duck pond after lunch."

"That's right. So I did."

"I'll go get Joey." She dropped Tamara's hand and started down the steps.

"Wait. Did his mother say it was okay?" Tamara asked.

Missouri halted and frowned back at them. "She's not home, but why wouldn't it be?"

Tamara exchanged a look with Stan, who shrugged. "I'd say if Joey's mom told him to stay put, put he'll stay. No harm in asking."

Missouri directed a puzzled look between them, then shrugged, too. "I'll be right back."

"Wait on the porch for me," Tamara called after her. "I need to have a word with your mother before we leave."

The look Tamara directed at Stan was grim. Despite her flippancy, the woman wasn't without feeling. She couldn't be looking forward to the coming confrontation.

Neither was he. He thought of Alcea's words.

The Florida I know is a fighter. You'd do well to re-member that.

From the bathroom where she'd just emerged from a shower, Florida heard her bedroom door open. She frowned, completely out of patience. First, Stan had acted like she had leprosy. Then her mother had pushed open the door without even knocking, sat down, and started in on some harangue that she'd had no intention of heeding. Tamara had barely gotten past a terse, "We need to talk," before she climbed out of bed, walked straight to the bathroom, and closed the door in her face. When Tamara had knocked, she'd only turned up the spigots in the bathtub. Tamara had given a sigh audible through the door and left.

And hopefully had the smarts not to come back. "Who is it?"

The bathroom door rattled. "Me. Let me in."

Not Tamara. Alcea. Her mood soured further. She unlocked the door, opened it a few inches. "Is knocking a lost art?" she said, voice acerbic.

Alcea didn't apologize. She pushed her way in. "You're not dressed? Well, c'mon, let's get going." Voice flustered, Alcea pulled on her arm.

What in blue blazes? Florida snatched it back. "I'll dress when I want to dress."

"You don't understand. Where's Stan? Or Tamara? I didn't see them when I came in."

Alarm started to surface under her anger. Alcea was acting strange. "Stan's at work. As for Tamara, who cares? What's going on?"

"It's Missouri." Alcea yanked on her arm again.

Alarm now complete, Florida let herself be hauled into the bedroom. "What about Missouri?"

"She's at the hospital."

"Omigod. Why? What happened?"

Alcea pushed her down on the bed and hurried to a dresser. In a moment, Florida saw a blur of her clothes as they flew through the air. "Put these on. We have to go. I'll call Stan."

Florida scrambled into her bra. "How badly is she hurt? Tell me!"

"No. Oh, Florida. My mind . . ." Alcea threw some shoes at her feet. "Missouri's not hurt. It's Joey. He and Missouri were on the dock at the duck pond. Missouri pushed him in."

Another tall tale from Barb Norsworthy. "Missouri wouldn't do such a thing. She'd never—"

"And he can't swim."

Florida felt the blood drain from her face. "Is he—is he all right?"

"Missouri jumped in after him, but got tangled in someone's fishing line. The Olausson brothers saw it all happen and pulled them out, but they had to call the paramedics." There was a world of worry in her tone. "Missouri's fine."

"Thank God. And Joey?"

"They think he'll be okay. But Florida . . ."

"What?" She shrugged into a shirt.

"The police came, too. They're waiting with Missouri at the hospital. They're charging her with assault."

Chapter 19

"Whatever happened to shake hands and make up? She's only nine, for God's sake!"

Sunday morning, next to Stan on one side of the kitchen table, Florida's face was anguished, dark circles under her eyes indicating she hadn't slept well. Neither had he; a dull ache throbbed at the base of his skull. The day had dawned as gray as his mood; the storms that had broken last night still hung heavy overhead, promising another day of rain.

On the other side of the table, a few cups of coffee growing cold between them, Florida and Alcea's attorney, Mel Murphy, dug through a briefcase. He'd given up Sunday brunch—"At the in-laws'," he'd said, "thank God you called"—to meet with them. For which, gratitude for saving him from his wife's parents or not, Stan was certain, they'd be charged two arms and two legs.

Which, given Florida's mood, she could have torn straight off of Tamara. Quite a few cross words had flown around since they'd gotten back from the hospital last night with a subdued and tearful Missouri. After a tense breakfast this morning, Julius had taken Missouri and the '66 Dodge Charger over to Alcea's to keep her out of the line of fire until the meeting with Mel was over. He didn't know where Tamara had gone. To hide, he supposed, from the murder Florida housed in her heart.

Mel pulled out a file. "Even though Joey Norsworthy is perfectly fine now, I'm afraid that, nine or not, what she did *is* considered a crime. You know Chief Spindle would've called it kid high jinks—"

"Because that's what it was!"

Mel moved smoothly over Florida's interruption. "But his hands are tied. The Norsworthys say she's gotten increasingly out of hand in the last month and they're concerned you won't pay attention if charges aren't brought. Emotions are running high." He shrugged. "After all, if it weren't for the Olaussons, their son could have died."

Florida flinched.

Mel flipped through some papers. "The police report says Mrs. Norsworthy specifically told Stan she didn't trust the grandmother's supervision. And that this was after your daughter, uh, exposed herself to young Norsworthy just two days ago?"

"*Exposed?* Oh, for God's sake. Barb Norsworthy makes her sound like next thing we know, she'll take up mass murder," Stan said.

Florida's lips were white. "I told Dak. I told Alcea. Tamara *isn't* a fit guardian for a child. But would anyone listen?"

"It's not Tamara's fault," Stan said.

"Not her fault? Of course it's—"

"Let's not take up Mel's time with family squabbles."

From the look on her face, surprise shut her up. Stan sighed. There was enough time later to blame themselves for the fact Florida had been so involved with herself and he so involved with Florida that they'd left their daughter—a daughter trying to deal with too-big emotions—largely in the care of a woman who, no matter how quick-witted she remained, wasn't so fast on her feet anymore. They'd even had the balls to disdain her presence, while the whole time, they'd left their most precious gift in her charge.

He looked at Mel. "Tell us what's likely to happen."

"Nothing for a while. You'll get some papers in the mail, probably within the next four to six weeks, and they'll give you a court date. I'd guess that'd be about another month out. At the hearing, because the witnesses . . ." He paged through papers again. "Ah, the Olaussons again . . . everyone knows them; nobody'll doubt their word. . . . Anyway, because the Olaussons saw Missouri shove the boy into the pond, I'd say it's useless—and might make the judge mad—if we tried to show otherwise. Nope, better we stipulate to the charges and take the consequences."

Stan loved this *we* bit . . . like Mel would serve time for their daughter? His stomach clenched. Would Missouri actually serve time? Assault sounded serious. Could they put her in some cold-hearted detention center somewhere?

"Sentence?" Florida's face was the color of chalk. He could see her thoughts had run along similar lines.

"Again, don't worry. We can claim a lot of circumstances to lighten the penalties. Up until now, she's been in no trouble. Does well in school. She's been under a great deal of emotional distress because of Florida's condition, but you've already lined up family counseling that I understand will start soon?" Mel looked up.

Stan nodded.

"Plus it says here that young Joey provoked a reaction from her. And, as you say, she's nine. I'm certain she'll be put on what's termed a diversion program. You'll pay a fine. She'll visit a probation officer once a month, if that, and the court will order a course of counseling for her. She won't even end up with a record, providing you make sure she fulfills the terms."

"Oh, thank God." Florida laid her head on her arms. She made no sound, but her shoulders shook.

Casting a compassionate glance at her, Mel

stood up and offered Stan his hand. "I'll give you a holler as soon as we've received notice the case is on the docket. In the meantime . . . take care of each other."

"We will." Stan saw him out the door. The dark underside of the clouds seemed to brush the rooftops. As he watched Mel walk to his car, it started to sprinkle. Off in the distance, thunder stirred. When he returned to the table, Florida still sat as he'd left her. He angled his chair next to hers and took her into his arms. "It'll be okay. Everything will be okay."

For long moments, she cried quietly on his shoulder as the rain pelted the roof. Finally, she pushed away and mopped at her eyes. "I—I'm sorry. I've got to stop this." She took a few deep shuddering breaths. "Anymore, it seems I'm more leaky than a rusty faucet. And just about as much fun."

"Give yourself a break. You've had a lot to leak about. You're mourning—loss of your sight, loss of the way you used to live."

"The return of my mother."

"You can't expect to just bounce right back. I don't care what philosophy your brother spouts. When bad shit happens, you've got a right to feel bad."

"Where'd you get so wise?"

He was quiet a moment. "Serena. When she was dying, after she was gone, there were days when I could hardly drag myself out of bed. But I learned to move through it."

"How?"

"Denial. A whole helluva lot of denial. I highly recommend it."

"But then you finally have to face what's happened."

"Yes, and the anger and grief that go with it. But not until you're ready." He rubbed a thumb over the tear tracks on her cheek. "Denial's a great insulator. It'll unravel when you're ready to handle more." The watch on his wrist caught his attention. "Damn. I hate to take off, but I promised Jess the afternoon off and need to get over to Strides."

She caught at his arm. "A few more minutes? There's something else I wanted to talk to you about."

It warmed him, her turning to him. "For you. Anything."

"Good."

She sat up straight. For the first time in weeks, he saw steel back in her spine. He would be glad—except for a sudden twinge of alarm that pinged in his brain. "You know, all that time upstairs, I was thinking. . . . I've been trying to figure out how to get my old self back. But yesterday I realized . . . there's no returning to the past. You can't go back."

"No, you can't."

"There is no old me; there's no returning to the old me. There's just . . . me. The way I am now. And you have to work with what you've got."

"True." Watching her, seeing a glimmer of her

old spirit, he felt his alarm fade under a swell of satisfaction. He'd known if they gave her time, she'd be back. Even her eyes sparkled.

"And in my case, there's not a whole helluva lot to work with. . . ."

The unease came back. "I wouldn't say—"

"So, this morning, thinking over everything that's happened, I made a decision."

"Which was?" Somehow he knew he wouldn't like what was coming.

"Missouri will go live with you."

Unable to see his jaw hit the floor, she took his silence for approval. "I knew you'd agree. Yesterday certainly proved Tamara can't handle her. I certainly can't." She gave a small laugh. "I can't even see her. More than that, though, it will get her out of the orbit of the Norsworthys."

The Norsworthys. Is that what this was about? He pulled his jaw back into place. "Florida, I talked with the Norsworthys last night. They were upset, yes. And maybe they have too much starch in their shorts, but they're not bad people. In fact, they still want Missouri and Joey to be friends. They just felt we needed a . . . wake-up call . . . where Missouri was concerned. I'm not sure they weren't right."

"Maybe they are." She waved a hand. "Don't worry, I'm not going to lob missiles across the street. I just think Missouri would be more comfortable without Barb Norsworthy glaring at her all the time. Then, after—"

"Missouri would be more comfortable? Or you

would?" With Missouri gone, Tamara could go, too.

"—after I'm out of—" Florida stopped, his words apparently catching up to her. "What do you mean by that?"

She looked so much her former imperial self, he hesitated, then came at her from another angle. "How do you think Missouri will react to this idea?"

"She'll love it. She'll move in with you and then—"

"She'd hate it." Away from her own room. From Joey. From Julius. From her aunt and uncle. And even from her Gram-Tam. Sure, she'd still see them all, but not all the time, not like she did now. And she needed them now. Especially Florida. She was already feeling rejected, neglected. Who needed a judge? She'd feel sentence had been passed and she was no longer welcome in her home.

"No, she won't. She loves you. She'll have that pool she's always wanted."

Had Florida lost her mind? "And you think a pool will replace her *mother*?"

"You sound like you think I'll like being away from her. I won't, but I'm not—"

"Explain that to Missouri," he muttered under his breath.

"Would you let me finish?" She actually stamped her foot.

He jumped.

"I'm *not* talking about forever. I'm talking just

a few months. Until Christmas. Until I'm out of Hope House. Then you and I can have a small holiday ceremony before y'all move in here. Or—wait a minute. Maybe you should just move in now." She thought for a minute. "Or maybe we should move in with you or all of us find somewhere else to live. I don't own this house and Alcea would probably prefer not having us as next-door neighbors. That would get Missouri away from Barb Norsworthy, too. Yes." She looked thoughtful. "That'd work the best, I think."

He blinked. Either he'd just heard a proposal or he'd gone fucking nuts. "A marriage of convenience?"

"No! It'd just be the *timing* that's convenient. But, of course, that's not the main reason. You love me, I love you, so . . . ?"

"Quit. You're embarrassing me with all the romance."

"C'mon, Stan," she wheedled. She leaned in, her lips brushing his ear. "Just consider it. It's a good plan. We could . . ."

A *good plan*? Christ. Florida was back with a vengeance. Steamrolling right over everyone. Over him. But as he listened to the murmur in his ear—the note of hope, the return of life, and a certain titillation that was sending some of his other body parts onto high alert—he didn't have the heart to squash her plans.

Instead he cleared his throat and, like the weenie he was, told her he'd like to think things over and they could talk about it tomorrow. As soon as the words left his mouth, anger rose in his throat. At her. But mostly at himself. God. What was he doing? He was complying like he was negotiating a purchase for a goddamn NordicTrack, not considering marriage.

As he left, he argued with himself. Why not just fall into line? It'd be easy enough, and it was what he wanted. He loved her. He loved Missouri. It'd make life sweet again if they could all be together.

Yet somehow he knew everything had just gone sour.

Chapter 20

Shortly after Stan left, Florida heard the breeze-way door open. A rain-scented breeze whipped through the kitchen, then fell still as the door banged shut again. Missouri and Julius had returned from Alcea's. When they came through the kitchen, she stretched an arm out toward the violet blur of Missouri's shirt.

"C'mere, honey. We need to talk."

But Missouri stepped out of reach. "I'm gonna watch TV."

Florida sighed and rose as the violet splotch moved into the great room. "Guess I'm still not forgiven."

Julius wheeled around toward his quarters. "And I'm gonna take a nap."

Her lips tightened to keep her chin from trembling. She felt his snub keenly, and not for the first time that day. All morning, he'd been subdued, keeping his speed under Mach three, the bicycle bell silent, and himself unresponsive to anything she said. She deserved his ill opinion.

Last night, she'd been scathing and none too quiet with her opinions of Barb Norsworthy, of anyone who had ever championed the idea of Tamara supervising Missouri . . . and of Tamara herself. Fortunately, she'd waited until they'd returned home from the hospital to launch into her rant. Unfortunately, she hadn't waited until Missouri was out of earshot.

Missouri had burst into tears—just after they'd finally subsided—and had run upstairs, refusing to come back down when Florida—deeply ashamed at her outburst even before Tamara had muttered, *Smooth move*—begged her to. Stan had been more circumspect than her mother. He'd only heaved a long-suffering sigh before going to their daughter. She'd sat in embarrassed silence long after Tamara had followed him out of the room. A silence that had given way to a long night of more measured thought.

But now, as she culled through what Mel Murphy had told them, and wondered how much to pass on to Missouri, her outrage stirred again. Good God. That something like this could come to courts and lawyers and . . . sentences? It was insane. Missouri was a child. A child in pain. She'd never intended to hurt anyone, let alone Joey, and she already felt repentant. Florida had heard it all morning in the shuffle of her footsteps and a silence broken only by an occasional sniff. What more did the Norsworthys want?

She took a deep breath, reining in her anger. If she wanted to blame anyone, she should blame herself. As soon as her disability had become evident, she should have gotten help for Missouri. She should have thought of her daughter instead of being so consumed with herself. Well, she might be a day late, but that would change. Beginning now.

In the great room, the television set squawked. Florida swept her gaze around the room, a quiet kaleidoscope of natural colors enlivened only by an occasional smear of decorator green or Chinese Red, since gray clouds still hung heavy against the windows. Rain pattered on the rooftop. Her eyes landed on a huddle of purple in the club chair.

Taking a circuit around the room, Florida stopped at the television and switched it off.

"Mom, what are you doing?"

Stepping carefully, she made her way to the club chair and lowered herself to her knees in front of Missouri. "This." Forearms flanking her daughter's thighs, she leaned forward until their noses nearly touched, ignoring how Missouri shrank back. "I want to be able to see you."

She didn't like what she saw. Missouri's dark eyes were wide and scared, red like her nose. Her hair fell over her shoulders in a wild tangle.

"Why?"

"Because I love you, honeybun. So very much."

At her words, Missouri's face crumpled and she pitched herself into Florida's arms. Florida held

on tight, crooning and rocking until the storm subsided. When Missouri's tears were reduced to
snuffles, Florida pulled back, but kept Missouri's
hands tucked in hers.

"Tell me what happened yesterday." She'd
heard the disjointed account Missouri had given
the police, as well as more than she wanted to
hear from Barb Norsworthy, but maybe if Missouri spilled it all again, she'd feel better. Maybe
they'd both feel better.

Missouri's voice was small. "We went to the
pond and out on the dock. Gram-Tam had bought
us some feed at Beadler's for the ducks, so we
were going to give them some supper. Gram-Tam
didn't go out on the dock; she said she was so
rickety she might fall in. But it wasn't her fault,
Mom. Really it wasn't. Even if she'd been out
there, I still would have done what I did. She
couldn't've stopped me."

"Okay, okay. Still. She shouldn't have let you
go out there if she couldn't be with you." Florida
realized she sounded as prim as Barb Norsworthy.
And about as smart. She knew Joey's accident
wasn't Tamara's fault; she even knew that under
more able-bodied supervision, the incident still
would have happened. But she wanted someone
to blame. She wanted Tamara to blame.

Missouri's silence let her know she didn't agree,
but she didn't defend her grandmother again.
Probably afraid of another scene.

Florida sighed. "I'm sorry. You're right." She
wasn't. "Go on."

Missouri lowered her gaze. "We were throwing food to the ducks. There were baby ones, and mama ones. Joey pretended he was one of the babies, and I picked a different one to be. And we tried to see if we could get the food to land just right so each of our babies could get it before the other ones. It was just fun." She stopped.

"Then what happened?"

"The food was all gone and the ducks started to swim away. And Joey pointed at mine and said that if that was really you and me, I'd be the one going first instead of the mama one, since my mom was blind as a bat. He was laughing." Florida heard a quiver start in her voice. "I know he didn't really mean anything—it was just a stupid thing to say—but I got mad. And I pushed him. I didn't mean for him to go in the water. I didn't mean to hurt him. I just didn't want him to laugh. What's happened to you isn't funny!"

Again Florida gathered Missouri into her arms. "Oh, honey. It's all right."

"And then I was so sc-scared." Missouri's voice was muffled against her shoulder. "He splashed around and then I couldn't hardly see him anymore and I jumped in, too, but then there was fishing line or something. . . . I thought we were going to d-die."

Oh, God. "But you're safe now. You're safe." And she'd stay that way. "And so is Joey. I know you didn't mean it. Joey knows that, too."

"But now I—I'm in a lot of tr-trouble. They'll send me to jail."

Florida squeezed tighter. "No, you won't go to jail."

"Joey said so!" It was a wail.

"Yesterday at the hospital? He was scared and mad, honey."

"But Mrs. Norsworthy also told me—"

Damn woman. "Shhh. You'll go to a judge, and the judge will be fair and tell you that you just need to talk to someone every once in a while about the things you feel bad about. We all need to do that. My accident has been hard on everyone, and we need some help to get everything straightened out again."

And then maybe Missouri wouldn't have to go before a judge at all. Maybe after the Norsworthys' initial outrage had passed and they knew the family was getting help, they'd turn reasonable, like Stan thought they would, and drop the charges. Or, if charges had to be pressed anyway, maybe they'd at least support Mel Murphy's arguments for leniency.

She thought ahead to Hope House and opened her mouth to tell Missouri she'd be living with Stan until she completed rehab, and then she and Stan would get married. That would make her feel better, wouldn't it?

But then she stopped. Stan hadn't actually agreed. She frowned. He had to agree. The image of Julius lying helpless in that alley, gasping for air and ringing that pip-squeak of a bell while she was unable to do anything to help, still terrorized her. Thinking of what could have happened to

Missouri or Joey was a frigging nightmare. Maybe it would have happened on anyone's watch, but if it happened on hers, she couldn't live with herself. Sure, they could hire a nanny or something, short-term, but even then, she wanted someone sighted around to see what was what. Not Julius. And *not* Tamara. Someone whole and healthy and possessed of some character, which definitely struck her mother from the list. When Florida felt better equipped to resume the task, she would. At least she hoped she *could*. She was sure Hope House would give her back a large measure of her independence, but there might be limitations she couldn't surmount.

"If I go to jail, Mommy, will you visit me every day?"

"Oh, no, Missouri. No jail, hon," she murmured, thinking of her earlier conversation with Stan.

She'd bungled it, she realized. He hadn't seemed angry that she'd made it all sound like a business proposition, but was it a wonder he wanted to think about it? She hadn't meant to be so, well, unromantic. And he was partially right. It would be a marriage of convenience in some ways. At least the timing would be. Given all the recent upheavals, even with them certain of their hearts, a quick marriage could make for a tumultuous first year or two. But she'd been panicked over Missouri, wanted to make things right for her, even while she knew they might be wise to enjoy a long courtship.

But, hell, she knew she loved him. Knew he loved her. Knew this was their second chance at a time when both of them were ready. So she'd assumed . . .

Missouri stirred and Florida pulled her closer, her thoughts stumbling.

Maybe she'd assumed far too much. Stan had whispered words of love, but never words of marriage. He'd had the opportunity in the past to make her his wife, but he'd chosen Serena instead. Because Serena wasn't as strong-willed or stubborn or—

Suddenly she felt the world fall out from under her feet.

Stan had been living out a fantasy. While she'd been lying in bed, while she'd been feeling helpless and hopeless, for a short while, he'd had Serena again.

A half an hour after Missouri had squirmed out of her embrace and headed for her room, Florida still sat in the great room, her thoughts catawampus. She'd pushed herself up to the ottoman in front of the chair Missouri had vacated, her face turned to the pale shimmer from the windows. The room was a chiaroscuro of shadow and light. Mostly shadow. Overhead, the rain still pounded.

She felt so alone. Just as Stan had replayed his part with Serena, had she slipped into his dead wife's role? In her neediness, had she grabbed on to him, like the only lifeboat available once Daniel was gone?

She'd thought she was sure about him, but . . .

What was she sure of anymore? What *could* she be sure of? Blindness had built walls. The people she loved stood on the other side, and she could no longer see them clearly—or the horizon that had once seemed so infinite.

The lethargy that had dragged her down started to creep back up her limbs, turning them leaden. Impatiently, she shook herself before tears could swell. Stan was right. What had happened was *bad shit*. She'd have good and bad days—good and bad *hours*. Sometimes she'd have to take things minute by minute just to get through. Hope House and counseling would help, but she supposed that on some level, she'd always feel separate, different.

A faint scent of oranges drifted into the room.

She wanted to screech with frustration. And some days she might even feel suicidal.

She turned her head toward the doorway, seeing movement, seeing a smear of the yellow that Tamara must be wearing. "What do *you* want?"

"Testy, aren't you?"

"What do you expect? My daughter was in your care yesterday and almost drowned."

"Oh, for God's sake. It was a dock on a duck pond, not a pier in the Atlantic. Even if I rivaled Maurice Greene, it wouldn't have changed anything that happened. The fine Mrs. Norsworthy's opinion to the contrary notwithstanding. And yours."

Florida followed Tamara's progress into the

room, over to the sofa, where she sat down. Florida stood, intending to retreat upstairs.

"That's some plan you've hatched for Missouri," Tamara said.

Florida stopped. She hadn't shared her plans with anyone except Stan. "So along with abandonment, you've perfected eavesdropping?"

"Pretty much. Although normally I wouldn't butt my nose in—"

Florida harrumphed.

"—but I want what's best for Missouri."

"And you're implying I don't?" Anger rising, she struggled to contain it. Tamara wasn't worth the energy. And Missouri was upstairs. "I'm only being realistic. I'm not a fit guardian now—look what happened with Julius. And you certainly aren't—look what happened with Joey. So, since Alcea is minding the store, that leaves Stan. His hours are flexible. He can be available when Missouri needs him. And he can keep a *sighted* eye on anyone he might have to bring in to help. Someone *trustworthy*."

"Maybe." Tamara didn't sound a bit fazed by the implication she wasn't. Maybe because she knew her own limits. "But Missouri will think you don't want her. You, of all people, should know about that."

"Stan's her father. What I'm doing can't hold a candle to dumping her on someone she doesn't even know. And you of all people should know about *that*."

"But you *are* dumping her."

"I'll be right here! We can see each other all the time. She just won't live with me, that's all."

"And you think that will sit right with her? You know, when I first started spending time with Missouri, I thought she did you credit as a mother. But now I wonder if you—"

"Don't you judge me. Don't you *dare* judge me. You had no excuse for what you did. You were an able-bodied woman; I'm legally blind. I'm in emotional pain. It'll get better, but right now I can't take care of her properly. I'm doing the best I can!"

"You think I wasn't?"

"Don't make me laugh."

"You know, you're awfully fast with the judgments yourself. I had reasons for what I did."

"And I'm sure they're doozies. Lay 'em on me. Go ahead." Florida's voice was scathing.

There was a pause. Then a blur as Tamara stood up and moved to the door. It slammed shut in her wake. *No!* She would not allow her mother to walk out on her, not ever again. Springing up, Florida strode to the door as quickly as if she'd been fully sighted, and followed her mother outside on the porch.

As she stepped outside, a gust of wind lifted her hair off her neck, chilling her despite the heavy humidity. The rain was drumbeats on the overhang. Absorbing what she could, she took a few steps, turning toward a column of yellow, still as a post. She blinked. Maybe it was a post. Then she heard the column exhale and smelled the smoke.

She lowered her brow. "Don't you run away from me. I want to hear your excuses. You owe it to me."

Another billow of smoke. "Sit down."

"Don't you—"

"Sit down, for Chrissakes, before you fall down. You're standing near the top of the steps."

Flushing, Florida moved to the wicker settee, guided by the blotches of red roses on its cushions.

"Did you ever ask yourself," Tamara said conversationally, "why, if I were so Goddamned eager to get rid of you, I waited till Dakota was sixteen and you were six?"

"You kept Dakota for revenge on his father. S.R. wanted him, so you kept him away until S.R. was dead."

"And you? Why'd I keep you?"

"Because . . . I don't know."

"Nice to hear you admit there's something you don't."

Florida stood up. "I'm not going to sit here and listen to—"

"Sit down," Tamara barked. "I'm getting Goddamned tired of your selfishness."

Startled, Florida sat down before she realized she'd done it. She straightened. "My selfishness? What about your—"

"*Yes*, I was selfish. I was selfish and a slut and all the other things you've always thought me. I did steal from Dak's father, and I did keep a step ahead of his detectives because I knew the man would destroy me for crossing him."

"And—"

"*And* because I knew he wanted Dakota and it was one way I could get even with him for lying to me and choosing someone else."

"I knew it." Florida thumped back, arms crossed.

"But that doesn't mean I didn't learn to love Dak."

Florida snorted.

"Unbelievable as you might think it, I did. And when you were born, I loved you, too. I'm not saying I had a clue in hell what to do with each of you. And I'm not saying I wasn't completely screwed up—I was still a slut, still did drugs, squatted in any commune or shelter that would let me stay for a while. It was probably a miracle that nobody took either of you away from me before I left you here."

"So you're going to tell me you left us for our sakes."

"Partly, I did."

"Only partly? Guess that's more honesty than I expected from you. And the other part?"

"I left you here because I was pregnant again."

"Figures. So where'd you dump him—or her? Where is this long-lost half brother or sister of mine?"

There was a long pause. "Dead. He . . . died last year."

There was a funny squeaking sound, some hacking. For a moment, she thought Tamara was choking. Alarmed, she half rose. Then sank back down as she realized Tamara wasn't strangling.

She was crying.

Slowly, disjointedly, between lighting up a half pack of cigarettes, Tamara spilled out her story. At thirty-six, she'd learned she was once again pregnant. At a free health clinic, one of the nurses talked her into an amniocentesis, where she'd learned the baby had Down syndrome. Back then, not only were abortions not as easy to come by; it was nearing the end of her first trimester and she couldn't bring herself to do it.

"I'd already started talking to him, singing to him. He was already real to me."

She couldn't abort. And she knew the chances of finding adoptive parents were slim. With no money saved, no job, no home, and not knowing if S.R. had ever called off his detectives, she came home.

"I didn't know what else to do. I'd decided to throw myself on S.R.'s mercy. I figured he had his reputation to think of, even if he could care less what happened to me. Surely he wouldn't hound a woman pregnant with a Down's child."

Florida's disgust that she'd hide behind her disabled baby must have shown on her face.

Tamara's laugh was dry. "That's right. Big surprise. I wasn't above using my child's misfortune to play on his sympathies. I wasn't above using anything that it took to make sure each of you were well cared for. If he still wanted Dak, then I'd give him Dak. And I hoped he'd take you on, too. Or maybe Cowboy would. I couldn't support all three of you. But I knew I was the only hope for my unborn kid. I had to keep him."

"But Dak was old enough to work."

"Dak was *smart*. God, was he smart. Once he learned to read, he hardly did anything else. I didn't have money for college. Not even an address to apply for a loan. But S.R. had both money and an address. A fancy address. Even Cowboy would offer him a better chance. And you—it wasn't too late for you to start school."

"So you were the paragon of altruism. Right."

"Hell, no! Did I say that? I had some good intentions, sure. But I can face the truth—unlike some people I know. I knew taking care of a Down's baby would use up every ounce of selflessness in me. There wasn't a lot to begin with. There wasn't enough left over for you and Dak. Satisfied?"

As a matter of fact, Tamara's admittance that she'd acted partly in selfishness *did* mollify Florida . . . somewhat. "Go on."

"When I got here, I found out S.R. was dead. And Cowboy—" She erupted in a coughing fit that Florida suspected covered her emotions. But when she spoke again, her voice was matter-of-fact. "He didn't want me. He said he'd take you both on, said he could do no less, since he knew I'd never be a fit mother, but *I* needed to hit the road, Jack. He didn't want to see anything more than the back of me. I couldn't blame him. I'd already caused him a whole truckload of heartache. Just like my mother."

So Tamara had left Dak and Florida with her father and had headed to the West Coast, where she'd heard welfare benefits were as generous as the sunshine.

"And I did it. I kicked the drugs, and I eventually got off welfare, and I made a life for Cal."

As Florida listened, her heart had thawed. A little. Not a lot. "Well, that's just dandy. But what about the children you'd left behind?"

Tamara's voice grew defensive. "I hardly made enough for two of us and the special programs Cal needed even with state help. Besides, by the time I was on my feet, Dakota had already graduated. You were nearly through elementary school. What was the point?"

"You were our mother. *That* was the point!"

Florida heard the ashtray rattle as Tamara stubbed out her cigarette. "I said I was selfish, all right? Do you need to hear it again? I was hurting and immature and *damnably* selfish. I admit it. It was easier *for me* to pretend you'd never existed."

"Then why'd you come back?"

"I changed. I know you don't believe it, but caring for Cal . . . he was so innocent. So accepting. Never saw anyone except in the best light. He was the best person I'd ever known— and he made me ashamed. He made me want to live up to his love. When he died . . . I couldn't stand the hole in my heart. I was lonely; it's as simple as that. So I decided to look up your brother."

"But not me."

"Oh, don't be so dramatic. I knew if I found Dak, I'd find you, too."

Florida thought over everything Tamara had said. There were still things that didn't make sense and she wasn't about to give her mother the benefit of any doubt. Why should she? She owed her nothing. "Does Dak know all this?"

There was the click of the lighter, another puff of smoke. "Yes."

"Then why didn't he tell me?"

"On that day I showed up at your door, he said he'd started to, but you were too upset to listen." Florida sensed Tamara's shrug. "Then you had the accident. Then he left on his trip. . . ."

Dak would try to dodge raindrops in a downpour. "And what's your excuse? You've had both the time and the opportunity."

"I didn't say anything because you would have thought it was just a shitload of excuses."

"And now I won't?"

"No."

Florida laughed. "And why is that?"

"Because you're about to do the same thing."

Florida went speechless for a moment. "It's not the same thing and you know it."

Tamara moved across the porch. Florida followed the glow of the ash as she flipped her cigarette into the wet grass. At the doorway, she paused. Florida could feel her mother's eyes boring a hole into her.

"Isn't it?" Tamara asked.

The screen door slapped shut behind her.

Chapter 21

When Stan stepped out of Strides late in the afternoon the next day, the rain was still falling as it had been since Saturday, sometimes in a slow drizzle, others with a clap of thunder that unzipped a torrent. The roads were slick, the ground was soggy, and some intersections were flooded.

Along with the basement at Strides. Fortunately, he used it only for storage, but unfortunately, the sump pump hadn't kicked in. When they'd discovered the rising water—probably due to a drainage backup somewhere—he and Jess had worked through the night moving supplies and equipment out of the water's reach, catching only a few catnaps on mats on the floor. He considered the flooding an act of divine intervention. He hadn't been ready last night to give Florida any answers, not that having more time to ponder their conversation had made much difference. He still wasn't sure what to do. Marrying her . . . making a home with her and Missouri . . . it was what he wanted. But . . .

But what? Something wasn't right. Whether it was his allowing her to ride roughshod over him yesterday or because he was looking for another Serena and had just discovered she wasn't it—or possibly both—he didn't know. And he really didn't know if whatever was wrong could be fixed. Or even if he wanted to try.

Throwing his gym bag into the back, he got in the Suburban and headed toward Florida's. But just before he turned the corner to her house, he changed his mind and steered toward Memorial Park instead. The familiar scenery was washed gray by low-hanging clouds and the unceasing rain. He followed the graveled curve around the duck pond to the rear of the acreage, traveled a short way along Navajo Creek, glad the roadway sat up high. The creek was swollen now; the little island in the middle had shrunk around the duck blind. The footbridge had washed away. After passing under a wrought-iron arch that marked the entrance to Cordelia's cemetery, he took the right fork, bouncing through ruts filled with water made rust by the red Missouri clay. Near the far side of the cemetery where the tended grounds met the snarl of the woods, he pulled to a halt and got out. Unerringly, he made his way to Serena's side.

Kneeling at her grave, uncaring of the water soaking into his sweats, he pulled at a slender weed, then dropped his hands on his knees and closed his eyes. Her image filled his head. Merry eyes and vivid smile and a way of tilting her head as she looked up at him that said she was confident he'd know what to do. He'd lived up to her expectations. He'd *grown* into her expectations, proving to her—and himself—that he wasn't the weak-willed weasel of his youth. He'd become the strongest and best man in her world, and her champion when she fell sick. Not because she'd shown him how, but because that was how she'd thought of him.

And what had he been thinking of Florida? What had he expected from her?

Although he was partially sheltered by the solid oak branching over Serena's grave, rain still pelted the back of his neck and ran in rivulets under his shirt. Still he waited for answers, for clarity. Slowly Florida's image glossed over Serena's. Chin tilted with determination, the confidence she'd built against the odds of abandonment reshaping itself until her spine was straight and her shoulders were squared.

That was the Florida he knew. That was the woman he'd fallen in love with so many years ago. And that was the woman he'd encouraged to be less than she could be so that he could live out a fantasy.

The one where his wife lived.

He tilted his head up and let the rain mingle with his tears as he silently poured out all the questions in his heart.

Expecting to hear the lilt of Serena's voice answer him, he was surprised when it was Alcea's that cut through his disjointed thoughts. *You've turned into a man who goes the distance.*

Florida's joined it. *There is no old me.*

And in his mind's eye, Serena smiled.

He stood up feeling as if a weight had been lifted. There was no old Stan. Only the one he was now. A man who was a helluva lot more than the one he'd once been. A man who could go the distance.

He brushed the top of Serena's headstone with his fingers. If he met her now, married her now, they'd no longer work. Just like he'd once allowed Alcea and Florida to run roughshod over him, he'd now do the same to Serena.

He now needed—and wanted—a woman who could meet him halfway. He wanted Florida. Not the old Florida. Nor the invalid. But the one he knew could be forged by her ordeal—if he'd let her. And if he'd stand up to her.

Turning his back on the grave site, he returned to his car and fired the engine. Skidding over the gravel, he steered toward Florida's.

He needed to tell her—forcefully—that they couldn't get married.

When he arrived at Florida's, letting himself in through the breezeway, despite the trill of Missouri's voice coming from Julius's quarters, the tension was as heavy in the house as clouds were thick in the sky. He found Tamara in the kitchen, slapping dishes into cupboards from the dishwasher.

She'd given him a sour look. "Great idea, Einstein."

"What's that?"

"My talking to Florida."

With all that had happened in the past few days, he'd forgotten he'd asked her. "Didn't go over, huh?"

"The upside is that I'm still alive. It's carried our feud to a whole new level."

"Where is she?" he asked.

"Right here," Florida answered from the doorway. She leaned against the jamb, arms crossed. "You put her up to that? You think I'm as bad as she is?"

"Yeah, I'm the devil incarnate." Tamara rolled her eyes to the ceiling. "I'll be with Missouri and Julius." Leaving the dishwasher door hanging open, she headed through the doorway to Julius's quarters. Moments later, he heard the adjoining door close and Julius's television fire up.

"I can't believe you—" Florida started.

"Sit down."

She blinked, but moved to the table. He seated himself across from her and took her hands. "Florida . . . this is all wrong."

"What's all wrong?"

"Everything." He took a breath, let it out. "Ever since your accident, I've tried to help you, but—"

"And you have." She loosened a hand and touched his face, hers going soft.

"But I've done too much."

She frowned. "What do you mean?"

"You haven't needed me. Not like you think. I've provided an illusion of strength."

She drew her hands away. "You're sounding like Dak."

By God, he was. Maybe he should listen to Dak more closely.

She continued. "You're the one who said it was okay to need people. Well, now I need you even more than before. Missouri needs you. I can't keep her, not like this. Not right now."

"Of course I could take her. Would love to, even. But . . . you *don't* need me. You're strong. Strong enough to do what's right. And this isn't right. It's what's easiest. For you. Even for me. Because I want what you're offering."

"So y'all do think I'm as bad as Tamara."

He blew out a breath, suddenly exasperated. "This has nothing to do with Tamara. It's about you. And me. And Missouri. I'm not marrying anyone, not even you, because it's *convenient*. This is nuts. Missouri needs you—now more than she ever has—and she doesn't care if you can see her or not. No matter what kind of light you put this under, you can't change that fact. So what if you can't be perfect? So what if you screw some things up? Who gives a fuck? You'll do more things that are right. And you can let the rest of it go."

There was a surge of sound from the television in Julius's room. Tamara must have turned it up to drown them out.

Florida stared at him, mouth agape. For a moment, he thought he'd reached her, but then she stood up. "Are you telling me you don't want to marry me? Or that you won't give our daughter a home?"

"I'm telling you I won't get married because it's a *good plan*." He stood up, too. "And, of *course*, I'll give Missouri a home if you won't. But would you stop and think what this will do to her?"

"Don't you remember what happened with Julius? What happened with Tamara? What it will do to her," Florida said, "is keep her safe."

He realized that she'd moved past reason and into that zone where she just wanted to be right, bless her mulish heart. But she no longer sounded so certain. And her expression was troubled. He *had* reached her. He just needed to give her some space to come to the same conclusions herself. He suddenly felt hope. This might work after all.

A noise came from the doorway. Glancing over his shoulder, his heart sank. That surge of sound hadn't been Tamara juicing up the volume of the television. It had come when Missouri had opened the door to Julius's quarters and slipped out. She'd taken a step into the kitchen, then halted. His mind traveled back on what she would have heard and he groaned. More than enough.

Eyes wide and fixed on Florida, she backed up

until she hit the doorframe. "Why do you want me to live with Daddy? Is it because I pushed Joey and now I'm going to jail?"

"Absolutely not! I love you. No matter what." Knocking a chair back in her haste, Florida reached for her, but Missouri sidestepped her grasp. "But until I'm better—"

"Missouri." Stan kept his voice calm. "Your mother just wanted to—"

Still staring at Florida, Missouri rode over his words. "Daddy told me your eyes *couldn't* get better. You're lying!"

"That's not what I meant. I meant—"

Before she could finish, Missouri ran past her toward the front of the house, probably headed upstairs.

"Where'd she go? Missouri!" Florida followed in her wake. *"Missouri!"*

They both heard the front door slam.

Not upstairs. Stan leaped forward. By the time he'd wrenched open the door and run out on the porch, he could no longer see her. She'd disappeared into the gloom.

Florida had moved up behind him. "Can you see her? Can you?"

"Stay here. I'll find her."

Without waiting for an answer, he ran down the walkway and toward the square. The rain pelted his face. This had to be the direction she'd chosen; the other way led into the hills. Pacing himself, knowing that she might be faster, but he could go farther, he jogged up Main. The square was largely deserted, the stores closing, their lights flickering off. Bent against the continuing downpour, a few people raced to their cars, their umbrellas providing scant cover. He glanced into storefronts still lit against the weather and stopped at Sin-Sational and O'Neill's Emporium to ask if anyone had seen her. At Peg's, a startled Alcea looked up from her pile of receipts when he stuck in his head.

"You seen Missouri?"

"No. What hap—"

But before she could get the rest out, he'd moved on, moving past Up-in-the-Hair, where Missouri had recently purchased that god-awful purple nail polish. A lump pushed into his throat and he pushed it back down.

Within thirty minutes, he'd covered the square and graduated to the warren of alleys that pushed up to its back sides and behind the old homes that fanned out at its edges. After another hour, still not winded but finally losing hope, he stopped.

Water running into his eyes, he trudged back down Main toward Florida's. The murk had deepened enough that the streetlamps had already sputtered on. In the growing dark, there were hundreds of places a little girl could hide undetected—from behind trash bins to doghouses to detached garages to tree houses. She wouldn't be found unless she wanted to be. Given that she'd be wet and uncomfortable, and soon hungry for supper, and scared—that lump rose again—that would be sooner rather than later.

Despite the lines he was feeding himself, his stomach stayed knotted. She was only nine. And she was upset. He turned and studied the square again, looking for movement. There was none.

But as he watched, the lights—those left in storefronts, the streetlamps, and even the one that lit up the bell in St. Andrew's steeple—all went black.

Chapter 22

Twenty-four hours after Missouri had run out the door, the electricity was still out. As were the phone lines. The rain hadn't slaked—the *Cordelia Sun* (at least the last issue they were able to print) reported the biggest downpour the region had ever experienced this late in the summer. Overflowing storm sewers, flooding creeks and streams, trees toppling from soggy roots and gusts of wind, water up past ankles in gutters, and many streets underwater had all hampered repairs.

And rescue operations. Most of the town had turned out to search for Missouri as word spread she was missing. Chief Spindle had successfully lobbied for an AMBER Alert as fears grew that someone might have picked her up. Fears that were bumping up against the ones that she might have drowned. Fears that nobody was expressing to Florida, although no one needed to.

Fear was as thick in her kitchen as the posse of people that trooped in and out.

Someone had brought over a generator, and the kitchen had been turned into an outpost for the posse looking for Missouri. The table was loaded with food from the Ladies' Auxiliary, mostly leftovers donated from residents' dark refrigerators. One electric cord was split between a coffeepot and the cell phone they wanted to keep charged for word from the police. But it had stayed silent.

Standing at the sink, Florida washed cups and passed them off to her mother, who was keeping them full for the searchers. Florida had her lip clamped between her teeth to keep from screaming. From terror: She felt like she'd aged fifty years since Missouri had disappeared. And from frustration: She couldn't do much to help. Not even pour a damned cup of coffee.

Someone touched her shoulder. She turned and was almost nose to nose with Alcea, close enough to see the deep sympathy in her eyes. "Stan just came in the front door. He wants to see you."

Without asking, Alcea tucked Florida's hand over her arm to lead her to the great room, and Florida let her. She needed the guide. With all the activity, the house was strewn with umbrellas and rain boots and slickers.

"Why'd he send you to get me?"

"He didn't say." In the alcove near the stairs, Alcea stopped and turned Florida to face her. "I want—no I need—to tell you I'm so sorry, Florida."

"I know; you don't have to say anything." Florida blinked, but the tears spouted anyway. She snuffled them back. If she started, she'd never stop.

Alcea hugged her. "Not about Missouri. I mean, of course, I'm sorry you're going through this— but kids run off all the time. They give their families heart failure, and then they return. It's a rite of passage. We'll find her. I know we will."

Florida gave a watery laugh. "And of course, you're always right."

Alcea's voice stayed serious. "Not about you and Stan. Maybe you and I linked up long ago over what a schmuck he was then, but our friendship's more than that now. Seeing the two of you together pushed a whole boatload of buttons, but your relationship with him is your business, not mine. And whatever that is . . . well, I hope you still want to be friends." There was a hitch in her voice. "Because it's been lonely without you."

"Oh, Alcea." Florida returned her embrace.

"And I am really, *really* lousy at bookkeeping." Swiping at her eyes, Alcea stepped back and gave her a little push toward the great room. "Now go. I think Stan can take it from here."

A minute later, all the warmth she'd felt at Alcea's apology had turned to ice. She sat on the edge of the sofa, where gravity had dropped her when her knees had buckled. Stan knelt beside her. Cupped in her palms, she held a Mary Jane

Croc. Purple. Missouri's name smudged on the bottom. One of the search team had found it not far from where Navajo Creek fed into the duck pond.

"With all the flooding," Stan said, "she could have lost the shoe somewhere else and it just ended up there. It doesn't mean anything."

But his breathing was ragged. They both knew that it did.

She thought of how much Missouri loved Memorial Park. How that damnable pond had always drawn her, how much she enjoyed skipping stones over its surface, or feeding the ducks, her dark curls hooked behind her ears, her eyes shining. It was a familiar, friendly place for her. A place where she might have sought refuge. A place where she might have . . .

She swallowed. "Did they find anything else? See anything else?" Her voice was high and thready.

"No. They searched around the pond, up into the woods, both banks of the creek. When the rain slows, they'll—"

He broke off. But she knew he'd been about to tell her they planned to drag the pond. From deep in her chest, a keening started. She held the shoe up to her cheek and rocked herself back and forth.

Stan pulled her against him. "We don't know anything for sure. Not for sure."

The ruins of the blind on the island in the middle of Navajo Creek had always fascinated Missouri. It was where she and Joey had gotten into trouble last spring. If she'd tried to use that rope swing over the creek . . .

Her heart ripped from its moorings. She sobbed. Stan gripped her so tight, her breath was constricted. But she didn't care. Without his embrace, she thought, she'd shatter into a thousand pieces.

"No," he suddenly said, his fierceness penetrating her misery. "No. She's not gone. I won't believe it. She's as stubborn as you are. Even if she's cold, wet, and hungry, she could still be hiding somewhere." He pulled back. "Like the duck blind. The creek's flooded. The creek's flooded, the footbridge washed away. It's so hard to cross, nobody would figure she'd try. But what if—"

Florida caught his hope. "What if she used the rope swing?"

"Exactly. I'd forgotten about the damn swing. She could be there. Hiding. Maybe she even heard people calling for her but wouldn't come out, afraid she'd be in more trouble." He stood up. "Let me go tell the others. . . ."

He loped off to the kitchen. When he returned, Florida was struggling into a slicker she'd found on the floor of the entry.

"Tamara says some youngster was spotted near the elementary school. Everybody's rushed off to comb the neighborhood over there." Apparently registering her intention, he stopped.

She could feel his indecision. And she waited for his objection. Not that it would matter. She didn't care what he said; she was going, too. She had to.

But he only reached over and pulled her sleeve into place. "I grabbed the cell phone. What're you waiting for?"

By the time they reached Memorial Park, dusk was closing in, an almost imperceptible shift in light as the clouds stayed thick overhead. In his rush, Stan had driven straight into a flood of water before they'd reached the cemetery gate and the engine had stalled. They'd had to abandon the Suburban and continue on foot. Although he'd left on the headlights and both of them brandished flashlights, Florida could see very little except a glow on gray cotton. Stan kept his beam pitched ahead; she kept hers directed on the movement of his feet, following him with complete faith, making sure she kept the same speed, which wasn't very fast. They were keeping to the gravel road, higher than the pathway around the pond, which was nearly underwater. The going was slippery.

Finally they hit the cemetery gates. Stan veered to the left and Florida followed. The oaks, branches hanging low and waterlogged, cast even darker shadows and she was afraid for a moment she'd have to stop or be rescued herself, but the image of Missouri drove her on. The closer they got to the island, the more certain she was that they'd find Missouri there.

And, pray God, still alive.

"Did you try the cell?" she called, trying to think of anything else they could do.

"Yeah, but nobody answered." They had a direct line to Chief Spindle, but Missouri wasn't the only emergency today. Some people were trapped in cars, some stranded in their homes and needing medical assistance; trees continued to lose their grip on the ground; accidents were legion. The small Cordelia police force had been over-whelmed. The state police were assisting, but the storms hadn't impacted only Cordelia. There was a whole county of towns needing help.

Stan stopped. Florida moved up beside him, feeling a subtle change under her feet. They were on more porous ground. She took a small step forward; wet grass brushed her ankles. She could hear water rush nearby.

"Are we there?" She'd had to yell to be heard over wind, rain, and the roar of the water. Stan could be right; Missouri might have ignored peo-ple hollering her name, but more likely, she sim-ply hadn't heard them. If she was there to hear them.

"Yes!" He yelled back. "I'm guessing the wa-ter's about thigh-deep, maybe less in some places." Normally the creek measured only a foot deep. "And it's moving fast." He hesitated. "I don't think you should try to cross."

Even though she wanted to, she wouldn't argue with him about her limitations. For the rest of her life, she'd face a balancing act between what she could attempt and what she shouldn't. This was a time when trying would be more than foolish; it could be deadly. Not just for her. For Stan. For Missouri.

"Just come back to me!" The idea of Stan getting swept away as he forded the creek had her heart in her throat.

He pulled her to him. His kiss was savage, his mouth wet and cold on hers. "I will. Wait for me." He released her as quick as he'd grabbed her, leaving her gasping for air but feeling more hopeful than she had felt all day. He moved away until the bulk of him faded into the surrounding grayness. The island was small; it would take him only a minute once he reached it to check the duck blind.

Straining, she tried to follow his progress, but the gallop of the elements was too loud.

"Mommeee!"

A thin, high-pitched whine, borne on the wind. Florida's heart stopped and she held perfectly still. Wishful thinking or—

"Daddeeee!"

Then Stan's voice. "She's here, Florida! She's here! Stay put, Missouri. Stay there, sweetheart. Let me come to you!" Stan's bellow was a low rumble, barely audible.

Sobbing, Florida dropped to her hands and knees and felt her way closer to the edge of the bank. "We're coming, Missouri!" She yelled in the direction of the island. "Daddy's coming!"

Afraid she'd lose her mind if she didn't know something soon, she waited, so tense she felt she'd shatter.

Suddenly Stan hollered, "Shit!" There was a loud crack, a whoosh, then only the sound of the water rushing past.

The bottom fell out of her stomach. "Stan!" Florida sobbed. "Missouri! What's happening? Omigod, *please*, what's happening?"

"Florida! It's okay, we're okay. But you have to go for help! Get help!"

Like a crab, she scrambled sideways, following the direction of his voice. "Where are you? What happened?"

"A tree fell. It's trapped Missouri's leg!"

He sounded closer. They were straight ahead. Ten feet? Twelve feet away? But all she could see was fog. She almost screamed with frustration.

"Get me! Take me to her. I'll stay. You get help. It makes more sense!" She spoke in short beats, hoping he could hear her. Wondering if he could see her.

"We're in the creek! Tree dragged her under." He spoke in the same rapid bursts. "I'm holding up her head. Can't free her. You aren't strong enough. Need help."

"Mommy! Help us!"

Florida looked behind her, at the gray mass that was ground, water, sky, trees. Despair swept her; she turned back to Stan. "The cell phone!"

"Gone. Lost . . . in the creek." Stan's breath had caught. He was an athlete. One with staying power, but even he couldn't last forever against the onslaught of water.

She took a deep breath. "I'll be back. Hang on! *I'll be back!*"

She had to do this. She had to.

*   *   *

Florida finally stumbled out of the park and onto Maple Woods Drive. The precious long minutes it had taken her to find her way out, helped by the headlights on Stan's car, and then by her flashlight once she got past it, felt like weeks. Once she hit pavement, she wanted to dash forward, but forced herself into a fast stride, hoping the stick she waved in front of her would let her know if an obstacle loomed. Stan's and Missouri's lives were depending on her. She couldn't risk falling.

Out here, despite the lack of streetlights, the light wasn't as dim. She kept to one side of the gray ribbon of street, stick out in one hand, fingers of the other trailing along the cars parked at the curb. She could hear the water gurgle past in the gutters, the rustle of the foliage of trees that arched inked fingers overhead.

"Help! Anybody? Help!"

Unable to conquer the weather, her voice couldn't reach the tall Victorians and sprawling bungalows that loomed around her. She'd have to try them until she found someone home. She moved to the other side of the row of cars, keeping to the grassy side of the gutter. She prayed no kid had left a bicycle flung on the ground, no gardener a rake tossed aside in haste.

She hit the first concrete walkway. The first house. But knowing it was Betty Bruell's, she skipped it and headed for the next. Betty wouldn't hear her no matter how hard she pounded. Concrete again met her footsteps and she turned, holding out one hand, swinging the stick in the other, resolutely keeping her feet on the pavement and not letting fear slow her down. After stumbling her way up the steps to the porch, she beat on the front door, but nobody answered. Moaning in frustration, she felt her way back down and moved on to the next.

Two more houses and no answers later, her breath was rasping. She stumbled, caught herself against a car. For a moment, she halted, fighting panic.

"Missouri . . . Stan." She breathed. "Missouri . . . Stan."

Setting her chin, she went on, chanting their names in a kind of mantra, first in a whisper, then yelling them like a madwoman, hoping someone would hear, that anyone would hear, until her voice was hoarse. That kept her going down the fourth walkway and heading to the fifth, but hope was losing out to despair. True to its nature, Cordelia had turned out in droves to help those in need from the flooding. . . .

And it seemed nobody, *nobody*, on this godforsaken street was still home.

How long had it been since she'd left Stan holding Missouri above death in the water? Thirty minutes? Forty? An hour? Oh, *God. Please.* A sob filling her lungs, tiredness buckling her knees, she misjudged and tripped over the curb, only narrowly saving herself from a nasty spill by catching herself palm down on the trunk of a car. She snatched back her hand before she set off the car alarm.

Car alarm. *Car alarm*! Idiot! Without a second's hesitation, she banged on the trunk, then scrambled around the car and yanked on the door handle. There was a satisfying screech as the alarm exploded through the gloom, as sweet as song. New hope building in her chest, she fumbled along the line of cars. With the growing yuppiefication of the center of town, half of them had to be newer models, and even minivans were equipped with theft deterrents. The third car she tried joined the shriek of the other. Two cars later, she'd set off another . . . and then another.

Within five minutes, she'd set off no fewer than a dozen alarms and had nearly reached Main. Behind her headlights flashed, horns blared, and alarms wailed in a cacophony that could wake the dead.

Nearing exhaustion, she staggered forward, crying. Finally, *finally*, God answered her prayers. Bursts of red light filled her vision as a police car swerved around the corner.

"Hurry! Hurry!" Yelling in a voice too raspy to be heard, she ran ahead, waving her arms. A siren sounded briefly; then the car skidded to a halt in front of her.

She collapsed on the ground, praying they weren't too late.

Chapter 23

The rescue squad that responded within minutes to Chief Spindle's radio call wouldn't let her go with them. They knew where the duck blind was. And they didn't want her to become one more person to rescue. At least that's what they said. But she knew, with the stark fear that had held her rigid ever since she'd collapsed on the street twenty minutes ago, that it was because they were afraid of what they'd find when they reached Stan and Missouri.

They must have been in the creek close to an hour. Stan was strong, but so was the water.

Refusing any ministrations except a mug of coffee that was growing cold, she sat on the back ledge of an ambulance that had pulled up to the park entrance, a blanket gripped closed at her throat. She knew another ambulance had moved in-

side the park perimeter. *Just in case*, she'd been told
by the emergency worker who had brought her coffee. Words that were meant to reassure, but didn't.

Behind her, headlights crisscrossed and red bea-
cons strobed. The worker had said police cars had
moved into place to keep one side of the street
clear and block the flow of anything but emergency equipment into the park.

Word of what was happening in Memorial Park
had carried on the wind and rain that blew through
Cordelia. With the same inevitability as locusts
swarming in summer, cars and trucks had paraded
onto Maple Woods Drive. People had piled out.

"What are they doing?" Florida had asked the
worker.

"Just standing there, ma'am."

She understood. They didn't know if they'd
come for a celebration.

Or for a dirge.

Dropping her head, she drew a ragged breath.
The emergency worker had hustled off to see what
else he could learn. Only sheer willpower was
keeping her from exploding into a million pieces.
Over and over, Missouri's and Stan's names
streamed through her mind as she continued the
mantra that had brought her this far.

"Florida!"

She raised her head.

"Florida!"

She whimpered, afraid she was hearing things.
Afraid that in the rattle of rain and rumble of
engines, she was only imagining Stan's voice.

"Mommy!"

She stood, the mug she was holding dropping from nerveless fingers to shatter at her feet. Oblivious to the wreckage, she crunched over broken crockery as she fumbled her way forward, aiming for those voices, still uncertain if she'd heard correctly or suffered a psychotic break. Her outstretched hands encountered the leather jackets of policemen, the stiff garb of firefighters, the wet suits of rescuers who milled near the entrance. They parted, hands reaching to guide her through the crowd. Behind her, the crowd buzzed with a low rumble of anticipation as word carried backward.

"Florida!"

It *was* him! It was! Laughing and crying, she lurched forward and finally, *finally*, she was in Stan's arms. He was soaked and shivering, trembling with exhaustion, but he was alive and uninjured and holding her so tight, she could hardly breathe.

"I think this belongs to you, ma'am."

"Mommy!"

A rescue worker paused next to them and Missouri launched herself out of his arms and into theirs.

Moving like a wave, the crowd behind them swelled into life.

Soon, the noise of a hundred car horns filled the night, overpowering the rain, blaring not with the urgency of alarm anymore but with the lighthearted merriment of jubilation.

Chapter 24

Three days later, on Friday evening, Florida and Stan sat as close as physics allowed on the wicker settee on Florida's front porch. As they'd recovered from their ordeal over the last two days, the rain had turned to showers, and the winds borne in on a new front had finally blown the clouds away. Electricity had been restored the night before last, the flooding had ebbed, and now the sun slanted low through the branches of her dogwood tree, warming Florida's lap.

A whoop came from the front yard, punctuated by the peal of the bicycle bell. Deciding they were well matched between Tamara's age, Julius's disability, and the new walking cast Missouri sported for a minor greenstick fracture—no more ballet lessons for the near future—Tamara and Missouri had launched some kind of game that seemed to meld soccer with a form of keep-away from Julius. Florida could see them only in a tumble of color and movement, so Stan had been calling a play-by-play.

"If Julius pivots any faster, he'll drill through to China. That is, if he doesn't get stuck up to the elbows in the ruts he's made in the yard." He paused, then spoke louder in faux-sportscaster voice. "And he's off! Hurling the ball at Missouri while Tamara takes the middle—"

"Can I play, too?" A new voice piped up.

"I'll be damned." Stan's voice dropped. "It's Joey Norsworthy. They must have decided Missouri's not an ax murderer after all."

"I'm sure it had something to do with public opinion," Florida replied drily.

The prosecutor had called yesterday to say he was dropping the charges. Missouri's rescue had provided a joyous note in an otherwise somber few days of flooding and property damage. Given the townsfolk's reaction, he was undoubtedly courting their continued goodwill. As were the Norsworthys.

"Your mom say it was okay?" Tamara called.

"Yep."

"Then get yourself on in here, young man. You'll play on Julius's team. But watch out, us girls are kicking ass!"

Joey snickered.

Florida sighed. As sure as the sun rose mornings, as soon as Cordelia's collective attention moved on, Barb Norsworthy wouldn't have to look far for a new grievance against *someone* in Missouri's family. Florida started. It was the first time she'd thought of Tamara as family. She examined her feelings. Nope, no overnight miracle. She hadn't forgiven her mother. Maybe she never would, at least not entirely. But after nearly visiting a similar hell on Missouri, she felt a new understanding. Perhaps that was enough to provide a bridge to the future.

Florida heard the gate open and close as Joey joined the game. In moments, it was bedlam again.

" '*A hit,*' " Julius crowed. The bells chimed. " '*A very palpable hit.*' And you, madam, are *it.*"

Stan sighed. "I'm afraid your flower border is history."

Tamara's voice rose above Missouri's giggles. "You're taking advantage of an old lady!"

Julius snorted. "Tamara, you're a danged youngster. You've no right to bellyache until you're my age. '*With mirth and laughter let old wrinkles come*'!"

She felt Stan's smile. He gathered her hand in his. "What do you say? Shall we grow wrinkles together?"

Her heart leaped. Content with being safe, they hadn't yet discussed the future. She knew her own heart, but hadn't been sure of his. Still, she hesitated. "I'm not Serena, Stan."

"Which is a good thing." The jocular note fell from his voice. "I loved her, Florida. But she belongs to another time and place. To a different Stan. You belong to this one. To my present."

Pressing something into her hand, he bent his head to hers. "And to my future."

"It's a miss on your part, madam!" The bells rang madly.

"Julius is twirling again," Stan murmured against her cheek.

The old mechanic suddenly howled.

"And there," Stan said as his mouth found hers, "goes the rosebush."

"That's okay," she whispered when he gave her a chance to catch her breath. "Roses may look fragile, but they're tough. They'll come back."

She ran her fingers over the object in her hands.

It was her Willow Tree angel, arms raised in victory.